FROGMORTON CULPEPPER

Frogmorton Culpepper didn't wa
expecting to save the world, not   .... to
prove out his environmental technology experiments to his
superiors first. The world had yet to provide any recognition of
his genius. His mother had yet to provide any recognition of his
ability to do anything. The girl of his dreams had yet to provide
any recognition of his existence. Some, if not all, of that changes
in *Frogmorton Culpepper Saves the World*, a work of the scientifically
fictitious that if it doesn't change your life forever, will at least
make you smile (a lot) .... and if you want to know why there's a
picture of a cleverly-folder origami rhinoceros on the cover, all
we can say is that you'll have to read the book.

KEITH TREZISE

Keith Trezise lives in Warwickshire, England and amongst other
things is a playwright and entertainer. His plays have been
performed worldwide, with his one act play *Duplex* winning a
Little Theatre Guild of Great Britain award. He has been a
member of a number of bands and is currently performing with
his one-man show as a guitarist and vocalist. *Frogmorton Culpepper
Saves the World* is his first novel.

BY THE SAME AUTHOR

PLAYS

Branching Out

Four Play

Duplex

Curtain Call

Dying to Be Heard

FROGMORTON CULPEPPER
SAVES THE WORLD

or

There's an Alien in My Microwave

Keith Trezise

Best Wishes

Keith

CORONA
BOOKS

First published in the United Kingdom in 2017
by Corona Books UK
www.coronabooks.com

An earlier version of this work was previously published by the
author under the title *Termination: Project Earth*

The moral right of the author has been asserted.

ISBN 978-0-9932472-5-5

Cover design and photography by Martin Bushell
www.creatusadvertising.co.uk

Origami rhinoceros designed and folded by David Brill,
Vice President of The British Origami Society
www.brilliantorigami.com

For my sons, Christopher and Adam
Thank you for believing

CONTENTS

Frogmorton Culpepper Saves the World is a unitary novel, but its chapters have titles.

CHAPTER ONE

The Environmental Technology Department's Most Menial Employee

For most of his thirty-two years, four months and seventeen days Frogmorton Culpepper had known space was big. After all, he'd read *Hitchhiker's Guide to the Galaxy* seven times, and whilst he was sure that most of the rest of it was made up, he was sure the bit about space being big, really big, was true. But he'd been thinking about space and its size a lot recently, and was thinking about it now as he lay flat on his back on the floor of his living room. He turned to Chloe, who was laying on the floor next to him, and said, 'Space is big.'

The news was no big deal to Chloe. She took it all in her stride. Space might well be big, but she had much more important things on her mind.

It might be worth mentioning that Chloe did not have much of an idea about the concept of space. Indeed, the subject rarely bothered her at all. Chloe only ever thought about two things - eating and sleeping. A boring trait in a woman, that is agreed, but nobody ever said that Chloe was a woman, did they? In fact, Chloe was Frogmorton's cat.

'Space is big,' Frogmorton repeated, in case Chloe had missed the enormity of the statement the first time around.

Chloe responded by stretching her paws out in front of her and, giving a huge yawn, curled up into a fluffy ball and went to sleep.

Frogmorton sprang to his feet and ran across to the window, which he flung open. He stuck his head out and gazed up to the heavens to make sure he hadn't been mistaken. The sudden movement was too much for Chloe, and, thinking at least a hurricane was about to strike, she dived for cover under the couch.

'See, it must be big,' he mused, 'otherwise you would be able to see the other end of it.'

'He's not still going on about space,' thought Chloe. Just because she had no concept of space didn't mean that she couldn't have an opinion. Many successful politicians have forged their careers using that principle.

'I mean, it would take an enormous amount of time to get all the way across it,' Frogmorton continued.

Chloe was getting rather fed up with all this talk about space, and took the opportunity to leave the room whilst her master was contemplating the cosmic navel.

Frogmorton stared up at the stars dancing motionlessly above him. He scoured the sky and found the Great Bear. That was easy to recognise. Then his eyes darted from constellation to constellation. There was Hydra. There was Leo. And Orion the great hunter. He singled out each of them in turn, calling their names out loudly in triumphant recognition, all the time gasping at the awesome spectacle above him. It was a pity he hadn't got a clue about astronomy and hadn't identified one constellation correctly. But he was keen and enthusiastic, and that must count for something in the great scheme of things.

It was being keen and enthusiastic that got Frogmorton his job. He worked at Dawson University in the Environmental Technology Department. Oh, sure, it sounds pretty impressive, but the truth of the matter was that Frogmorton was nothing more than a laboratory assistant, which in effect meant he was little more than a janitor sweeping up the mess left over when the scientists had finished a project and were satisfied (or not) with the results.

He had written to the Head of Department, shortly before receiving his exam results from school, saying how much he loved the environment and how he wanted to work towards a better place for future generations to live. The Head of Department wrote back and told him that if he obtained good grades in his exams, he could be considered. However, the results were not quite what Frogmorton was expecting and the Head of Department turned him down. Undaunted, Frogmorton wrote relentlessly to the Head of Department saying that he would take any job offered in order to work with the environment and, eventually, his persistence paid off and he was given the job he has now - mostly because the Head of Department was fed up with all the letters and certainly not because of any aptitude Frogmorton may have had towards working with the environment. Nevertheless, Frogmorton felt that he was contributing to the salvation of the planet and it made him feel good. Besides, he didn't intend being a laboratory assistant for the rest of his life, and was taking an Open University degree in order to gain promotion. With a degree he felt he could really make a difference. People might start to take notice of him. He would be able to communicate his ideas to the world - make people aware that they had it in their own hands to stop the rot that was gradually taking over and destroying the planet.

The following morning was going to be the starting point of his future career. The following morning he was going to get the results of his Open University degree course. The following morning he was going to ask the Head of Department for a real job in the Environmental Technology Department.

He had already been working on a project in the Environmental Technology Laboratory with the, albeit reluctant, permission of the Head of Department. It formed part of his course. It was not a set project; it was an idea of his own and he was very excited about it indeed. He called it 'Project Earth' and he was aiming to show how the greenhouse effect could be reversed and how the ozone layer could be replenished.

Frogmorton was starting to feel dizzy looking up to the heavens. He sighed at the incomprehensible vastness of it all and said, with a smug feeling of total comprehension, 'Space is bloody big.'

* * *

Of course, Frogmorton was quite correct. Space is a pretty large chunk of real estate with plenty of room to build an extension. You don't get a lot of noise from the neighbours either. As a matter of fact, you hardly ever see them. But his last statement was not quite as accurate as it might, at first glance, appear. You have probably heard the argument that space is relative and, I dare say, it is. Who are we to doubt the words of scientists? But do any of us really know what it is relative to?

'Time!' I hear you all shout in unison. Well, that's a pretty vague statement. It's as if we are all programmed to respond to the question 'What is space relative to?' by shouting out 'Time!' like a bunch of demented parrots. The fact is that 'time' is a word landlords use when they want to close the bar and send everyone home so that they, the landlords and their chosen few, can start the serious business of after-hours-drinking. Time is a device bosses use to measure how effectively employees are performing their jobs - or not, as the case may be. Time is a man-made thing. It's our way of measuring the passing of day to night and season to season. I don't doubt that those things are relative to space, but hours and minutes are synthetic. They don't really exist outside the ticking of someone's watch - but I digress. As I have said, space is relative. We don't have to know precisely what to. Let's just accept the wisdom of science.

So Frogmorton's claim as to the size of space was a bit rash. He didn't qualify his statement and, therefore, it was a little flawed.

E⌾ PAYMENTS
INTERNATIONAL

HUNT'S
9 HIGH STREET
Rugby CV21 3BG
TID: 25806214   Receipt no.: 001400
MID: GB0000000067220
**** **** **** 2699   Valid to: /
AID: A0000000031010
Visa Contactless(B)
Visa payWave)))

Sale

TRANSACTION AMOUNT   **GBP**
                                8.99

RECEIPT FOR CLIENT
SIGNATURE NOT REQUIRED

Authorisation code: (1) 007634
ARQC: 8233A83C783CD49B

DATE: May 14, 2021   TIME: 10.21.13
                                 App. ver.: 7407

Of course, if you're sitting in a space capsule hurtling towards the moon at God knows what speed, knowing that a decimal point in the wrong place in your trajectory could make you miss your target by several thousand miles, space is, indeed, very big.

If, on the other hand, you are trying to thread a needle, you will notice that the space through which you are trying to push the thread is not that big at all and that a decimal point in the wrong place in your trajectory could make you miss your target by several thousand miles. Or, at least, that's how it seems.

It is thought in some circles that contemplating the size of the Universe - which includes quite a bit of space, I understand - can send people mad. I cannot fully agree with this theory as I personally used to think about the vastness of the Cosmos quite often as a youth.

Frogmorton pulled his head back inside. He could not see very far in the night sky and was straining his eyes. (Although, it could be argued that, because some of the stars Frogmorton had been looking at were several hundred light years away, he could actually see very far in the night sky.) He noticed that Chloe had left the room. She always seemed to do that when he wanted to have a chat with her. It was as if she sensed that he had something he wanted to get off his chest, and so she would run off and find a hiding place until he had forgotten what it was he wanted to say to her. She could be very selfish at times.

The only other person he could talk to was his mother, but she wasn't interested in any of the things he was. The only thing she seemed concerned about was finding Frogmorton a wife. If she was so interested in seeing him married, what the hell did she give him a name like Frogmorton for?

He had asked her about that many times, but she would never tell him. It remained one of the great untold secrets of the Universe.

He thought that, maybe, he was named after one of his grandfathers, but research showed him that that was not the case. Frogmorton, indeed! What a ribbing he used to get at school. He imagined, perhaps, that the name might have been some fantastically hilarious joke his mother was playing on his father, but dismissed that idea, because his mother was devoid of a sense of humour. However, no matter how he came by the name, he was stuck with it. Everyone knew him by that name so there was no point changing it now, not after thirty-two years, four months and seventeen days.

He always believed that he suited his name, though. Especially the 'Frog' bit. Mind you, at times, he felt the 'mort' bit to be quite reflective of not only the way he felt, but also his social life. It was not easy, being a spotty spectacle wearer, to attract females in his youth and, although now his spots had long disappeared, so had his self-confidence. Consequently, he still felt ill at ease with girls.

Whenever his mother described him to an eligible young lady, she would always highlight his strong points, which didn't usually take her many minutes to do. If he only thought about it more, though, he could make himself quite presentable.

Frogmorton closed the window and drew the curtains. It was late and he had a busy schedule ahead of him the following day. He walked through to the kitchen to make himself a bedtime drink, and there was confronted by his nemesis.

His mother sat at the kitchen table, a picture of refinement with her legs up on the table picking dead skin from between her toes.

'Mum! Do you have to do that?' he pleaded.

'Are you going to do it for me?' she asked. Quite a relevant question really.

'But do you have to do it on the kitchen table? We have to eat off there.'

'Oh, and so you expect your poor mother to bend down and reach her toes now! You know what my back's like.'

'Mum, there is nothing wrong with your back.'

'No, I know. And that's because I don't go around bending over to touch my toes all the time. I look after my body, I do. You ought to do the same. It's no wonder you're not married, the way you neglect your body.'

'I do not neglect my body.'

'Well why aren't you married by now then? I was married with five kids by the time I was your age.'

'No you weren't. I'm an only child.'

'No thanks to your father. He was always after it, he was. Dirty old sod! If I'd given in to him every time he wanted a bit, I'd probably have had a dozen kids.'

'Do you mind putting your feet away, Mum? I want to get myself a bit of supper before I go on up to bed.'

His mother did mind, but grudgingly put away the offending appendages and went off to bed, all the time mumbling about what a randy devil Frogmorton's father was and how she couldn't even do whatever she liked in her own kitchen any more. Staring at the retreating figure of his overbearing mother made Frogmorton realise that marriage would not be a bad option after all.

He went to the cupboard to get the cocoa and found only an empty tin, so decided to settle for hot milk. As he made his way to the microwave with his mug of milk, Chloe decided to return home with some supper of her own and darted through the cat flap at just the right moment to send Frogmorton sprawling across the kitchen floor. Amazingly he managed not to spill a drop of milk and, as he lay there on his stomach, Chloe proudly laid her offering about half an inch from the end of his nose. It was a mouse.

Chloe was a strange creature. She very much enjoyed the hunt. Her instincts were in perfect working order. She would stalk her prey with great patience, and would pounce at just the right moment. She would spend the required amount of time toying with her catch, but then, perhaps because of being pampered by her human companions so much, she would not eat her quarry unless it was hot. She wanted her meat cooked - albeit done rare. In order not to keep Chloe waiting too long, Frogmorton usually microwaved her little titbits. Three minutes on full power for a mouse or vole, four minutes for a rat or small bird and ten minutes for the likes of the occasional seagull.

He picked the dead creature up by its tail and headed for the microwave. He opened the door of the appliance and put his mug of milk inside, closed the door and set the timer for one minute. Oh, don't worry about hygiene. Frogmorton had a second microwave just for Chloe, and he didn't even keep it in the kitchen. In fact, it was hidden out of sight behind the television cabinet in the living room. A series of beeps gently reminded Frogmorton that his bedtime drink was now warm and he retrieved it from the microwave, and took it and the mouse through to the living room. Chloe was frantically rubbing around his legs as he passed between the two rooms, and it was a miracle that he didn't end up on the floor in a heap again. Frogmorton placed his mug on the coffee table and went behind the television cabinet to cook Chloe's supper. As he bent down to open the door of Chloe's microwave, he noticed a peculiar purple light emanating from within. He pressed his nose up against the glass door to observe this phenomenon more closely and could hardly believe his eyes. Standing there inside Chloe's microwave was a four-inch-tall humanoid figure bathed in a purple glow. Chloe arched her back and spat, narrowly missing

Frogmorton's face, which he had turned towards her as if to ask her for confirmation of that which he had just witnessed. He looked back at the microwave. There was no glow this time. Everything appeared normal. Frogmorton tossed the mouse inside and set the timer to three minutes. He thought he had better get off to bed - he must have been more tired than he felt.

Isn't fate funny? Things invariably happen either when we least expect them or when we've turned our backs or left the room just for a couple of seconds. Like when your favourite football team is playing a televised live match and you have to leave the room half way through the first half because of an urgent call of nature. You can bet your bottom dollar that the moment you leave that room the deadlock will be broken by one or other of the teams sinking the ball into the back of the net. And when you're out and about on holiday, for instance, you know that the moment your battery goes dead in your camera, Elvis Presley will walk by hand in hand with Lord Lucan.

Such a case of peculiarly bad timing occurred at NASA's SETI installation at Ames Research Center near Palo Alto, California. For the briefest of moments the instruments picked up a particularly strong and localised signal. Further investigations would have revealed that the signal had been aimed at somewhere in the UK. However, at precisely the same moment Gavin Woosner, the operative on duty at the time, decided to sneeze. It wasn't, of course, a conscious decision and, if he had had the choice, he would probably have preferred not to bother, but the event did distract him from observing the first real contact with extra-terrestrial life this planet would have. He did, of course, notice the incident on the print-out, but, thinking the anomaly was caused by his nasal ejaculation, his reaction was to say, 'Man! When I sneeze, I SNEEZE!', and then he continued to ignore it. If Gavin Woosner had been able to make arrangements to sneeze at a later date, he could have made a name for himself at NASA.

CHAPTER TWO
Life on Erith

As we have already mentioned, space is big, or at least relative to you and me and our conceptions of space and time, space is big. It should, therefore, come as no surprise that we are not alone in the Cosmos and proof of this fact, if proof were needed, embodied itself in the shape of the inter-galactic StarDestroyer Blagn'k as it sped along at velocities that we can only dream of. Its crew consisted of StarFleet Admiral Kratol and SpaceTrooper (Fourth Class) Domr'k. Although the star-shaped vessel was the size of a small city, a larger crew was unnecessary. The two aliens hailed from the planet Braakl'g and they were in the employ of a highly-developed life-force known as The Source, who used them to do some of the more mundane tasks associated with being Controllers of the Universe.

The Source had been in existence long before what we regard as the Universe, although they had limited knowledge of events preceding the Big Bang or, as they called it, the Medium-sized Pop. They evolved over the millennia into a single entity embracing the whole of their civilisation whilst, somehow, retaining the individuality of each constituent part. A hard concept for us to grasp - agreed, but take my word for it. What reason do I have for lying to you?

This single entity had no physical form and relied on using lesser species to perform any actions that were on a lower plane than pure thought. That was where Admiral Kratol and Trooper Domr'k came in to the picture. Oh, sure, the fact that Kratol was an Admiral sounds very impressive, but the rank was automatically awarded to any officer of the Braakl'gian Space Navy who was in command of a StarDestroyer. The truth of the matter was that he and Domr'k were nothing more than inter-galactic janitors sweeping up the mess left over when The Source had finished a project and was satisfied (or not) with the results.

The mighty StarDestroyer Blagn'k slowed to below light speed in order that Domr'k could send the statutory warning message to the inhabitants of the planet Erith. They had to drop below light speed or the communications accelerators would not function correctly and they would probably arrive at their destination before the message. The message gave the inhabitants a chance to put their case to the Justice Council. It gave them the opportunity to avoid annihilation if they could convince the council that they were a viable civilisation that would be able to enrich the common being of The Source and/or Universe. The name 'Justice Council' sounded grand and important, and that's why Kratol used it. The truth was that there wasn't a council at all, but Kratol believed himself to be fair and compassionate.

'Whoops!' said Domr'k.

'What do you mean "Whoops!"?' demanded Kratol.

'It's alright, Your Excellency. I have corrected my mistake.'

'Your mistake? What mistake?'

'The warning message, Your Excellency. I accidentally transmitted it to the wrong planet.'

'The wrong planet? There is only one planet within a radius of twenty light years. I hope the communications accelerators didn't kick in.'

'I'm afraid they did.'

'In that case, if the "wrong" planet is within a million light years, they will have already received the message. It will throw the entire population into a state of chaos and anarchy. Where did you send the message to?'

'Earth.'

'Earth? Well, that's not quite so bad. The population there is already in a state of chaos and anarchy.'

'It's an easy mistake to make, Your Excellency. The planet has got such a similar name to Erith.'

'You've got to be more careful. We'll just have to hope they think it's a hoax.'

'It only transmitted for a few seconds. They might not have noticed.'

'Enough! There's nothing we can do about it now.'

'Yes, Your Excellency.'

'So, if it's not too much trouble, do you think you could send the message to the planet Erith now?'

'Of course, Your Excellency.'

Domr'k took great care in feeding the correct data into the communications computer, and checked everything twice before executing the transmission.

'It is done,' said Domr'k.

The four-inch-tall humanoid figure, bathed in a purple glow, materialised in the main chamber of the Queen's domain and started, dutifully, to impart its sombre message to the inhabitants of Erith.

Erith was a beautiful planet. It was rich in the Universe's most precious resource - water - which took up nearly nine-tenths of the surface. The seas and oceans were teeming with life at all stages of the evolutionary process. Here creatures did not leave the water to colonise the land, maybe because it was in such short supply or perhaps just because they preferred the vastness of the oceans.

In fact, the only land dwellers on Erith arrived here quite by accident, clinging to an asteroid which bounced off their home planet scooping them up and depositing them here. Hardy little blighters, aren't they? With no competition from indigenous species, these land dwellers flourished and spread across the entire landmass. They soon adapted their diet to make the most of the varied plant life they encountered and developed a way of farming their favourite crops. These land dwellers resembled ants in the way they behaved socially and, indeed, in the way they looked. If we had come across them in the Amazonian rain forests, we would have definitely declared the discovery of a new species of ant. Because these land dwellers were alien to the planet, Project Erith had become unstable, because life had not developed there naturally from the primordial soup. Erith civilisation had been contaminated by alien life forms, and so the great experiment that The Source was conducting was flawed, and now Kratol and Domr'k were being sent there to sweep it all under the cosmic carpet.

The four-inch-tall humanoid figure, bathed in a purple glow, was, in fact, a holographic projection of Admiral Kratol. He decided at the outset that he was the only one fit to deliver the message. It was, after all, a very important message and Kratol was, in his eyes at least, a very important being. I suppose he was a very important being in Domr'k's eyes as well, but then, when you only hold the rank of Space Trooper (Fourth Class), even a Braakl'gian ooze beetle was a very important being.

'Inhabitants of Erith,' the message began, 'pay heed to this message. After all, this is a very important message.'

The inhabitants of Erith didn't pay much heed to the message at all. For one thing, the real inhabitants were too busy in the oceans running their everyday lives to be bothered with a four-inch-tall humanoid figure, bathed in a purple glow, going on about the impending doom of the planet. And another thing, the hologram was projected into the Queen of the alien land dwellers' chamber, so the real natives of Erith never got to see it anyway. Sure, the ant-like aliens saw the hologram, but they didn't pay it any attention at all. They preferred to go about the business of grazing on the plants they had farmed and making sure the Queen was doing her bit in the reproduction of their species.

Although Kratol was convinced about the very important nature of the message, it was hard to understand why he relied on a four-inch hologram, bathed in a purple glow and projected at the planet's surface more-or-less at random, to provide an opportunity for the inhabitants of that planet to defend themselves. If he had looked back at the past records of the message's effectiveness in providing that opportunity, he would have seen that, out of the two and a half thousand or so planets that he had sent it to, only four had responded and none had been successful in their attempts to avoid oblivion.

It may be of some interest to you to know why Kratol and Domr'k are hurtling through the Cosmos laying waste to thousands of planets. They are not merely intergalactic vandals, far from it. As I have said previously, they are, in fact, glorified janitors in the employ of The Source.

Here on Earth we have always been fascinated about where we come from. Were we created by a Supreme Being or did we evolve from simple one-celled organisms millions of years ago? Well, I'm not one for controversy, but I can reveal, here and now, that both schools of thought are correct. Yes, we can have our cake and eat it. Mind you, there would be no point having the cake in the first place if we had no intentions of eating it.

So, all the arguments that have raged throughout the ages concerning the origins of mankind could have been avoided. We did evolve from one-celled organisms - but it was a Supreme Being who created them, The Source.

You see The Source is very old, very wise, but very frustrated. They themselves, although they are a Supreme Being, are plagued with the same question that has been hounding us. They want to know where they came from. Were they created by an even more

Supreme Being, or did they evolve from the lowly one-celled organism like the rest of us?

In order to try and solve this ancient riddle, The Source had created life in its simplest form on all planets in the Universe that were capable of sustaining it in whatever form it might develop, and were keeping a watchful eye on the evolutionary processes at work to see if life would evolve into a carbon copy of themselves. Time was of no concern to The Source and, as it is a man-made phenomenon anyway, they weren't even aware of it. The only thing of importance to The Source was finding their - well, their source! They were interested in nothing else. Well, being a single entity, they wouldn't even be interested in sex, would they? (But I don't know that for certain, so don't quote me.) Mind you, if one of those life evolution experiments worked and created a second Source, sex might be on the cards.

However, getting back to the plot, The Source was anxious that their experiments were conducted under the best possible conditions and would not tolerate interference from any outside influence. This showed a flaw in their approach, as far as I'm concerned, but- hey - what do I know? I'm not a Supreme Being; I'm just a writer. Far be it for me to say that I've ever created something from nothing.

Consequently, if any project was under threat from any contamination, or even any deviation from its anticipated course, it was terminated. Enter Kratol and Domr'k stage left. They were The Source's instrument of termination. It was their job to roam around the Universe tidying up all the failed projects. They were damn good at it. Their brief was not to destroy a planet wholesale, but to make it devoid of all life forms ready for the project to be started all over again. The Source was clear in its instructions to the two Braakl'gians. After all, it wouldn't do to go around blasting planets out of existence. That would upset the fine balance of the Universe, and would have an impact on all the other projects. All they had to do was make sure each failed project was cleansed and made devoid of all life, but only after the message had been sent, in case the life forms had any reason for being allowed to survive. Just wanting to live was never really a great defence, as the four planets that responded to those messages discovered.

Three days later the StarDestroyer Blagn'k entered a very close orbit around the planet Erith, its huge star-shaped hull casting a gargantuan shadow over the world below. The communications lock had pinpointed the exact location of Kratol's hologram, which had just finished delivering the message. Not only was the message very important, it was also very long. The sudden arrival of the huge craft did nothing more than arouse a passing interest in most of the more trendy worker-ant-like beings, but they shrugged the apparition off and continued with their daily chores. A few of them, however, did get a little excited about it and made up their minds to inform the Queen.

Domr'k announced the StarDestroyer's arrival to his commanding officer, 'We have arrived at Erith, Your Excellency.'

'Domr'k, your ability for stating the obvious never fails to impress me.'

'Why, thank you, Excellency.'

'Have we received any communication from the Eritheans?'

'Not yet, Excellency. Should we prepare to go down to the surface to meet them face to face?'

'I don't think that would be a good idea. Remember what happened on Gweelox 4.'

'Well, we did threaten to annihilate them, Your Excellency.'

'That's no excuse. We threaten to annihilate the inhabitants of all of the planets we visit, and we generally do annihilate them, but none of the others turned nasty on us. They just accepted it and let us get on with it. There's absolutely no reason to take things out on us. It's not our fault if they don't know how to evolve properly.'

'Quite so, Excellency.'

'No, if the inhabitants of this planet can't be bothered to listen to our message and respond to it, they deserve to be wiped out. I don't see why I should go over it all again with them. Why do you think we send the message ahead of us in the first place?'

'I don't know, Excellency.'

'That's what I like about you Domr'k. Your complete lack of any intelligence whatsoever. Prepare the De-populator Device. I shall be resting in my quarters if you need me. Don't disturb me until the device is ready for deployment unless you hear from anyone on the planet.'

'Yes Excellency,' Domr'k said as he prepared the De-populator Device for deployment. Not that there was much preparation involved. He merely had to flick a switch to turn it on. Then he had to wait whilst the device prepared itself for activation.

The De-populator Device worked on a very simple principle. Firstly, it would scan the planet and register all life forms and then it would analyse each one and isolate all of the requirements necessary for its existence, for example, what it ate, what it drank, what it breathed, etc. Then it would use the StarDestroyer's replicators to produce chemicals that would neutralise all of those requirements. These chemicals would then be deployed on the planet via light pulse carrier waves as digital information which would be received and decoded by each individual creature. Once decoded, the chemicals would act immediately, bringing every living organism on the planet to a swift and untimely demise. Neat, don't you think?

It's amazing! For three days the four-inch-tall humanoid figure, bathed in a purple glow, went about its task of explaining what was going to happen to life on Erith unless somebody came up with a jolly good reason for leaving the planet in peace. For three days the ant-like alien land dwellers dutifully ignored the hologram's very existence. They would walk round it rather than through it; but they were damned if they were going to listen to it. Then it stopped talking and fizzled out. That's when the ant-like land dwellers noticed it. The Queen summoned one of her workers who happened to be near to the hologram when it disappeared.

'What did you do to that light-being?' she demanded to know.

'Nothing, Your Majesty,' he replied quite honestly.

The Queen was quite ready to carry on with the interrogation when she was interrupted by one heck of a commotion at the entrance to the colony. Workers were running here, there and everywhere, excitedly shouting things like, 'It's here!' and 'It's back!' as they witnessed the arrival of the StarDestroyer Blagn'k, mistaking it for the great asteroid that had transported their ancestors to Erith all those centuries ago. All at once, the ant-like alien land dwellers discovered religion.

'It's the prophecy!' cried out one of the workers with the kind of enthusiasm that is expected when proclaiming the coming of anything described in a prophecy.

'What prophecy?' the Queen enquired, quite rightly, as there had never been any prophecies in their culture. The workers had always been too busy working to have the luxury of just sitting around wondering about the Universe and working out prophecies that may or may not come true. Still, just because there hadn't been a prophecy in the past, the workers didn't see why they couldn't have one now.

'The prophecy of the return of the asteroid!' cried a second worker with suitable gusto for the occasion.

'Who prophesied that?' asked the Queen.

'He did,' said the second worker, pointing at the first worker with his antennae, 'just now.'

'Well, that doesn't count. Prophecies have to be announced well before an event occurs; otherwise it wouldn't be a prophecy, would it?' the Queen retorted. She was feeling a little uneasy at the prospect of having her authority undermined.

'Who says?' came a voice from the crowd, which had come to a standstill by now.

The Queen was shifting about uncomfortably. She could see she was onto a loser, but she stuck with it. 'You can't have something happen and then say, "Oh, by the way, we knew all along that that was going to happen." Any fool could do that.'

'But you can't deny that the prophecy has happened,' said the first worker. 'Look at the sky above. There it is for all to see. The return of the asteroid.'

'Yes, I know it's there,' continued the Queen, 'but you didn't mention anything about a prophecy until after the asteroid had arrived. How do you account for that?' She knew she had them stumped with that one. The whole colony gazed skyward and racked their brains for the answer. This was a dangerous time for the Queen. None of them had ever stopped to think before. If they continued to go on like this, the next thing they'd want to do would be to form a government.

The Queen, unnerved by the sound of silence as the colony concentrated on the problem, tried to push home her advantage and said, 'Well?'

The first worker was struck with inspiration and held his head high to announce, 'We forgot to mention it before.'

'You forgot to mention it?' mused the Queen. 'You forgot to mention something as important as the prophecy of the return of the asteroid?'

'Yes, that's right. We forgot to mention it,' said the second worker.

This was met with great murmurs of approval from the other workers. The first worker was gaining in confidence now that his newly-found memory and religion started to kick in, and said, 'We've been working non-stop all our lives and we were always so busy it just slipped our minds. But, now the prophecy has come true, I declare today a holiday.'

The crowds of workers erupted into spontaneous applause and cheering at the prospect of having a holiday. Somewhere near the back of the throng, one worker turned to his neighbour and said, 'What the hell is a holiday?'

'Who cares?' came the reply. 'But we're having one.'

The Queen was right to be worried. Her subjects were starting to think as individuals for the very first time. The normal running of the colony ground to a halt as workers split up into groups to hear stories of the prophecy being told by self-appointed holy men. Some workers began to compose music and create elaborate sculptures as they discovered the Arts; however, they were grossly under-funded. Other small groups would sit around in circles and develop philosophies. One of the greater minds amongst them came up with the shatteringly simple philosophy that 'I think I am, therefore I might well be.' None of the others had a clue what he was going on about, so they declared him to be the greatest philosopher they had ever known.

I think it's probably time to put your mind at ease about the way in which the ant-like alien land dwellers arrived on Erith. I know you're wondering how these creatures managed to survive the impact of an asteroid hitting their home planet and also the endless trek across the stars clinging to the aforementioned chunk of rock for countless generations and, finally, how they came to be deposited on Erith itself. At this rate, if I keep explaining everything to you, there will be no mystery left in the Universe. Of course, I can't possibly know the exact details; I can only offer you a theory.

Have you ever been out in the garden on a summer's day, tip-toeing merrily through the tulips, when you come across a swarm of ants marching across the garden path? No? Well, you ought to get out more then! Those of us who have encountered this phenomenon will, invariably, try to kill all the little ants by crushing them underfoot. However, no matter how hard you put your foot down, when you lift it up again there are always one or two ants that you've missed. How, you may ask? Easy - they were hiding in the tread on the sole of your shoe and then came out when you lifted your foot. That is my simple theory. When the asteroid hit the ant-like alien land dwellers' home planet, a whole bunch of them hid amongst the cracks and crevices on the surface of the asteroid. Obviously, because of the force of the impact, they were probably winded and couldn't come out of hiding straight away and were trapped on the asteroid when it bounced back into space. Of course, the force of the impact would have meant that part of the home planet's surface, including lots of plants, would have stuck to the asteroid as well, thus ensuring a source of food for the hapless creatures kidnapped by the great rock. As for the reproduction processes required to maintain the population aboard the asteroid as it sped across the Universe - well, I don't think I need bore you with the details of that! The depositing of the ant-like alien land dwellers on the surface of Erith is also easily explained.

When the asteroid bounced off their planet, its trajectory was set, unwittingly, for a collision course with Erith. Had Erith been a planet much less endowed with water, the asteroid would probably have hit the surface and, because the last contact it had made with a planet had damaged the internal structure of the asteroid, it would have shattered into millions of pieces, killing all of its reluctant passengers. However, when it finally did hit Erith, it touched down in the sea, skimming along the surface like a World War II bouncing bomb, slowing down considerably as it journeyed on. When it reached the shore, all the ant-like alien land dwellers decided to get off the asteroid whilst the going was good. A wise decision, because, owing to the scarcity of land, it ended up rolling into the ocean on the other side and sank out of sight below the waves.

Life amongst the ant-like alien land dwellers had reached new levels of spiritual attainment. In the few hours since the prophecy, they had formulated a new society where the individual was more important than the whole, and they all revelled in their new-found freedom from the shackles of perpetual labour. There was joy and celebration wherever you looked and, for the first time ever, they were experiencing happiness.

Aboard the StarDestroyer Blagn'k, Domr'k hailed his commander on the communicator. 'It is ready, Excellency,' he announced.

'I'm on my way,' Kratol replied.

This was the bit that Kratol really enjoyed. This was the moment when he assumed the role of Saviour or Destroyer. If the inhabitants of the planet came up with a good reason for allowing themselves to live, he would graciously reprieve them from their fate. If however, as had actually happened every time heretofore, they had no good excuse for evolving wrongly, he would wipe them from existence and try not to smile whilst he was doing it. He strode along the corridor on his way to the bridge with all the dignity of a triumphant emperor marching into a recently conquered city, cursing his luck that there was no one around to see him. As he entered the bridge, Domr'k stood up and saluted as a mark of respect and Kratol ignored him. He marched up to the De-Populator Device and, with his finger hovering above the activator said, 'Any messages from the planet?'

'No, Excellency.'

Kratol smiled and stabbed his finger down on the activator.

The ant-like alien land dwellers below looked up as the light pulse wave carriers shot out in all directions from the mighty StarDestroyer/asteroid. The first worker was about to inform his fellow creatures of the prophecy of the strange lights from the asteroid, but was unable to impart this wondrous knowledge, because a split-second later he, and indeed the rest of all life on Erith, ceased to be. They no longer thought and they no longer were.

'Right,' said Kratol, 'plot a course to the next planet on the list.' And then he went back to his quarters for a well-earned rest.

CHAPTER THREE

The First Day of the Rest of Frogmorton Culpepper's Life Begins

Frogmorton Culpepper managed to wake up at the most annoying time known to man - one minute before his alarm clock was due to go off. It wouldn't have mattered if he had overslept by an hour, or even if he had woken up a couple of hours early - he could have coped with that, but that one minute deficit really made him cross. That single minute would have made all the difference to the outcome of his dream. A mere sixty seconds stood in the way of him climbing into the jacuzzi with the gorgeous, naked, Elaine Markham, the Head of Department's twenty-six-year-old, beautiful, single daughter. But wasn't that always the way with dreams? Didn't they always end just before the good bits? Either that or the good bits would slowly start to turn into bad bits. Like the time when he dreamt that he was swimming with Elaine, racing to the island in the middle of the lake, knowing that victory meant that she would do whatever he wanted her to and how, when the shore was in sight, he heard his mother calling him for help. She was drowning in another part of the lake. That dream had real promise. There he was, about to make love to the girl of his dreams whilst listening to his dreadful mother drowning in the background - true bliss, but it wasn't to be. His mother started to shout louder and louder until he could bear it no longer. He awoke with a start, realising that his mother really was calling out for help. She sounded quite distressed and so, half an hour later, sensing that it might be urgent, he went to investigate. The sound was coming from the bathroom. His heart sank as he entered the bathroom and there he was confronted by the sight of his naked mother wedged in the bath like some bloated elephant seal demanding that he should free her, and, with the help of a bottle of washing-up liquid and the A-frame from his garage, he did.

However, no amount of thought regarding the oddities of dreams was going to change the situation. Frogmorton was awake, and so he thought he might as well drag himself from under the duvet. He swung his legs out of bed and fished hopefully with his feet for his slippers, only to find that Chloe had already found them. 'Why can't she use a litter tray like any other cat,' he mused. He removed his foot from the damp and smelly slipper and hopped to the bathroom to take a shower.

He liked a hot shower first thing in the morning. Mind you, with thoughts of Elaine Markham lingering in the back of his mind, it might have been more appropriate for him to take a cold shower.

He had fallen in love with Elaine the moment she first walked into the university's Environmental Technology Laboratory some six months ago. She had all the things he was looking for in a woman - two arms, two legs, all her own teeth. He wasn't too fussy. But then, on top of all those basic requirements, she was gorgeous. He had spoken to her many times about his project, Project Earth. He had told her how he hoped one day to reverse the greenhouse effect and to plug the holes in the ozone layer. Every time he saw her he would try to impress her with his scientific know-how. He hoped that, one day, she might even take time to listen to him.

The sad fact was that, as far as Elaine Markham was concerned, Frogmorton Culpepper didn't exist and, if he did, he was probably that funny little laboratory assistant chap who swept up in the lab. Still, Frogmorton didn't allow any of these thoughts to dampen his enthusiasm. He knew that when the postman came and delivered his exam results and when the Dean gave him a research post in the Environmental Technology

Department, then he would stand a real chance with Elaine. He let his mind wander as he smothered shower gel all over his puny body. He imagined what it would be like conducting all those Earth-shattering environmental experiments with Elaine at his side offering assistance and the occasional kiss on the back of the neck. He lingered over the last thought for a little longer than he intended and couldn't help noticing that he was lathering up the shower gel on a certain part of his anatomy with much vigour and gusto. Just as he was about to complete his soap-frenzy the bathroom door was flung open and in marched his mother who flung down the toilet seat, flung up her nightie and deposited her carcass onto the aforementioned seat with an ear-splitting display of anal music in the form of a military fanfare.

'Mother!' Frogmorton protested. 'Do you mind? I'm in the shower.'

'What of it? Nnnngh!' she replied. 'You haven't - nnngh! got anything I haven't seen before.'

'That's not the point.'

'I've seen plenty in my time - and not just your father's. Randy old devil he was.' This she said to the accompaniment of the unfinished concerto for derriere and other wind instruments.

'Will you just hurry up and do what you've got to do and leave me in peace?' Frogmorton pleaded. 'I would like to take a shower without interruptions from you.'

'If you found a decent girl and got married, you wouldn't get interrupted by me.'

'I couldn't count on it.'

'It's not natural, a boy of your age - single.'

'Alright, Mum! I'll see what I can do. If you'll only vacate the bathroom and let me finish this shower.'

'I haven't finished yet. You'll just have to wait - nnnngh!'

Despite performing some very difficult orchestral pieces, Frogmorton's mother was unable to complete the first movement and, amidst a flurry of toilet tissue and thunderous applause from the cistern, she took her bow and left the room.

Isn't plumbing fascinating? Have you ever noticed that plumbing is, without exception, temperamental? The older the plumbing, the more grumpy it becomes. You can't even empty the sink without the pipes groaning about the task of carrying the used water down to the sewer. Also, no matter how hard it tries, it has great difficulty in mixing hot water with cold to provide running water that is a comfortable temperature for the human body to tolerate. Mixer taps, especially in older systems, can be a nightmare. Swilling your hands can take up to fifteen minutes just to get the mix right. Then, just as you manage to get the temperature exactly right, what happens? Yes, someone turns on a tap somewhere else in the house (or even somewhere else in the street with some systems) and all the balancing between hot and cold goes down the drain - you end up getting scalded. The same thing happens in the shower if someone flushes the toilet.

'Aaaaargh!' Frogmorton squealed with an enormous amount of passion as he leaped out of the boiling shower. He stepped onto a wet patch and felt his feet slide from underneath him. He let out another yell as he performed a double back somersault, ending up in an untidy heap on the floor. He lay there for a few moments, making sure that the room wouldn't attack him again, but then, before he could regain his composure, the bathroom door swung open again and his mother tossed in a hefty envelope which landed on his manhood in a far from friendly manner.

'Postman's been,' his mother informed him, and then she

turned and left the bathroom, leaving behind the lost chord in her wake.

This was it. This was what Frogmorton had been waiting for - his results. If they were good enough he could make a name for himself in the world of environmental technology. He would be taken seriously at last. Why, he might even receive government funding to continue his Project Earth on a larger scale. Good Lord! He could even envisage a Nobel Prize.

Frogmorton studied the envelope in great detail, turning it this way and that, the way most of us do when we receive mail, looking intensely at the outside of the envelope in the vain belief that this will somehow reveal the contents to us. After studying it this way for about ten minutes, Frogmorton realised that the only way he was going to be able to read the contents of the envelope was to open it, and so he did. For some strange reason, the ability for him to read and understand the English language disappeared. The text became blurred and indecipherable. Then he realised that water was dripping on to the paper from his body, dissolving the ink where it fell. He quickly grabbed a towel and dried himself off before continuing to read his mail. He read swiftly through the preamble and soon got to the important bit. Yes. There it was in black and white. He had passed. He now had a degree. He could put letters after his name. More importantly, he could now approach the Dean for a real job.

Frogmorton jumped to his feet excitedly and ran from the bathroom, frantically waving his piece of paper for all to see. He ran into the kitchen and announced in a loud voice, 'Look what I've got!'

Now, you must remember that our hero had dashed straight from the bathroom floor to the kitchen and, therefore, was as naked as the day he was born. His mother was noticeably unimpressed with the arrival of her naked son into the room. After all, didn't she herself admit to having seen plenty in her time? Unfortunately, Mrs Douglas from next door, who had come to partake of morning coffee with Frogmorton's mother, was not so well travelled and, despite having had six children, had never set eyes on the male reproductive organ in her life before. Consequently, Frogmorton's sudden arrival in the kitchen, shouting, 'Look what I've got!' came as something of a shock to the poor woman. Not realising that Frogmorton was referring to the piece of paper in his hand, Mrs Douglas took stock of Frogmorton's prowess, let out a shriek that would have made a banshee proud and fled hysterically from the house, not looking back once.

Frogmorton's mother looked on incredulously as Mrs Douglas ran into the road causing several vehicles to swerve dangerously and said, 'Hasn't that silly cow seen a letter before?'

'I've passed!' Frogmorton cried, unperturbed by the Mrs Douglas incident, but only because he had been so engrossed in his own good news that he hadn't even noticed her.

'Passed what?' his mother enquired.

'My exam.'

'What exam?'

'Mother!' Frogmorton said, feeling quite upset by her apparent lack of understanding of the entire issue. 'Don't you pay any attention to me at all? My Open University exam. I've passed it and now I've got a BA. Do you know what that means?'

'Bugger all?'

'It's a Bachelor of Arts degree!'

'I never knew you wanted to be an artist.'

'I don't.'

'Then why have you got a degree in Art?'

'I haven't got a degree in Art. I've got a degree in technology.'

'You just said you've got a Bachelor of Arts degree.'

'Yes that's right, but in technology.'

'I didn't know you could do painting.'

'I can't.'

'Well what sort of art is "technology" then?'

'It isn't any sort of "art" - it's a sort of "science"!'

If Frogmorton's mother wasn't confused up to this point, his last statement really did it for her. She furrowed her brow and thought long and hard before coming up with the following question, 'Why haven't you got a Bachelor of Science degree then?'

The moment had been lost. Frogmorton realised that no matter how much he explained the situation, his mother would never grasp the concept and, even if she did, she probably wouldn't even care.

'Never mind,' he said as he turned and headed back to the bathroom to get a towel to dry himself properly.

His mother called out after him, 'With a bum like that you shouldn't have much trouble finding yourself a wife. Your father had a bum like yours. Randy old sod, he was.'

Frogmorton went into the bathroom, picked up a towel and took it into his bedroom to dry himself off. What the hell was his mother going on about? Her words echoed around his head - 'With a bum like that you shouldn't have much trouble finding yourself a wife.' How on Earth would that help? He could just see it now. Him walking into the Environmental Technology Lab, sidling up to Elaine Markham and dropping his trousers so that she could appreciate the finer points of his posterior. Yes, very impressive. How could she resist?

It's not as if Frogmorton didn't want to get married. In fact, he quite relished the idea, not least because it would be an escape from his mother. It was not the sort of thing he ought to rush into, though. He had to make sure that the woman that he chose to spend the rest of his life with was the right one. What a ghastly mistake it would be if his wife turned out to be as bad as his mother. The more he thought about it, the more he was sure that Elaine Markham was the one. All he had to do now was convince her that he was the right one for her. That was going to be the hardest bit.

Frogmorton finished drying his important little places and tossed the wet towel into the washing basket, and then got dressed and went down for breakfast.

'Boiled eggs, this morning,' his mother informed him as he sat down at the breakfast table.

He was just about to reach for his spoon when his mother said, 'Hold on,' and then she picked up his egg spoon and proceeded to insert the handle of it into her ear.

'What are you doing?' Frogmorton asked in wonderment.

'I've got a bit of wax I need to shift,' she explained, digging deeper and deeper with the spoon handle.

Frogmorton got up from the table and began to brush his hair.

'Aren't you going to eat this egg?' his mother asked.

'I'm not feeling that hungry anymore.'

'I'll have it then,' his mother said. 'I'd hate to see it going to waste.'

'I thought you didn't like eggs.'

'Oh, I like eggs. Trouble is they give me wind.'

Frogmorton's mother removed the spoon handle from deep within her cranium, wiped it clean on her petticoat and then started to devour the egg.

'Have you seen Chloe this morning?' Frogmorton enquired.

'Yes,' his mother replied, spraying albumen and yolk across the table. 'She was in here earlier with a dead thing. I put it in the microwave for her.'

When his mother mentioned the microwave, it reminded him of the incident the previous night, when he imagined he had seen a tiny purple alien creature in there.

'Really?' Frogmorton said. 'Did you notice anything odd

about it?'

'About what? Chloe, the dead thing or the microwave?'

'The microwave.'

'Not that I know of,' said Frogmorton's mother. 'Should I have?'

'You didn't notice anything inside it?'

'Only the dead thing and I put that there. What's this all leading to?'

'Probably nothing. Only last night I could have sworn that I saw something purple in there.'

'You ought to clean it out more often.'

Sensing that the conversation was going nowhere, the usual route it took when his mother was involved, Frogmorton said no more and left for work, making sure that he had his exam results with him.

CHAPTER FOUR
A Message to Muridae

Far away in the vastness of space, the mighty StarDestroyer Blagn'k continued on its relentless mission to tidy up the Universe. Secretly, Admiral Kratol seriously doubted whether The Source would ever get the experiment right. He hoped that they wouldn't. After all, if his masters ever did get it right, he would be out of a job - he and all the other StarDestroyer Admirals.

What's that? You thought that Kratol was the only one going around removing failed life forms from the Universe? For your information, and in case you missed it earlier in the story, space is big. Even at the incomprehensible speeds that the StarDestroyer Blagn'k reaches it could never span the Universe; after all, the Universe is even bigger than space. Kratol and his StarDestroyer are merely an infinitesimal part of the fleet that The Source employs. There are thousands of billions of StarDestroyers hurtling around the Cosmos laying waste to planets.

Kratol's doubts were probably well founded. The Source, despite being a Supreme Being and possessing all the knowledge in the Universe - except things occurring before the Medium-sized Pop AKA the Big Bang, of course - had, without exception, messed up every experiment they had ever conducted. No life form had ever evolved to the high plain upon which they existed. This was very annoying to them. If only they could find the missing link that would solve the one remaining mystery of the Universe and complete the last chapter in their vast book of knowledge.

These doubts were still nagging at Kratol when, over the

intercom, Domr'k's voice invaded his space, cutting into the silence of his quarters like a chainsaw through a blancmange.

'Excellency, we are ready to send the message.'

'Alright, Domr'k. I'm on my way.'

As Kratol strode onto the bridge he couldn't help noticing the pained expression on Domr'k's face and, fearing his underling might be ill, asked, 'Are you in pain, Domr'k?'

'No, Your Excellency,' came the honest reply.

'Then why are you screwing up your face in that ridiculous manner?'

'I was just thinking, Excellency.'

'Thinking?!' Kratol echoed, barely concealing the disbelief in his voice. 'Where does it state in your job description that you are required to think?'

'I didn't mean anything by it, Excellency.'

'Good, Domr'k. Don't do it again.'

'No, Your Excellency,' Domr'k replied with something that appeared to be a sulk in his voice and in his expression.

There followed a prolonged, uneasy silence. It was finally broken by Kratol.

'Alright,' he said, 'out with it.'

'Out with what, Your Excellency?'

'Whatever it was you were thinking about.'

'I don't know if I dare utter it, Excellency.' Domr'k felt somewhat uneasy about sharing his thoughts with his commanding officer.

'Well if you don't get it out of your system, I fear you will be unable to carry out your duties properly. So get on with it so that we can get down to work again.'

Domr'k felt his knees start to shake. He was very worried that Admiral Kratol might take what he had to say as a personal criticism and feared the consequences. Then again, he also feared the consequences if he didn't say anything, now that he had caused all this fuss and bother.

'It's about the message, Your Excellency,' Domr'k said at last.

'You haven't sent it off to the wrong planet again!' Kratol shouted.

'No Excellency, nothing like that.'

'Well, what is it then?' Kratol had very little patience and it was starting to show.

Domr'k cringed. He knew there was no going back now. 'It's just that I thought ...' he began.

'Thought what?'

'That, perhaps, the message was a little too long.'

'Too long?!' Kratol roared. He had always been under the impression that the message was too short. After all, it was a very important message. Probably the most important message that anyone could ever receive. He was furious with Domr'k for thinking such a thought. He did toy with the idea of vaporising the ungrateful SpaceTrooper (Fourth Class) there and then, but then realised that if he did, there would be nobody under his command to sweep up the remains.

As if sensing his superior officer's murderous intent, Domr'k tried to justify his statement. 'I'm not saying that it is not a great and noteworthy message, Your Excellency,' he blurted out in an effort to save the situation. 'I have never in all my life heard a more stirring and important message.'

'Quite so,' interrupted Kratol.

'But I fear, Excellency, that the recipient creatures cannot fully digest and interpret your noble intentions with enough time to spare to formulate a case for their defence.'

'What foundation is there for this belief?' Kratol demanded to know.

'The last planet we visited, Your Excellency.'

'Erith?'

'Yes, Excellency. Erith,' Domr'k said. 'I noticed that the message only cut out seconds before we arrived above the planet.'

'Your point being?'

'The inhabitants of that planet may have had a valid reason for not being wiped out.'

'Well, they should have presented their case to me then.'

'But, as I said, Excellency,' Domr'k continued, 'they did not have time.'

'So what do you suggest then? Should we leave them to evolve in their own misguided way, just because our message is so important that it doesn't finish until a split-second before we arrive to wipe them out?'

'Of course not, Excellency,' Domr'k said in his best grovelling voice, 'but don't you think that, perhaps, a shorter message, repeated several times might make as much of an impact and also give time for a response?'

'A response, you say?' Kratol said.

'Yes, Excellency, a response.'

'Do you know, Domr'k, you might be right. Goodness knows we've had very few, if any, responses in all the time we've been doing this job - apart from Gweelox 4, of course. Yes, a shorter message repeated several times. I'm glad I thought of that. Brilliant. No wonder I'm an Admiral and you're just a StarTrooper (Fourth Class).'

'Yes, Excellency,' said Domr'k, cursing his luck that he was a mere StarTrooper (Fourth Class) and Kratol was a StarFleet Admiral.

It was pure luck, after all, that decided what rank the two Braakl'gians were awarded. There were only two ranks in the Braakl'gian Space Navy with no prospects of promotion and, as neither of them required any particular qualifications, they were usually awarded on a 'first-come-first-served' basis.

Unfortunately for Domr'k, on the morning he was due to enrol his alarm clock failed to go off.

Aren't alarm clocks infuriating devices? Isn't it strange how we all hate them, but we've all got them? I wonder how people used to manage to get up in the morning when all they had to tell the time with was a sundial. And how on Earth could they tell the time at night? Mind you, we're all supposed to have internal clocks, aren't we? Something gifted to us by the Gods.

However, yet again, I digress. We were supposed to be exploring the realm of alarm clocks and why we are seemingly ruled by them. As I have briefly touched upon earlier, time is of great importance to the human race, despite the fact that it is merely of our own invention. The trouble is that when we originally invented time we didn't put enough hours in the day. Either that or the amount of hours we did need just wouldn't fit. I suppose we could have made the hours shorter to fit more in, but then they wouldn't really be hours any more, would they? Therefore, we had to devise a way of utilising the small amount of hours that we were able to stuff into a day (twenty-four as a rule). This is why we invented alarm clocks, to measure that precious commodity and enable us to get out of bed in the mornings with plenty of time to spare - if only we could remember to set the damn things, or if only we could resist using the snooze button, the worst feature we ever incorporated into alarm clocks and an absolutely excellent way to make oneself late.

Space Admiral Kratol wasted no time in recording his shorter message on the hologram projection unit. He found that he was able to put more dramatic bits in it, to drive home his main points more - well, dramatically. When he was done, he played back the hologram to see if anything needed changing, but the whole thing seemed so perfect he didn't want to change one word. He copied and pasted the whole thing many times to bring the overall message duration up to its previous length and, satisfied beyond any reasonable expectations, uploaded the new shorter version of his 'doomsday' speech onto the communications computer. He paged Domr'k on his communicator.

'I've uploaded the new, shorter message, Domr'k. Prepare to send it to the next planet on the list.'

'Yes, Excellency,' Domr'k said. He logged in to the communications computer and fed in the data for the next target, and then slowed the StarDestroyer down to below light speed in order to send the message on its way to Muridae, the next (fortunate?) planet on the StarDestroyer Blagn'k's itinerary.

By some strange quirk of fate, the four-inch-tall humanoid figure, bathed in a purple glow, appeared in the office of the High Commander (Space Defence Corps) on Muridae. The High Commander was busy with one of his aides and was reaching a very important stage in the intercourse he was having with her, when Kratol's hologram appeared on his desk a couple of inches away from the end of his nose. If you think I'm about to go into full pornographic detail here, I'm afraid you'll be disappointed. The intercourse I mentioned just now was social, not sexual.

Kratol's hologram said, 'This is a short, but very important message. We are on our way to wipe out all life on your planet. If you can come up with a pretty good reason why we shouldn't, please leave a message after the tone.....beep..... This is a short, but very important message. We are on our way to wipe out all life on your planet. If you can come up with a pretty good reason why we shouldn't, please leave a message after the tone.....beep..... This is a short, but very etc., etc., etc.' Well, he didn't really say 'etc., etc., etc.'; I put that bit in so that I didn't have to carry on writing the full text of his message for several days. It would have been very boring for you to read as well.

The High Commander was quick to react. His entire career had been spent waiting for the threat from outer space to come. His whole being had been geared up to respond to a possible alien invasion. He had been trained to deal with this situation with military precision and, with true military precision, he responded by messing his pants.

Kratol's hologram droned on and on. The High Commander watched in awe at the four-inch-tall humanoid figure bathed in a purple glow. He tried to touch it and pulled back in surprise as his hand passed right through it. He was about to say something to his aide, but realised she had fallen to the ground. He supposed she had fainted with the shock; the truth was that the smell from his nether regions had overpowered her.

The High Commander stabbed his finger at the intercom. 'Patch me through to the Space Defence Listening Post.' His voice was a little shaky; the smell was getting to him as well.

'Listening Post,' his intercom informed him.

'Are you getting this incoming message?' the High Commander bellowed.

'Incoming Message? No, sir. We're not picking up any radio signals at all.'

'I don't think this is a radio signal. It seems to be made up of light. Can you trace it?'

'I'll try, sir.'

'Good. And be quick about it. We're under attack.' The High Commander stabbed at the intercom again. 'Get me Space Defence Flight Control.' He was put through straight away.

'Flight Control.'

'Scramble the Elite Squadron. We have an incoming.'

Look, Martak! I'm not falling for that one again.'

'What are you talking about?'

'That old "scramble the Elite Squadron" gag. You had me going the last time, but I'm wise to you now.'

'Listen, you idiot! We are under attack. Now, scramble the Elite Squadron!'

'Who do you think you are? The High Commander?'

'That is exactly who I am. Now, unless you want to go on report for the rest of your natural days, SCRAMBLE THE ELITE SQUADRON!'

'So, you're the High Commander, are you?'

'Yes!'

'Martak, you don't even sound like the old fart. Now be a good fellow and stick your head up your ...' The sentence ended there, because at that precise moment Martak walked in to Flight Control.

'Up my what?' enquired the High Commander with real interest. There was no reply, because the embarrassed operative broke the intercom connection and pressed the button that activated the 'scramble' klaxon in the Elite Squadron ready room.

It took a few minutes for the sound of the klaxon to register with Squadron Leader Fligg. He had only ever heard it once before when it went off by accident following an overdue maintenance check shortly after he had first arrived at the Elite Squadron Base. He remembered asking about it then and, although he couldn't quite recall what it was for, he was sure it was probably important. After a while, mostly because the sound was beginning to irritate him, he decided to contact Flight Control to see what all the fuss was about.

'What's all the fuss about?' he asked Flight Control over the intercom.

'The High Commander has ordered a scramble. He says we're under attack.'

'Are you sure, Flight Control?' Squadron Leader Fligg queried. It seemed a reasonable question. After all, he had spent half of his life attached to the Elite Squadron and there had never been such an order before.

'Quite sure, sir,' came the reply from Flight Control.

'Ah, well! I suppose I'd better get the ships launched then,' said Fligg.

Fligg began to feel very excited. The only reason for the Elite Squadron to be scrambled was the threat of alien attack. Invaders from space. It seems that most intelligent civilisations in the Universe are worried about interstellar conflict, and the Muridaens refused to be an exception to that rule. They were as paranoid as the rest of us.

The Elite Squadron consisted of five Asteroid Class Deep Space Medium Armoured Interceptors piloted by the best of the Muridaen Space Defence Corps and, once the initial confusion was over, they scrambled and reached high static orbit above Muridae within five minutes, their long-range scanners set at five million km.

Back in the High Commander's office, his aide had started to regain consciousness and the High Commander began to regain his composure, helped mainly by a swift shower and change of uniform. Kratol's hologram droned on.

'What is it?' the aide asked, indicating the four-inch-tall humanoid figure, bathed in a purple glow, and almost fearing the answer.

'Something we've been dreading for a very long time. A message from some savage alien race who want to destroy our planet. An alien race that will stop at nothing. They'll burn our cities. Rape our women. Slaughter our babies. They are demons who will not be satisfied until Muridae is laid to waste and the ashes of our brave soldiers are scattered to the twelve winds. They won't be satisfied until our crops are rotting in the fields and our livestock are driven so insane that they will start to devour each other.' The High Commander felt very strongly about the situation.

'Is it serious then?' asked his aide who, although she worked for the Space Defence Corps, didn't really believe in aliens.

'Deadly serious. I've launched the Elite Squadron. They should be able to deal with the threat long before these aliens get close enough to Muridae to cause us any real problems.'

'Are you sure they'll be able to stop them?' the aide asked. It's funny how one's disbelief in aliens diminishes in direct proportion to the proximity of them to one's own planet.

'Well, that's the theory,' the High Commander said with less conviction in his voice than the aide wished to hear.

'Theory?' she said, losing confidence in a successful outcome by the second. Kratol's hologram droned on.

The High Commander listened to the message more intently, trying to formulate an alternative plan in the event that the Elite Squadron couldn't live up to their name and be elite. His eyes lit up slightly when he heard the bit in the message that said for the several-thousandth time, 'If you can come up with a pretty good reason why we shouldn't, please leave a message after the tone.'

'That's it!' he cried. 'I'll send them a message in return. I can avoid terrible carnage by communicating with them. Reasoning with them.' And then he pulled a High Command pencil from his drawer and started composing a reply to Kratol's message. A reply that would convince the alien aggressors to leave Muridae alone.

With this thought in mind, the High Commander opened his High Command notebook, placed the end of his High Command pencil in his High Command mouth and sat motionless with writer's block for several hours.

CHAPTER FIVE
Project Earth

Meanwhile back on Earth, Frogmorton Culpepper travelled to work at the Environmental Technology Department at the university with a very self-satisfied smirk on his face. At last he was somebody. A Bachelor of Arts in Technology, no less. There was absolutely no reason now why he couldn't be given a proper scientific job to do now, instead of cleaning up after everybody else. He had reached a watershed in his life and career. Not only was he newly qualified, but he was also ready to demonstrate his experiment, Project Earth, to the Head of Department. He couldn't see how he could fail to impress. That Nobel Prize was getting closer all the time.

Frogmorton couldn't wait to tell someone about his degree. He felt so elated that he must have been walking several inches above the pavement. When he reached the university he climbed the stairs to the Environmental Technology Laboratory at least three at a time, bounded along the corridor at a pace that would have demanded a drug test at the Olympics and hurtled through the door like he was a horizontal jack-in-the-box, the latter action with such force that he knocked the Head of Department flying on to the floor.

'Sorry!' Frogmorton proffered in a vain attempt to avoid his superior's wrath.

'Sorry?!' the Head of Department spluttered, trying hard to keep his cool under very trying circumstances.

'There's no need for you to apologise, Professor Markham. It really was all my fault,' Frogmorton said as he tried to help the Head of Department to his feet.

'Leave me alone,' Markham insisted. 'You'll only make

matters worse.'

'Don't shout at the man, Daddy,' said a voice from behind Frogmorton that almost made our hero throw up. It was Elaine. It was the girl who made Frogmorton quiver every time he thought of her, a strange habit, but harmless.

'Stay out of this, Elaine,' Markham growled sweetly to his daughter.

'You're always picking on Frogmorton, Daddy. It's not fair. And you make the poor dear nervous. It's no wonder he's always having accidents and knocking things over when you're around. You can be so intimidating.'

To be fair, Frogmorton was also always having accidents and knocking things over when Professor Markham wasn't around, but he wasn't about to point this fact out. He just couldn't believe what he was hearing. Was the love of his life really sticking up for him? Did she really refer to him by name? He didn't even know she knew his name. Things were certainly going well on this wonderful day. Nothing could possibly go wrong. He knew Project Earth was going to be successful. He knew that he would be offered that real job. He knew it was only a matter of time before he got that Nobel Prize. He knew that Elaine Markham was going to fall head over heels in love with him. What could possibly go wrong?

Markham looked at his daughter with a wry smile and said, 'Darling, I promise I'll never intimidate Frogmorton again.' And then, with the same smile forming a jolly frame around his slightly discoloured teeth, he turned to Frogmorton and said, 'You're fired!'

That is what could possibly go wrong. Frogmorton felt a lump come into his throat. He felt so humiliated. Especially in front of Elaine. All his hopes, dreams and aspirations had been shattered with those two simple words, 'You're fired!'

'But you can't fire me, Professor Markham,' Frogmorton

pleaded, 'not today of all days.'

'Just watch me,' Markham said, still not shaking off that smile, which was now in danger of making him look slightly manic.

'Daddy, don't be silly,' Elaine contributed to the debate. And to be fair, she had a good point. It was not an easy matter for anybody to be fired from a university's employ. Short of an employee having murdered the Vice-Chancellor in front of hundreds of witnesses and been convicted for it, there would need to be complaint procedures, written warnings, meetings, appeals etc. etc. etc. before anybody could actually be fired.

'Alright,' said Markham, 'I'm a fair man. I can be magnanimous. I can overlook past mistakes. If you can come up with a pretty good reason why I shouldn't fire you, I won't. And don't just say you need the job. That's not good enough.'

Frogmorton's eyes started to glaze over. How could he possibly come up with a good reason for the Head of Department not to fire him? He racked his brains. He couldn't think of a single reason, despite the fact that something was nagging him at the back of his mind. He looked at Elaine for inspiration. Her beauty was so awe-inspiring that he forgot what he was supposed to be thinking about.

'Well, have you thought of a reason for me not to fire you, Frogmorton?' goaded Markham.

Suddenly, Frogmorton remembered. It all came flooding back to him as his memory began to open the sluice gates of his mind. He recalled the scalding shower, his mother's impromptu concert in the bathroom and the look on Mrs Douglas's face as he ran into the kitchen stark naked brandishing his good news. There must have been a good reason for all that somewhere.

'I do have a good reason, Professor Markham. I've passed my Open University degree course,' Frogmorton said at last.

'Congratulations, Frogmorton,' said Elaine as she patted him on the back. He felt his face redden at the touch of her hand on his body.

'And I'm also ready to demonstrate my experiment,' Frogmorton continued.

'What experiment?' Markham asked.

'Project Earth. I had your permission to conduct it,' Frogmorton replied proudly.

Elaine smiled at him and said, 'Project Earth? That sounds intriguing. What's it all about?'

'I think I've solved the problem of the greenhouse effect and the depletion of the ozone layer. I've set up an experiment in an old fish tank and I'm ready to show that my theory works.' Frogmorton was so excited at sharing this information with Elaine, that he nearly wet himself.

'Ridiculous!' said Markham. 'How on Earth do you think you can solve such complex problems in an old fish tank? Why, the solution to those problems has evaded even the best-equipped scientific establishments in the world. Whoever gets to the bottom of it is guaranteed a Nobel Prize. I sincerely doubt that a laboratory assistant with an Open University degree is up to that sort of research.'

'I tell you I've solved the problem and I intend to show the Dean today.'

The Head of Department didn't like the thought of it. But, somehow, it could be true. After all, some famous discoveries from the past had been made through chance, like when Alexander Fleming found that a penicillium mould had accidentally contaminated a staphylococcus culture and stopped the bacteria's growth. That had given birth to antibiotics and also won Fleming a Nobel Prize. If Frogmorton really had discovered how to reverse the greenhouse effect and fix the hole in the ozone layer, he would take his place in history alongside the scientific giants - Newton, Einstein, and Oppenheimer. Markham's head began to swim with jealous thoughts. It just wasn't fair. Why should Frogmorton get the credit? He was only a janitor for goodness sake. The credit mustn't go to Frogmorton. At all costs the credit mustn't go to Frogmorton. Markham felt that he should be the one to receive the accolades of the scientific world. If Frogmorton was right and he really did have all the answers, Markham would have to get the credit. But how? He would have to devise a way to discourage Frogmorton and take over the experiment himself - after Frogmorton had done all the groundwork, of course. It shouldn't be too difficult. Frogmorton wasn't the brightest person that Markham knew.

The Head of Department turned to Frogmorton and, replacing his wry smile with a friendly one, said, 'Alright, Frogmorton. I'm willing to give you the chance to prove yourself. Set your experiment up and I'll have a look at it at two o'clock this afternoon.'

'Will you invite the Dean along, Professor Markham?' Frogmorton asked hopefully.

'No,' said Markham, 'let's wait until you've perfected it. We do want to make the right impression on the Dean, don't we?'

'Oh, Daddy,' remarked Elaine, 'you can be almost pleasant sometimes, when you put your mind to it,' and she kissed her father on the cheek. Frogmorton watched on in the vain hope that Elaine might favour him in the same manner, but instead she just left the room.

'Well, Frogmorton,' the Head of Department said, 'you'd better get off and prepare that experiment of yours.'

'Yes, of course, Professor Markham,' said Frogmorton, and he went off into the back room of the laboratory where he kept all his cleaning materials and his precious fish tank containing Project Earth.

When Frogmorton was out of sight, Markham jumped to his feet and rubbed his hands together in glee. Life was taking a turn for the better. Whatever happened, he was going to profit from

Frogmorton that day. If the experiment turned out to be a damp squib he would take the steps necessary to terminate Frogmorton's contract. If, on the other hand, the experiment was a success he would have to somehow sabotage the results and then temporarily terminate Project Earth, until a later date, possibly after he had terminated Frogmorton - and I'm not talking about merely his contract.

* * *

I imagine you are wondering about Project Earth. I know I would be if I were in your position. After all, Project Earth is what this story, or at least this chapter, is all about, isn't it? I am talking about Frogmorton's Project Earth at this point. Well, let's face it. We already know what The Source's Project Earth is. You don't? Well pay more attention, will you? Honestly, I don't know why I'm bothering to tell you this story if you're not going to take notice of the plot.

Alright! For the benefit of those of you didn't manage to pick it up from the storyline earlier on, The Source's Project Earth is us. Well, not only us, as in the human race, but us, as in the denizens of Planet Earth. Every living creature that ever was. Evolved from the simple one-celled organisms that were created by the Supreme Being (The Source) millions of years ago as some kind of evolutionary experiment. Frogmorton's Project Earth is an environmental experiment that he is conducting inside an old fish tank in order to solve the problems of the greenhouse effect and the depleted ozone layer.

I expect most of you are on the Head of Department's side on this one. Thinking that such a problem is far too complex for a laboratory assistant with an Open University degree to solve. Think again. In fact, if any of you had just taken the trouble to think about it, you might have been up for the Nobel Prize instead of Frogmorton. The answer to the double problem of greenhouse gases and ozone depletion is really quite simple and involves the use of a high-altitude aircraft, large sacks full of soot, iron filings and a powerful laser beam.

The idea came to Frogmorton when he was browsing Wikipedia one day and came across the word 'buckminsterfullerenes'. Well, isn't that the sort of word that would make you sit up and take notice? A buckminsterfullerene is a curious, perfectly spherical carbon molecule formed at very high temperatures that contains sixty carbon atoms, and when it encases a metal atom it becomes a superconductor. 'So what?' I hear you say. Well, by some strange coincidence, the next item that Frogmorton browsed was 'ozone' and he found out that it was formed when stable oxygen (O_2) is zapped with ultraviolet (UV) radiation or electrical discharge. This started Frogmorton's brain off on a thought frenzy. He asked himself the question, 'If ozone can be made by zapping oxygen with a high electrical discharge, why don't we just zap the ground with a great big laser cannon in order to warm up the air quickly and create a thunderstorm that would create an electrical discharge in the form of lightning?' Then he went on to wonder if he could use the oxygen tied up in the carbon dioxide which is causing the greenhouse effect in order to help restore the ozone layer whilst reducing the amount of greenhouse gas in the atmosphere. He reckoned he would need an immense electrical discharge for that, and thought that the buckminsterfullerenes encasing a metal atom would do the trick by providing a superconductor for the lightning. You've got to admit that the boy is a genius! However, there was a problem in as much that you can't just go to the local chemist and ask for a packet of buckminsterfullerenes. You had to make those yourself. So how would he go about doing that? Easy. Zap some soot and iron filings dropped from an aircraft with a great big laser cannon in order to form the buckminsterfullerenes encasing a metal atom. The force of the blast would also be sufficient to dislodge the carbon atom from the oxygen molecule in the carbon dioxide in the atmosphere, releasing plenty of oxygen for the lightning to turn into ozone. Of course, the carbon that was released would also react to the very high temperatures generated by the lightning, and these would react with the soot and iron filings to form even more buckminsterfullerenes encasing a metal atom and provide more superconductors to react with the lightning causing further chain reactions with the carbon dioxide, lightning, soot, etc.

So, the method was simple. Drop your soot and iron filings and zap them with your laser to start off the buckminsterfullerenes encasing a metal atom chain reaction, then shoot your laser at the ground to conjure up your thunderstorm to provide the lightning required to ensure the chain reaction continues. Perfect. All Frogmorton had to do then was set up a laboratory experiment to test his theory. Hence the fish tank.

In case you're wondering, buckminsterfullerenes got their name because they resembled the geodesic dome structures designed by US architect and engineer Richard Buckminster Fuller. Try and work that one into the conversation at the next cocktail party you attend, always taking care not to Spoonerise the second and third constituent parts of his name.

Tucked away in the back room of the Environmental Technology Laboratory, Frogmorton Culpepper felt very good indeed. Not least, because Elaine Markham had taken notice of him. That would have been fantastic in itself, but to actually get the opportunity to perform his experiment was the icing on the cake, and some piping, strawberries and silver cake-decorating balls to go on top of that. He busied himself with the preparations with so much enthusiasm that he failed to notice when someone came through the door behind him.

'I'm sorry about the way Daddy treated you just now.'

It was Elaine Markham. Frogmorton's body stiffened - some parts of it more than others.

'Elaine!' His heart began to pound out a samba beat.

'He really is quite sweet, most of the time. I know you probably don't think so; but he does seem quite keen about your Project Earth. Maybe that will help you to win him over.' Saying this, Elaine placed her hand warmly on Frogmorton's arm. His skin tingled beneath her touch. Things seemed to be going too quickly for Frogmorton to take it all in. Elaine had said more to him in the last sixty minutes than she had done over the last six months. Where would this mad, giddy, roller-coaster existence lead to?

'Do you think so?' he said, hoping that he wasn't blushing.

'Are you blushing, Frogmorton?' she said in a teasing manner.

'No. It's just a little warm in here, that's all,' he lied. He continued to prepare the experiment, very conscious of the fact that Elaine, someone who had hardly paid him any attention at all over the last six months, was watching every move he made with what he hoped was admiration.

CHAPTER SIX

The Muridaen Elite Squadron Strikes Back

Squadron Leader Fligg sat in the cockpit of his Asteroid Class Deep Space Medium Armoured Interceptor and strained his eyes as he scanned the depths of space ahead of him. Quite a futile gesture really, when you consider that his long-range scanners showed nothing on the screen, and they were set to detect incoming alien vessels at a range of five million km. However, no matter how pointless the gesture, it made Fligg feel as if he were carrying out his duties efficiently and that made him feel more at ease.

Fligg was the very best officer in the Space Defence Corps and, being commander of the Elite Squadron, that meant that he really was the elite of the Elite. No other officer had ever scored so high on the training simulators, both in astro-navigation and in space combat. The only regret he had was that he'd never tested out those simulator results in a real-time situation. But then no Space Defence Corps officer had ever had to employ the skills of astro-navigation or space combat in real life. Fligg just hoped that the simulator programmers hadn't made it easier than it would actually be. He was just re-enacting a particularly difficult simulated encounter in his mind when the intercom interrupted his train of thought. It was the High Commander.

'Fligg,' said the High Commander through the miracle of long-range communications technology, 'have you established any contact with the alien threat yet?'

'That is a negative response, sir,' replied Fligg in what he believed to be a suitably military manner in light of the current situation. 'Was that supposed to mean "no", Squadron Leader?'

'That's right, sir. We have no contact with the alien threat either visually or on our long-range scanners.'

'Well in future, Fligg, if you mean to say "no", why don't you just try saying, "no". I think you'll find it that much easier.' The High Commander was under a great deal of stress and, like so many other leaders, felt it most appropriate to take it out on those whom he led. 'Keep your wits about you and let me know the moment you do make contact.'

'That is an affirmative response, sir,' said Fligg, who strained his eyes yet again to see if he could see anything that his long-range scanners might have missed. After a few minutes peering out into the void, he decided to give his long-range scanners a kick, in case they were playing up. This turned out to be a bad mistake, because immediately after receiving the benefit of Fligg's heavy space boot, the long-range scanners sparked and fizzed and the screens went haywire. They suddenly acquired what seemed to be over a hundred targets moving in at great speed from a distance of about fifty km.

'Elite Squadron! Elite Squadron! We're under attack!' he screamed into the inter-ship communicator. 'Break formation and pick your own targets.'

As I have said, Fligg was the best. He hit the afterburner and had rolled his craft to manoeuvre himself behind the leading attacker even before he had finished shouting his order to the rest of the squadron. He immediately acquired a missile lock and sent off an image recognition missile. The enemy seemed to come from nowhere, but his quick thinking and lightning-fast reactions would save the day.

It had all happened so quickly that the missile found its target at precisely the same moment that Fligg's second-in-command shouted back over the communicator, 'Sir, stop your attack! You are firing on your own squadron! There is no enemy contact! I repeat. There is no enemy contact!'

'Oh! Sorry,' said Fligg as he broke off the attack and re-joined the formation.

The Elite Squadron now consisted of four Asteroid Class Deep Space Medium Armoured Interceptors piloted by the best of the Muridaen Space Defence Corps, and they maintained their static orbit above Muridae and waited for the alien invaders who were coming to destroy them.

* * *

Space Admiral Kratol's slumber was disturbed, yet again, by Domr'k's voice as it poured out of the intercom.

'Estimated acquired orbit around Muridae will be achieved in half of one hour,' the Space Trooper (Fourth Class) said to his superior officer.

'I'm on my way to the bridge,' said Kratol and, true to his word, he was.

It was about a quarter of a mile from Kratol's quarters to the bridge and so he used a little runabout to ferry himself backwards and forwards. In an effort to break the monotony of the journey, he would often drive a slalom course through the dozens of service droids he always encountered in the corridors. He wasn't terribly good at avoiding the little fellows and, invariably, he would run into two or three of them on the way, partially destroying them. He didn't worry too much about this, because the surviving service droids always picked up the pieces and repaired their fallen comrades.

The service droids fascinated Kratol. He had no idea how many of them there were on the ship, but he was awfully glad they were there. If anything went wrong with the StarDestroyer, he knew that they could be relied upon to put things right almost immediately a problem occurred. And with a ship the size of a city, the two crew members needed all the help they could get to keep it maintained properly in between services.

It's quite true that the StarDestroyer did not need to be quite as big as it was, and Domr'k had quite often remarked about this to Kratol. 'Why does the ship need to be this big when there are only the two of us aboard, Excellency?' he would say.

And, of course, Kratol knew the answer. 'To make us look important,' he would reply.

The truth of the matter was that Kratol had no idea why the ship was so big. But it really did make him feel important being the commander of such a huge vessel, and that made him feel very good indeed. In fact, Kratol was right. The reason that StarDestroyers were the size of a city was, primarily, to make them look important. After all, if they were going to go around the Universe threatening countless life forms with extinction, they could hardly expect to be taken seriously if they arrived in a two-seater space jalopy.

Kratol came to a halt in the main corridor, scraped off a couple of broken service droids from the front of his runabout and strode purposefully onto the bridge.

* * *

The High Commander sat back in his chair and examined the text of the message that he intended transmitting to the alien invaders, all the time keeping a watchful eye on Kratol's hologram as it continued its monotonous prophecy of doom. He flicked the switch on the intercom and asked his aide to step into his office. He thought he'd try it out on her first and see what she thought of it. He found it a very difficult message to write. He'd never had to do anything quite as important in his entire life before. If he'd got it wrong, the consequences would be final. When his aide entered, he asked her to take a seat.

'What I have to say to you is very important,' he said to her, wearing a grave expression on his face. 'We are faced with a deadly threat from an alien enemy. I have scrambled the Elite Squadron, and they are in readiness in a static orbit above the planet. We don't know the strength of the aliens or the seriousness of their intentions, but we do know that they want to give us the opportunity of communicating with them before they wipe us all out. I intend to make a representation to them in order that we may avoid annihilation. To that end, and in acknowledgement of the fact that the Elite Squadron is standing by, I have decided to transmit the following statement to the alien invader. I would appreciate your reaction to what I have to say.'

'Yes, sir.'

'Right. I'll read you the statement,' the High Commander said, clearing his throat in a vain attempt to make his statement sound more important. 'Alien Invader, this is a statement from the High Commander (Space Defence Corps) on Muridae. We are in receipt of your message informing us of your intentions for our planet and, quite frankly, we are singularly unimpressed. If you think that you can walk in here and take over our lives, you've got another think coming. We have space flight capabilities too, you know. And highly advanced weapons. We warn you now that we will not tolerate any threat to our planet, and will treat any contact between our civilisations as an act of aggression on your part, which will be dealt with accordingly. Do not underestimate the power of our forces. If you come too close to our planet we will destroy you.'

His aide didn't utter a word, but the High Commander waited for a response, hoping, perhaps that she would praise his hard work and bravery. After a brief moment, that seemed to last an eternity, she finally voiced her opinion.

'You imbecile!' she cried. 'You're going to get us all killed!'

'You didn't like it then?' the High Commander queried.

His aide rolled her eyes skyward in disbelief at the apparent lack of command of anything the High Commander possessed.

'Maybe you're right,' he continued. 'Maybe I am being a little too hasty. After all, their weapons are probably far superior to ours. They'll probably wipe us out in seconds. I'm glad of your input on this one. I might have made a big mistake by threatening them like that if you hadn't contributed to the debate in the way you did. I think a more subtle approach is called for.'

The High Commander flicked the switch on the intercom.

'Patch me through to Deep Space Communications,' the High Commander commanded.

The voice on the other end of the intercom said, 'Yes sir!' and executed the command that the High Commander had commanded in the hope of being commended.

When the link had been made, the High Commander proceeded to send his new 'subtle approach' type message to the alien invader.

He said, 'This is the High Commander (Space Defence Corps) on Muridae. We are in receipt of your message informing us of your intentions for our planet. In response to your obvious threat to our existence, I only have this to say,' he paused for greater effect and then wailed like a baby, 'I don't want to die. Please don't kill us! We surrender!'

Obviously, subtlety is in the eye of the beholder.

Squadron Leader Fligg was trying to decide how best to write up the unfortunate little incident involving the destruction of one of his own vessels in the space log. Shooting down part of your own squadron was always a tricky situation to deal with, not least because it seriously weakened the firepower of the squadron and, more importantly, involved masses of paperwork after the mission was over. The boffins who programmed the simulators had never come up with that situation in training either. Mind you, it was always better to be the one who had to fill out the paperwork rather than be the one who the paperwork was being filled out for. Nevertheless, that didn't make the task any easier. There was always a fuss made by relatives as well. They always seemed to think that it was a deliberate act of aggression when you vaporised one of your own ships with an image recognition missile. Anyone can make a mistake. Especially in a combat situation. And the High Command wouldn't hand out the rank of Squadron Leader to someone who couldn't handle killing a few of their own men in the course of duty either. It was a very responsible position. So much so that High Command usually allowed a Squadron Leader to kill at least a dozen of his own men during training before they even asked whether or not it was necessary. The men expected it too.

After considerable thought, though, Fligg decided he would write it up as a training exercise accident. That would look better on his record than 'I shot him down in cold blood after I had kicked seven bells out of my long-range scanner and acquired hundreds of false targets and panicked.' It had always worked for him in the past.

Fligg was just writing 'training exercise accident' in the space log when he heard the outgoing message from the High Commander in his headset.

'What?!' he cried in disbelief. 'Surrender?!' Fligg was very concerned. From the text of the message, it was obvious that the High Commander had cracked under the pressure. Space Defence Corps Directive 74(b) was quite clear about what action should be taken 'in the event that the High Commander had been killed, maimed, taken prisoner, gone insane or otherwise become unfit to carry out his/her duties'. It was up to him now to take complete control of the Elite Squadron. He had no further need to clear every order through Space Defence Corps High Command. The feeling of absolute power surged through his body. He liked the way it felt. There was no way that the Elite Squadron was going to surrender. The High Commander may have buckled under the pressure, but the Elite Squadron would see the job through to the end. The alien invader would not penetrate their defences and get through to destroy Muridae. Fligg addressed the other members of the Elite Squadron.

'Comrades,' he said, 'it is my sad duty to inform you that the High Commander has had to relinquish his authority, and now we alone stand in the way of the threat from the alien invader. We must prepare to lay down our lives in defence of our glorious planet, Muridae.'

'Oh, shit!' the words echoed through his headset from more than one of his fellow space pilots.

'Do not fear, comrades,' was his response to that outburst. 'We will overcome the odds. We will neutralise the enemy and counter any attack they mount.' Squadron Leader Fligg was the eternal optimist.

Fligg was just about to deliver a rousing speech to bolster the morale of his troops when the long-range scanners beeped to indicate they had picked up a target. The Squadron Leader glanced at the screen to visually confirm the bleep, but found that he didn't need to.

Because of the incredible speeds that the StarDestroyer Blagn'k was able to achieve, it arrived in orbit above Muridae at almost the same time that the Muridaen long-range scanners first picked it up. The vast size of the vessel seemed to invoke a strange chemical reaction in the stomachs of the Muridaens and they found themselves throwing up all over the place. Fligg, however, managed to keep his composure.

'This is it!' he screamed over the communicator. 'There only appears to be one ship. This is going to be a piece of cake.'

'A very bloody large piece of cake,' said one of the others in between stomach convulsions.

'Break formation and attack!' commanded Fligg.

There didn't really seem to be much reason for breaking formation, due to the overwhelming size of the target that presented itself before them. In fact, the target was so big they had absolutely no chance of missing it, even if they fired with their eyes closed.

Fligg let off a whole string of friend-or-foe missiles and pulled back to watch the enemy's destruction from a safe distance.

Down below on the surface of Muridae, the High Commander watched on in horror as he witnessed Fligg's onslaught on his monitor. What was going to happen to them all now? What did Fligg think he was playing at? Who gave him the order to attack? So many questions that he was afraid to answer. The alien invader was going to be really pissed off now. They would not look favourably on the High Commander's surrender whilst the Elite Squadron of the Space Defence Corps were conducting target practice on the mother ship. Then a new and more horrible thought struck the High Commander. What if this wasn't the mother ship? What if this was only a scout craft sent to test the planet's defences and report back the strength of the resistance it encountered. The High Commander didn't think that four Asteroid Class Deep Space Medium Armoured Interceptors piloted by the best of the Muridaen Space Defence Corps were going to make much of an impression. The more he thought about it, the more he wondered if the Muridaen government had really ever taken the threat of a possible invasion from outer space seriously. After all, five (now four) Asteroid Class Deep Space Medium Armoured Interceptors piloted by the best of the Muridaen Space Defence Corps wasn't much of a defence plan. And it did rather detract from the importance of the Elite Squadron, the fact that they were the only squadron. And it was rather short-sighted of the government to have the entire Space Defence Corps made up of only the Elite Squadron. The High Commander decided that when this was all over, he was going to write a strong letter to the government asking for more funds and resources.

* * *

On the StarDestroyer Blagn'k, StarFleet Admiral Kratol and StarTrooper (Fourth Class) Domr'k stood on the bridge preparing to activate the De-populator Device.

'Are you sure we have had no communication from Muridae, Domr'k?' Kratol asked.

'Well, we might have, Excellency,' Domr'k stated in a rather subdued tone.

'We might have!' spluttered Kratol. 'What in God's name is that supposed to mean? We have either received a communication from the Muridaens or we haven't. There's no "might have" about it. Please explain yourself.'

'Well, Excellency. A communication might have been received when I had to leave the bridge to attend to a call of nature.'

'You mean to tell me, Domr'k, that the Muridaens might have missed the chance of salvation from certain annihilation because you were too busy peeing on your boots to receive their message?'

'I couldn't wait, Excellency. I'd been hanging on to it for at least two light years. I had to go.'

'Oh, well, of course, your personal comfort must always come before the future of an entire civilisation. How selfish they must have been to wait until you'd excused yourself from the room before sending their message.'

'I did make sure the recorders were on-line before I went, though.'

'Oh good,' said Kratol. 'I'm so glad you eventually got round to sharing that piece of trivial information with me. Perhaps then, before I press this button and send them all into oblivion, you could play back the recording and see if we should spare them.'

'Yes, Your Excellency,' Domr'k said as he searched the communications folder for any incoming messages. After a few seconds he found it. 'Here it is, Excellency. The Muridaens did respond to the message we sent. I told you a shorter version would get more results.'

'Alright, Domr'k. Don't gloat; just play back the Muridaens' communication.'

Domr'k executed the order and the two Braakl'gians listened intently to what the High Commander (Space Defence Corps) had to say for himself. They were unimpressed.

'We surrender?!' mimicked Kratol in disbelief. 'Does this fool think we're at war with him? What possible reason would we have for declaring war? We have no quarrel with the Muridaens. We're just here to destroy them.'

'Well, Excellency,' explained Domr'k, 'in some cultures, the intent to destroy someone could be misconstrued as an act of war.'

'Them misconstruing our intentions is of no concern to us. And wanting to surrender is certainly no reason for us to spare the Muridaens. If they can't come up with something better than that, they're in a sorry state.' Having said that, Kratol raised his finger above the button on the De-populator Device. He looked at Domr'k with a satisfied smile on his face as he stabbed down his finger, but as he was about to press the button the ship shuddered as Fligg's friend-or-foe missiles struck home.

'Earthquake!' Domr'k shouted in mistaken confusion.

The force of the blast was enough to knock Kratol off balance, and instead of activating the De-populator Device, his finger hammered down on the button next to it.

'Shit!' said the StarFleet Admiral in a tone that worried Domr'k considerably.

'A direct hit!' cried Squadron Leader Fligg in a voice that conveyed his exhilaration accurately over the intercom and into the High Commander's office.

This news helped to snap the High Commander out of his self-pity and put him on a higher plane of thought. A state of optimism even. Fligg was winning. The alien invader might yet be defeated and sent home with its tail between its legs. And he, the High Commander, was solely responsible for the victory. He alone ordered the scrambling of the Elite Squadron. His determination and resolve was going to win the war and, perhaps, fame and fortune. He could see it all now. There he was, on the platform outside the palace receiving the Muridaen Exceptional Order of Bravery from the President herself. Garlands of flowers were being placed around his neck by beautiful women. The crowd was cheering and singing songs about the brave deeds that he had done, and he was just about to accept a gift of hundreds of huge cases of precious gems when Squadron Leader Fligg's voice boomed out over the intercom again.

'The alien ship is undamaged!' he cried.

* * *

'Excellency,' said Domr'k, 'what exactly do you mean by "shit"?'

'The movement of the ship knocked me off balance,' explained Kratol. 'I missed the De-populator button and hit the Destruction button.'

'Shit!' said Domr'k.

'You'd better set a course to a safe distance,' Kratol said a little uneasily. 'What idiot designed this ship so that the De-populator and Destruction buttons were so close together?'

Domr'k punched a set of coordinates into the navigation computer and the mighty StarDestroyer turned and headed off into space.

From his vantage point, the sudden shift in direction from the alien invaders' craft led Squadron Leader Fligg to believe that it was retreating. Maybe his friend-or-foe missiles had done the trick after all. They may not have compromised the integrity of the hull, but they may have caused damage to the interior of the ship. This idea filled Fligg with confidence. He had to decide whether to let the alien invaders retreat peacefully, or follow them and finish them off. There was really only one decision he could make. He had to finish the job he had started. If he let the alien invaders retreat, they could regroup and come back in numbers to attack. With only four Asteroid Class Deep Space Medium Armoured Interceptors piloted by the best of the Muridaen Space Defence Corps standing between the alien invaders and the planet, that was an option he was not prepared to take, and so he issued the command to pursue and destroy them.

The High Commander was overjoyed to hear that Fligg had caused the alien invader to retreat and was in hot pursuit of them. He turned to his aide to give her the good news. He was about to impart it to her when the Braakl'gian Destruction Device kicked in.

* * *

Fligg was the first one to spot the orange beam emanating from the star-shaped alien craft. He ordered the Elite Squadron to take evasive action, and all but one of the squadron managed to do so. The unlucky pilot was vaporised with his ship instantly, and the beam carried on towards Muridae.

The Elite Squadron now consisted of three Asteroid Class Deep Space Medium Armoured Interceptors piloted by the best of the Muridaen Space Defence Corps, and they continued in pursuit of the alien invader as it sped through the Cosmos and away from their home planet which disintegrated behind them as soon as the orange beam hit it.

CHAPTER SEVEN
A Reversal of Fortune

It was almost two o'clock and Frogmorton Culpepper was only a matter of seconds away from going down in the annals of history. Difficult though it was, he was able to put Elaine Markham out of his thoughts long enough to get the experiment ready. Project Earth was about to be tested properly for the first time. Frogmorton had conducted the experiment many times using computer models, and preliminary results had been quite encouraging. Now the time had come to turn theory into reality. If Project Earth was successful, it would be the most significant environmental technology breakthrough this century. He already had plans for expanding the project once he had proved its worthiness and received backing from the government. He wanted to extend the experiment to the atmosphere on Venus. Goodness knows, you couldn't get a bigger and better greenhouse effect than the one enjoyed on that planet. If it worked on Venus, we could probably set up colonies there. Imagine the benefits of being able to colonise another planet. It would solve another environmental problem for the Earth, that of overcrowding. At this rate Frogmorton Culpepper was in danger of solving all the problems that faced Planet Earth single-handedly, but he felt that he could live with that.

The hands of the clock on the wall of the Environmental Technology Laboratory decided to advance to two o'clock at the exact moment that the Head of Department walked through the door accompanied by his beautiful daughter Elaine.

'Well, Frogmorton,' he said, 'let's see what you've got to show us.'

Frogmorton got to his feet and walked over to his precious

fish tank. Pulling back the old tea towel that obscured the view, he announced dramatically, 'Welcome to Project Earth.'

He let the tea towel fall to the floor and awaited a response from the distinguished audience. There was silence.

After a few moments Markham, stifling his laughter, eventually said, 'Where is it?'

'What?'

'Project Earth.'

'It's here,' Frogmorton said, pointing pointedly at the fish tank.

Markham's scepticism could be well understood by the likes of you or me. We, perhaps, do not have the first idea about what a greenhouse effect and ozone depletion experiment should look like. But Frogmorton was a little put out by the Head of Department's seeming lack of comprehension.

'Where?' said Markham.

'In this fish tank,' Frogmorton replied, indicating the fish tank again in case Markham hadn't noticed it already.

Mind you, the fish tank didn't immediately jump out at you as though it were the hot bed of a ground-breaking environmental technology experiment. In fact, it just looked like an empty fish tank - apart from the four tiny fans strategically placed inside on the bottom facing upwards and several spark plugs arranged around the top of the tank and connected to a car battery.

'Let me explain,' said Frogmorton. 'This experiment, by its very nature, can only be conducted as a simulation of the real thing. I couldn't, of course, put a real cross section of our atmosphere into this tiny fish tank. All I can do is provide a close approximation to show the likely outcome if this process were repeated on a larger scale.'

'Yes, yes!' said Markham somewhat impatiently. 'We know all that; now get on with it.' He felt that perhaps he was wasting his time after all and that he should have got rid of Frogmorton earlier on when he had his chance.

Frogmorton continued, 'Now, I will show how we can reverse both the greenhouse effect and ozone layer depletion using the same process. In order to do this, I am going to be using some very simple things.'

The audience of two watched on as Frogmorton produced a bag of soot and some iron filings from a cupboard. Frogmorton turned on the fans in the bottom of the fish tank.

'Because the soot and iron filings will be released at high altitudes, these fans will simulate the length of time that the particles will be airborne, long enough for the process to take place.'

'What process?' interrupted Markham.

Frogmorton pulled back the cover from a laser that was positioned above the fish tank pointing down into it. 'I'm going to release the soot and iron filings into the fish tank, and then fire this laser beam at the particles suspended in the air by the fans, producing a quantity of buckminsterfullerenes enclosing a metal atom. These will act as superconductors which will intensify the electrical discharge from the spark plugs, which I am using to simulate lightning. The fish tank contains a large percentage of carbon dioxide which will react with the laser, lightning and superconductors, separating the carbon atoms from the oxygen molecules. The carbon molecules will form more buckminsterfullerenes, whilst the oxygen molecules will react with the lightning to make ozone. And that, in a nutshell, is Project Earth.'

Markham did not share Frogmorton's enthusiasm. 'You're quite mad,' he said. 'This ridiculous experiment is a waste of time and the university's resources. You had your chance to keep your job, Frogmorton, but this crazy scheme has only served to convince me that I was right to fire you this morning.'

'Daddy,' Elaine said, 'at least let Frogmorton demonstrate the thing before you dismiss it out of hand.'

'If he shoots off that laser in here, we'll be lucky to get out alive.'

'Don't be so dramatic, Daddy. This is the university's Environmental Technology Laboratory, not the latest set from some James Bond movie. Let Frogmorton do the experiment.'

'There really is no danger, Professor Markham. I've run extensive tests using computer models and I know it works,' Frogmorton added helpfully.

'You see, Daddy. There's nothing to worry about.'

Markham looked at his daughter and saw that she really believed there to be no danger and, with the thought of what he could achieve in the unlikely event that the experiment were successful, he decided to let Frogmorton proceed.

Frogmorton carefully introduced the soot and iron filings into the fish tank, making sure that none of it was blown back out by the fans and that there was only a minimal leakage of carbon dioxide. Once the soot and iron particles were floating freely, Frogmorton turned on the laser beam and then sent power to the spark plugs. The buckminsterfullerenes formed quickly around the iron atoms and reacted with the electrical discharges from the spark plugs.

Very gradually, the air inside the fish tank started turning pale blue as the ozone was being formed. The electrical discharges from the spark plugs began to grow in intensity, aided and abetted by the ever-increasing numbers of superconductors being produced. The spectacle was one to behold, but very soon it was clear that the chain reaction was getting out of hand. The experiment was working, up to a point, and this interested Markham greatly, particularly the tiny, sparkling objects that appeared to be falling out of the soot cloud. They were probably some form of pure carbon and that thought excited him. But, things were starting to look dangerous, and he had no option but to evacuate the laboratory. As they all got outside and closed the door behind them there was an explosion and the fish tank, unable to cope with the massive amounts of gas being produced, gave way to the inevitable.

'Not dangerous, you say?' Markham was enjoying Frogmorton's moment of humiliation. However, he had seen enough before he left the laboratory to realise that Frogmorton was really on to something. All that was left for him to do was to get rid of Frogmorton and iron out some of the problems. There were bound to be notes on the experiment; he just had to make sure that he didn't give Frogmorton time to pick them up on his way out.

'That never happened with the computer models,' Frogmorton pleaded. 'There must have been a variable in there that I hadn't provided for.'

'You're through, Frogmorton,' Markham said with great pleasure. 'You had your chance just now and you literally blew it. I should never have let you talk me into allowing you to proceed with this insane project. I should have thrown you out on your ear when I first had the chance this morning.'

'Daddy!' Elaine protested.

'And that's quite enough from you, young lady. I only gave this moron a chance for your sake. He let you down; so don't start trying to defend him.'

'But, Professor Markham,' Frogmorton started to say.

'Enough! Just get out of my sight. I'm terminating Project Earth. You're suspended immediately and I'll see you officially fired before you can say "buckminsterfullerenes". I want you off the campus immediately before I send for Security to take you away forcibly.'

Frogmorton was totally devastated. That was it. The end of what could have been a promising career. Humiliated in front of the girl he loved.

He couldn't understand how things had gone so terribly wrong. All the computer models worked a treat. Every one of them had ended in success. Frogmorton hung his head and left, completely dejected. Elaine went with him, but he was so downhearted that he didn't even notice.

Markham waited until they both disappeared out of sight and then went back into the laboratory. There wasn't too much of a mess to clear up. The explosion sounded much worse than it actually was. He started to cough as he breathed in the excess ozone hanging in the air, and started to look around the laboratory floor. He hoped he hadn't been seeing things earlier on. He hoped he would be able to find those tiny, sparkling objects that fell from the soot cloud. He got down on his hands and knees and sifted through the debris, being careful not to cut himself on the tiny slivers of glass everywhere. Then he found what he had been looking for, a very useful form of carbon indeed - a tiny, sparkling, beautiful diamond.

Frogmorton was still feeling despondent when he arrived home. Such a promising day had turned into a disaster, and he had no idea how he was ever going to make things right again. He could not believe that all the work he had put in on Project Earth was for nothing. He knew that he had the answers and today's experiment was merely a setback. All he had to do was check his computer models and find the variable that caused the explosion. He had not had time to retrieve his USB drives from the Environmental Technology Laboratory, because Markham had sent him packing without letting him collect his stuff together. He just hoped that he still had the backup files in his bedroom.

Frogmorton arrived home to be confronted by the sight of his mother sitting on the stairs, stripped to her bra, scraping large tufts of hair from her armpits with a blunt razor.

'What the hell are you doing?' he asked, quite understandably, of his mother.

'Taking pride in my appearance,' she replied, 'and if you did the same you'd have got yourself a wife by now.'

'Don't start all that again, Mother. I'm not in the mood.'

'Oh, "not in the mood", are you, eh? Where the hell do you think you'd be today if I'd told your father that I was "not in the mood"? I'll tell you. You wouldn't be here, would you? Mind you, your father was a randy old devil. Always after it. My ...'

Frogmorton interrupted his mother's sexual reminiscences before it got any worse for him to listen to. 'What are you doing sitting there like that?'

'Shaving under my arms. Doing a bit of personal hygiene,' she said whilst poking her little finger up her left nostril in order to retrieve something unsavoury.

'But why just there? You can see you straight through the front door.'

'Best bit of light in the house, just here,' she explained.

'But if the postman comes and sees you through the door, he'll have a bloody heart attack.'

'Well he should mind his own business then. Anyway, I'm not expecting any mail, are you?'

'That's not really the point, Mum. All I'm saying is that you ought to do that sort of thing in the bathroom.'

'It's really come to something when you can't do as you please in your own house!' Frogmorton's mother said, lifting the left cheek of her bottom in order to pronounce her own brand of exclamation mark. 'Anyway, what are you doing home so early?'

'I've been fired.'

'Fired? How are you going to support a wife with no job?'

'I'm not married, Mother.'

'It's just as well, isn't it? You'd really have let a wife down by losing your job. Goes to show that a fancy education does bugger all for you. Poncing about in here this morning, showing your credentials off in front of Mrs Douglas. Didn't do you any good at all, did it?'

'No, Mother.'

'And you're not going to get much of a job now that you're an artist. Not much call for Post-Impressionists down at the Job Centre these days, I'm told.'

'I'm not an artist, Mum; I'm a scientist.'

'Oh, that's alright then. I've heard that Sainsbury's are advertising for nuclear physicists to work on the fish counter. You'll be alright there,' she said, peeling off another strip of skin and hair with the dull blade.

'If anybody wants me, I'll be in my bedroom,' Frogmorton said. He had already suffered enough without all this abuse from his own mother.

As he disappeared upstairs, his mother shouted after him, 'Don't worry, Son. I'll get them all to form an orderly queue and I'll send them up in alphabetical order.'

Frogmorton slammed his bedroom door behind him, and his mother tore another strip off herself.

In the relative sanctuary of his bedroom Frogmorton began to go back over the events of the day in his mind. Everything had started off well enough. The exam results, the chat with Elaine and the experiment. Why had it all literally blown up in his face? The answer had to lie somewhere in his computer model experiments. He switched on his PC and, whilst the machine booted up, searched in his desk drawer for the USB drives he had backed up his simulations on. He didn't find the backup drives he was looking for, but he did find an old game he used to like playing. He installed Wing Commander II and spent the next couple of hours knocking seven bells out of the Kilrathi, an alien race descended from cats. He hadn't played it for quite a while, because it used to upset Chloe.

I have a theory about computer games. Especially those that simulate space combat. I believe that they are really designed by the government in order to prepare us for a possible invasion from outer space. It's a plot to get us all trained up in case the alien invader rears its ugly head. And isn't it funny how alien invaders always do have an ugly head? I reckon that our government is exactly the same as the one on Muridae. They're training us up to face the alien invader on a simulator, and then the best of us will be selected to join the Elite Squadron. But the joke is, they're not spending any money on the training programme - they're making us pay for it. We go out and buy all these space combat games and all the time we're training up to meet our Maker somewhere out in the void when our reflexes aren't quite as good as the Kilrathi. And don't let games like Mario and Pokémon fool you either. They're still getting us to manipulate strange looking creatures.

Frogmorton was still destroying Kilrathi ships when Chloe came through his bedroom window and jumped up onto the computer keyboard. She managed to kick in the afterburners on Frogmorton's spacecraft, sending it straight into the path of an oncoming Kilrathi fighter, destroying both ships in the process. The funeral of Frogmorton's character was quite moving as he watched the coffin drift off into space. Frogmorton looked at

Chloe. He was sure that she was a Kilrathi spy.

Chloe purred affectionately and rubbed her body against Frogmorton's skin. He knew she wanted feeding. She was never affectionate unless she wanted something. He picked her up and took her downstairs to the kitchen to see if he could find her any titbits in the fridge.

CHAPTER EIGHT

'Whump! There Goes Another Planet'

StarFleet Admiral Kratol was not used to having his StarDestroyer fired upon. He was very cross with the Muridaens. As he watched their planet disintegrate in the rear viewing screen, he was not entirely sorry. The cheek of it all. Firstly, the Muridaens accuse him of being at war with them just because he intended to destroy them, and then, to top it all, they have the audacity to shoot at him. It was certainly not in his job description to be a target.

He looked back at the empty space that used to be the planet Muridae and said, 'Serves you right!'

'What have we done, Excellency?' Domr'k asked, displaying a degree of fear in his voice.

'We've taught the Muridaens a valuable lesson, Domr'k;' Kratol said, 'that's what we've done. We can't have them thinking they can shoot at us just because they don't like what we were going to do to them.'

'But we've destroyed their planet, Excellency,' Domr'k remarked.

'Yes, well. I don't suppose they'll be needing it now. I shouldn't concern yourself on that score. I don't think the Muridaens will be worrying us anymore.'

'It's not the Muridaens I'm worried about, Excellency. What's going to happen to us when The Source finds out we've destroyed a planet? That will upset the balance of the whole Universe.'

'We'll have to make sure they don't find out then. What they don't know about can't hurt them.'

'But they're bound to find out. A whole planet blowing up is bound to attract some attention.'

'Yes, but no one needs to know that we were to blame.'

'We, Excellency?' Domr'k enquired. 'It was your finger that pressed the button.'

'Careful Domr'k, what you're saying almost amounts to mutiny. And you know the penalty for mutiny.'

'It's not half as bad as the penalty for destroying a planet.'

'But nobody needs to know. Planets are being destroyed all the time. One misplaced comet or asteroid hurtling through the Cosmos and whump! There goes another planet.'

'That's accidental. It's pure chance whether or not a comet or asteroid hits a planet and destroys it. Muridae wasn't an accident.'

'Yes it was! I went to press the button on the De-populator Device, but when the Muridaens shot at us I was knocked over and hit the Destruction Device button by accident.'

'Well that might not count as accidental.'

'How can an accident not count as being accidental?'

'The Source are very strict about not upsetting the balance of the Universe, Excellency. You and I both know that the destruction of Muridae was an accident, but they might not see it that way. It would have been different if it had been caused by a comet or an asteroid or something.'

'Well if we don't tell them, they won't know any different. Goodness knows it would only be a matter of time before some heavenly body or other crashed in to the damned planet. We've just saved it the bother.'

'Alright, Excellency,' said Domr'k graciously, 'if you don't tell them I won't.'

'Good man!' Kratol said. 'Now, set course for the next planet.'

'Yes, Excellency,' was Domr'k's reply.

Kratol was just preparing to leave the bridge when Domr'k made an unfamiliar sound. The SpaceTrooper (Fourth Class) actually laughed.

'Have I said something amusing, Domr'k?' Kratol said a little self-consciously.

'No, Excellency,' Domr'k replied, stifling a smirk with some difficulty.

'What is so funny then?'

'It's the next planet we are to visit, Excellency.'

'Why should that amuse you?'

'I think that they may already be expecting us.'

'Why should you think that?'

'It's the Earth.'

Domr'k could not fight the laughter back any longer and, seeing the funny side of it too, Kratol joined in.

* * *

Squadron Leader Fligg and the other two remaining members of the Elite Squadron looked on in horror as their home-world disintegrated in front of their eyes. There would be no going back now. Going back would be pointless anyway, now that their planet wasn't there to go back to any more. The last communication they had with their own kind was when they heard the High Commander shout, 'We're winning' ecstatically over the intercom a split second before the end. At least he went out on a high note.

Fligg called his pilots into close formation. He was determined that the alien invaders would pay the price for what they had done. If it took until eternity, Fligg and his Elite Squadron were going to track down the home planet of the alien invader and subject it to the same fate that befell Muridae. He would have his revenge. He knew that the alien invaders' ship was able to reach speeds beyond the capabilities of an Asteroid Class Deep Space Medium Armoured Interceptor piloted by the best of the Muridaen Space Defence Corps, so he decided that the only course of action open to him was to fire tractor beams at the alien invaders' ship and follow it through space like a trio of water skiers. He just hoped that the tractor beams would hold out long enough.

'Elite Squadron,' Fligg announced over the communicator, 'prepare to fire tractor beams at the alien invaders' ship.'

'Sir,' a worried voice replied, 'the three of us will never be able to pull a ship of that size in.'

'We're not going to pull her in,' Fligg said, 'she is going to pull us in.'

'What's your plan, sir?' the other Muridaen pilot enquired.

'We're going to get her to tow us through space to the alien invaders' home planet.'

'And then, sir?'

'And then we're going to blow the crap out of that planet, the way they did to ours.'

The two other Elite Squadron members cheered their commander, and locked on to the mighty StarDestroyer with their tractor beams. Moments later they found themselves hurtling through space at speeds they would have preferred not to experience.

* * *

Kratol and Domr'k were still chuckling to themselves about heading off into space to destroy all life on the planet Earth when Domr'k noticed that the mighty StarDestroyer was not responding to the set coordinates properly. There appeared to be a decimal point in the wrong place in their trajectory which could make them miss their target by several thousand miles.

'Excellency,' Domr'k said, the laughter in his voice had been replaced by concern, 'there appears to be a problem with the astro-navigation computer.'

'Are you sure?'

'Yes. The coordinates that I programmed in do not correspond to the present course. It looks like there's a decimal point in the wrong place in our trajectory.'

'That means that we could miss our target by several thousand miles,' said Kratol.

I can't help thinking that the two Braakl'gians have read my book.

'Yes, Excellency.'

'Can you compensate?'

'I can try, Excellency, but first I must run a systems diagnostic to see why the error has occurred.'

'Do you have any theories, Domr'k?'

'Well, the first thing that springs to mind is that the mass of the StarDestroyer Blagn'k has changed in some way.'

'What does that mean in layman's terms?'

'It means, Excellency, that I think either a bit of our spaceship has broken off or something has attached itself to us.'

'Well, check it out, Domr'k. We can't have bits of the ship dropping off. It's no longer under warranty.'

'Isn't that always the way?'

'Run your diagnostic and report to me when you've got a result. I'll be in my quarters,' Kratol said, and he left the bridge and climbed into the runabout he had parked outside. He drove to his quarters at breakneck speed, only managing to destroy one service droid in the process.

On the bridge Domr'k started the systems diagnostic. It was a very lengthy process and tied up the ship's computer ninety percent, the remaining ten percent being used to maintain life-support systems and critical repair tasks. Usually if something was wrong on board the StarDestroyer, Domr'k and Kratol wouldn't get to hear about it, because the service droids would track the problem down and fix it before it got too serious. That's why Domr'k had this theory about something happening on the outside of the ship, because if there was an external failure a repair has to be instigated by the crew, except in the case of a hull breach which is automatically sealed from within by the nearest service droid - provided it hasn't been sucked out into the endless void. Domr'k slowed the StarDestroyer to below light speed whilst the system diagnostic was running, partly to free up part of the mainframe and partly so as not to compound the error in their trajectory. All he could do now was wait.

* * *

When the StarDestroyer slowed down Fligg gave the order to disengage tractor beams and home in on the alien invaders' planet and take it out with their Armageddon missiles. The Elite Squadron pilots zig-zagged here, there and everywhere, checking their monitors and long-range scanners, looking for their target, but none was to be found.

'What are they playing at?' one of the pilots shouted over the communicator.

'Steady, Elite Squadron,' Fligg said reassuringly to his men, 'it must be around here somewhere. We'll just have to look a little bit harder. We might have missed it.'

'Missed it, sir?' a pilot said. 'How can we miss a planet?'

'I don't know,' came the reply. 'Maybe it's only a small planet. Look for it again.'

'But it doesn't show on the monitor or on the long-range scanner, sir.' This pilot was persistent and would probably have gone far in the Muridaen Space Defence Corps, if more of it now existed than just the three of them.

'Maybe the monitors and long-range scanners have been affected by the speeds we've just experienced. They weren't designed to take that sort of stress.'

'Well, I can't see any planet through the cockpit window either, sir,' said the persistent pilot. 'Maybe we weren't designed to take that sort of stress either.'

'It could be some sort of trap,' said the other pilot.

'Alright, Elite One,' Fligg said addressing the persistent pilot, 'you and I will maintain station here and keep an eye on the alien invaders' ship, whilst Elite Two makes another combat patrol of the immediate vicinity to see if he can locate the planet.'

'I'm on my way, sir,' said Elite Two, and the brave Muridaen pilot flew off in search of the elusive home-world of the alien invader, whilst Squadron Leader Fligg and Elite One kept guard over the mighty StarDestroyer Blagn'k.

* * *

Not long after Domr'k had slowed the ship down to below light speed, the error in the StarDestroyer's trajectory seemed to correct itself. It was as if whatever had fallen off the ship had reattached itself or whatever had attached itself to the ship had fallen off. Providing Domr'k's theory was correct, of course. However, Domr'k decided to wait until the diagnostic had finished, just in case the computer had a theory that was better than his. When the results came through Domr'k allowed himself a self-satisfied smile. The computer had agreed with him. The error in trajectory, it concluded, was caused by the StarDestroyer's mass being increased. It went on to state that the ship's mass had now returned to normal and that it was safe to proceed on the computed course. Domr'k informed Kratol of the results.

'Excellency, I have the system diagnostic result,' said Domr'k over the intercom.

Kratol got up from his bed, swearing that he would get rid of that lousy intercom one day.

'Good,' he said. 'Have you been able to resolve the problem?'

'I'm pleased to report, Excellency, that the problem appears to have resolved itself.'

'How come?'

'It would appear that when we left Muridae some debris attached itself to our hull causing an increase in the ship's mass, which had a critical effect on our trajectory.'

'And?'

'And now it's fallen off.'

'Fallen off?'

'Yes, Excellency.'

'Are we now in a fit condition to reach our target?'

'Yes, Excellency. I only await your order to punch in the coordinates for Earth again and we can resume the mission.'

'Then consider the order given.'

'Yes, Excellency,' said Domr'k and he punched in the coordinates and the mighty StarDestroyer resumed its mission.

* * *

Blissfully unaware of the fact that he was only thought of in terms of 'debris', Squadron Leader Fligg nearly missed the departure of the StarDestroyer. Had it not been for the eagle-eyes of the persistent pilot in Elite One, the Braakl'gian ship would have disappeared unnoticed and Fligg would have missed his opportunity for revenge. What with space being so big, it would have been practically impossible to track any ship through the void.

'The alien invader is leaving, sir,' said the persistent pilot. 'Should we lock on our tractor beams?'

'Affirmative, Elite One. Lock on tractor beam,' said Fligg decisively. 'Elite Two! Break off your mission and re-join the formation. Bring your tractor beam to bear on the alien invaders' ship.'

'Conforming, sir,' said Elite Two. And if he had responded a split second earlier, he might well have conformed. As it was, when the StarDestroyer turned on its hyperdrive Elite Two just happened to be in the wrong place and was vaporised by the blast from the StarDestroyer's engines.

The Elite Squadron now consisted of two Asteroid Class Deep Space Medium Armoured Interceptors piloted by the best of the Muridaen Space Defence Corps.

CHAPTER NINE
Rheingold

Gavin Woosner arrived at NASA's SETI installation at Ames Research Center near Palo Alto, California with a strong feeling that something was going to happen. Gavin had worked there for five years and every week, without fail, he would arrive at work with a strong feeling that something was going to happen - it never did. And in any case, the day something did happen he was so busy sneezing that he didn't even notice it.

In case you hadn't already guessed, NASA's SETI installation at Ames Research Center near Palo Alto, California was not dedicated to the study of Seti I, the son of Ramses I, and who was the second king in the Egyptian 19th dynasty whose tomb can be found at Thebes. I mean, what possible interest would all of that be to NASA? As you know, NASA's interests lay out there. The final frontier. That big stuff - space. What relevance is Egyptian history to space? Well actually, it might have quite a bit of relevance if you subscribe to the theory that the Great Pyramids are, in fact, giant astronomical observatories. (Incidentally, I do not use the word 'astronomical' in the previous sentence to indicate the size of the pyramids; I use it merely to indicate the function of the pyramids.) Or if you subscribe to the theory that the only way that those pyramids could have been built was through the help of visitors from the Cosmos. But no, NASA's SETI installation at Ames Research Center near Palo Alto, California had nothing at all to do with Egyptians ancient or modern (except for Yousaf Ben Nadir who was on attachment from Cairo University). The installation was there to search for extra-terrestrial intelligence.

Mankind has long pondered the question 'Are we alone in the

Universe?' It is with little wonder, therefore, that the human race has set up establishments to try and settle this far-reaching issue. The question of our uniqueness in the Universe is being tackled by the countless SETI programs in operation throughout the globe.

Many people believe that the Earth's history is peppered with examples of intervention by creatures from other worlds, but the modern era of space watching really began in 1947 with Kenneth Arnold's well-documented sighting of 'flying saucers'. This term quickly entered the vernacular, and hundreds of other people claimed sightings. That's when the search for intelligent alien life started in earnest.

NASA's SETI installation at Ames Research Center near Palo Alto, California began in 1992 and managed to operate for two years without the benefit of Gavin Woosner's help. Gavin came to NASA straight from Caltech, where he had been studying astrophysics and advanced origami. A strange combination, I know, but - hey - this was California. Gavin's prime reason for joining NASA was that he wanted to ride the space shuttle. He wanted to follow in the footsteps of all the great astronauts. He wanted to be out there, floating free, looking down on the planet we call home, seeing its smallness against the backdrop of the great void. Unfortunately for Gavin, his problem with asthma ensured that he would never go into orbit. Instead, he settled for the challenge of searching for new civilisations on far away worlds in distant galaxies.

Gavin sat at his desk and logged on to his terminal, and then sifted through the masses of data collected since his previous shift. There was so much to look at, but as usual so little to see. He often wondered if it was all worth it. What was the point scanning the heavens for signs of intelligence when there was so little of it in evidence in our own back yard? The SETI programme was being targeted in another round of cost-cutting exercises, and where was the intelligence in that? Okay, so we might be alone. There might not be any other intelligent beings in the whole of the Universe. In which case, cutting back on the SETI programme made good sense. But the truth was, we don't know for sure that we're alone and, if we're not, we certainly need to know. If alien intelligences were benign, there was much we could learn from each other. Sharing our knowledge of the Universe. Exploring our diverse cultures for the good of alien- and mankind. A coming together of vastly different civilisations with the sole purpose of enhancing our understanding of peace, beauty and serenity. And if, on the other hand, they were hostile, we could nuke the bastards!

The telephone rang on Gavin's desk and, believing it to be the best way of stopping it ringing, Gavin answered it.

'Hello,' he said, rather unimaginatively.

'Gavin, this is Mr Rheingold's secretary,' Mr Rheingold's secretary said. 'The Director would like to see you right away.' Then he, the secretary, rang off.

The Director, Mr Rheingold, only ever wanted to see people for two reasons. The first reason was to reward competent staff with a raise and/or promotion, and the second reason was to fire them. In the light of the current economic gloom that hung over the programme, Gavin was not expecting to be moved into a bigger office.

It took a matter of two minutes to reach the Director's office. If Mr Rheingold's secretary had wanted to, he could have just opened his door and called for Gavin, but he preferred to use the phone, because it seemed more professional. As Gavin entered the Director's inner sanctum, Mr Rheingold was on the phone, and so Gavin stood in the doorway until the call was completed - it was one of the longest half-hours that he had ever experienced.

Eventually Mr Rheingold cradled the telephone and indicated that Gavin should sit in the chair across the desk from him.

'Ah, there you are, Gary,' Mr Rheingold said, with more familiarity in his voice than Gavin felt comfortable with.

'Er - it's Gavin, Mr Rheingold.'

'What is?'

'My name, sir.'

'Yes, well I don't doubt it. Not if you say so.' Mr Rheingold paused for a moment with a blank expression on his face. 'So,' he continued, 'what did you want to see me about?'

'I didn't want to see you about anything, sir,' Gavin replied honestly.

'Well, what the hell are you wasting my time for? I'm a busy man, Garth.'

'You asked to see me, sir. And it's Gavin.'

'What is?'

'My name, sir.'

'Wanted to see you, eh?'

'Yes, sir.'

'What about?'

'I'm afraid I don't know, sir. But your secretary said you wanted to see me right away when he called me.'

'When was that?'

'About half an hour ago, sir'

'Well, if your idea of "right away" is half an hour, you've got a lot to learn, Kevin.'

'It's Gavin, sir.'

'What is?'

'My name, sir.'

'Right. Well I'm afraid I've got some bad news and some good news. Bad news is that we are about to be hit pretty severely by the latest round of government penny-pinching. Those goddamn sons-of-bitches always take it out on us. And do you know why? Because we're an easy target. Not tangible. Not sexy enough for those chowder heads on Capitol Hill. They just think that we're a bunch of computer nerds sitting on our cans doing sweet Fatty Arbuckle, whilst all the glory goes to those adolescent morons jockeying the space shuttle. They don't realise the significance of the work we do here. Christ, even I don't realise the significance of the work we do here, and I've been in charge of the goddamn programme for the past three years. And now, because of some knuckle-dragging politicians kicking up a stink about the decline in the economy and the impending recession, they tell me I've got to cut back. They ought to be voting me more money for our research. We should be expanding our program not shrinking it. What do you say to it all, Ian?'

'Gavin, sir.'

'What kind of a comment is that?'

'My name, sir.'

'Goddamit, Kenny, here I am telling you that I've got to fire you and you stand there with an identity crisis.'

'Fire me?'

'That's the bottom line.'

'But there are guys here who have put in less time than me. Shouldn't they go first, sir, in any cut-backs that take place?'

'Probably, Jerry. I don't know. I only run the place for Chrissakes. Look, someone's got to go. I ran all the names through the computer and picked one out at random - just like the lottery. You won the lottery.'

'I don't think much to the first prize.'

'I know it's a tough break, but - hey - you're a young guy. You're talented. You're gonna do alright for yourself out there,' said Mr Rheingold as he started to lead Gavin to the door.

'What was the good news?'

'The what?'

'The good news. You said you had some bad news and some good news.'

'Did I?'

'Yes, sir.'

'Well if I said it, it must be true. I wonder what it was.'

'You don't remember what it was?'

'No. Do you?'

'Hardly.'

'Well it must have been no news, and you know what they say?'

'What's that, sir?'

'No news is good news' Mr Rheingold found the funny side to that remark.

'When do I have to leave, sir?'

'The end of the week.'

Gavin left the office feeling rather depressed. It was not nice not being wanted or appreciated. If someone had to go, it ought to have been that idiot Rheingold.

Mr Rheingold opened the door Gavin had just shut behind him, and shouted after Gavin, 'Hey, Colin! I've remembered the good news now. If you can establish contact with an alien intelligence before the end of the week, we can keep you on.'

'It's Gavin!' Gavin shouted back. 'My goddamn name is Gavin!'

Mr Rheingold went back into his office mumbling, 'I've never known a guy so goddamn tetchy about his name.'

Kratol was getting increasingly fed up with the intercom - and Domr'k's voice. There was just one interruption after another on what was really supposed to be a straightforward leap across the Universe.

'What is it now?' he demanded.

'Our trajectory is wrong again, Excellency. We must have

picked up some more space debris, but I have instructed the astro-navigation computer to compensate for the discrepancy.'

'And you felt that you needed to disturb my rest to inform me that you have a problem but it is under control?'

'I thought you needed to know, Excellency.'

'Domr'k,' Kratol said, trying not to show too much anger, 'if the ship is about to enter an asteroid belt which threatens the very fabric of our being, I need to know. If we are under attack by some ungrateful species that has failed to evolve properly, I need to know. However, if everything is running as it should, either because of or in spite of your best efforts, I don't give a toss for the situation. Do I make myself quite clear?'

'Yes, Excellency.'

'Good.'

'Excellency,' Domr'k said after a brief pause.

'What?'

'It's time to send the message.'

'Slow us down to below light speed, I'm on my way.'

Kratol jumped into his runabout and scored a lucky seven droids on his way to the bridge.

* * *

Squadron Leader Fligg felt that this time more caution should be exercised. The alien invaders' mighty ship may be slowing down just to shake them off the trail again. He ordered Elite One to maintain tractor beam acquisition. He was not going to let the alien invader get away now. It was crucial that the alien invaders' home-world was found and destroyed to make amends for the injustice that had been dealt the planet Muridae.

The memory of his beautiful planet Muridae brought a lump to Squadron Leader Fligg's throat. He remembered the valley where he had grown up with its long, winding river and wild,

wild woods. The pool where he used to swim after school, where he promised himself he'd build a house when he was an adult. He could see the mountains and the seas as if it were only yesterday. Now they were all gone. Mind you, if it were only yesterday, they'd all still be there and the accursed alien invader would not yet have arrived. Deep within his memories Fligg thought he heard someone calling him, then realised that it was Elite One speaking in his headset.

'Elite One to Squadron Leader.'

'Go ahead, Elite One.'

'No sign of any planet on the scanners, sir.'

'I think they're trying to ditch us, Elite One. We're going to stick with them though, right until we get their home-world in our sights.'

'Do you think we'll be able to destroy their planet, sir?'

'We have our Armageddon missiles. Our most powerful weapon.'

'How many do we have, sir?'

'Two each. The Elite Squadron carries enough potential to destroy a planet. Didn't you pay attention to the recruitment video?'

'Yes, sir. But the Elite Squadron used to consist of five ships and ten Armageddon missiles; we now only have two ships and four Armageddon missiles.'

'Ah!'

'So now we'll only be able to destroy a bit of their planet.'

'Well that's better than not being able to destroy any of their planet.'

'I suppose so, sir.'

Fligg hadn't thought of that before. He had been so looking forward to getting his revenge, and now it was spoilt. What good was destroying a bit of their planet in retaliation for them destroying all of his? Whoever said revenge is sweet certainly must have had a full complement of Armageddon missiles or they didn't know what they were talking about. It just wasn't fair. There must be something he could do with four Armageddon missiles. They weren't exactly distress flares; they did have some poke.

In case you're wondering, Armageddon missiles were more than just guided bombs. Of course, they did contain vast quantities of explosive materials, or they wouldn't have been any fun, would they? The clever bit was the way in which they worked to bring about the destruction of a planet. Your normal bomb or missile only serves to cause damage to structures or life forms on the surface. Armageddon missiles carry powerful drills that penetrate deep down under the mantel of a planet releasing powerful sonic charges at regular intervals which create geological faults in the fabric of the planet. The drills keep going until they get to the planet's core, and then they deliver the final blow in the shape of a nuclear blast that sends the core material shooting out of the newly made faults, effectively turning the planet inside out. Computer models had shown that in order to destroy a whole planet between eight and ten Armageddon missiles needed to be deployed. Fligg had only four. He needed to come up with a way of deploying those four so that they produced the same effect as eight or ten. He put the problem to his tactical computer, but it was unable to help him, because it needed specific data from the target planet to predict the answer. This gave Fligg some encouragement. After all, the computer didn't dismiss the problem out of hand. All he needed to do now was to locate the alien invaders' home-world, feed the scanner data into the tactical computer and see what it could come up with.

CHAPTER TEN

So That's What Happened to the Dinosaurs

There was nothing in the fridge for Chloe, and Frogmorton noticed with some despair that there was nothing in there for him either. Chloe jumped from his arms and darted out of the cat flap and started to hunt for her supper. Frogmorton wished that he could do the same sometimes, but then he'd never really developed a taste for small rodents. As an alternative, he settled for going round to the local corner shop for something more palatable. But then again, if you've ever used any of the small corner shops that I have, you'll probably question whether or not Frogmorton will find anything there that is as tasty as a small rodent.

It was a short trip to the shops, but Frogmorton wished that he'd stayed at home. As soon as he entered the store he saw his mother talking to the shop assistant, a pleasant looking girl in her late-twenties.

'Talk of the devil,' Frogmorton's mother declared in a loud voice. 'I was just telling this young lady all about you, Son.'

The shop assistant tried to stifle a giggle.

'I told her what a gorgeous hunk you were and how you were still footloose and fancy free.' Frogmorton's mother turned to the shop assistant and leaned across to impart the next bit of information confidentially. 'He's just like his father, you know. A randy old devil he was. Couldn't keep anything in his trousers for more than five minutes.'

'You'll have to excuse my mother,' Frogmorton said to the shop assistant, 'she's not feeling herself.'

'No! And you wouldn't have to feel yourself much longer if you got yourself a decent woman. She could do that for you.'

'Mother! Do you have to?'

Frogmorton's mother confided to the shop assistant, 'Saw his tackle in the shower this morning. It'd bring tears to your eyes. He's going to make some girl very happy indeed.'

'Have you got what you came in for, Mother?'

'Yes.'

'Good. Now why don't you go home?'

'I don't know why you're so horrible to me. All I ever do is think of your happiness, and this is how you repay me.' Frogmorton's mother turned to the shop assistant and said, 'It's probably just as well he's not married. If he'll treat his mother like this, how would he treat his wife?' The shop assistant was clearly embarrassed, but that didn't deter Frogmorton's mother. 'Are you married?' she continued. 'A nice-looking girl like you could do a lot worse than my son here. He's still a virgin, you know.'

'Mother!' Frogmorton exclaimed, hoping that the ground would swallow him up right there and then. If he had thought about it, he would have realised that it would have been far better for everyone concerned if the ground had opened up and swallowed his mother. Mind you, it would probably have spat her right back out again.

'Alright, I'm going,' Frogmorton's mother said at last. 'I only came out to get something in for your supper, and you treat me like dirt.' She left the shop, drowning out the sound of the bell on the door as she broke wind.

'That was your mother?' the shop assistant asked Frogmorton, not quite believing what she had seen.

'Yes. A sweet old lady, isn't she?' Frogmorton said as he was leaving the shop.

'No wonder you're not married. Who'd want that as a mother-in-law?'

'Quite.' Frogmorton followed his mother home at a safe

distance. He wondered what she might have got him for his supper. He hoped it was bacon.

Frogmorton walked through the kitchen door at exactly the same moment that Chloe came back through the cat flap carrying her supper in her mouth. It was her favourite food - mouse. She laid it down on the floor by Frogmorton's feet, and sat there looking up at him with soulful eyes. 'Feed me,' they said. How could Frogmorton argue with that? With Chloe following behind in close procession, he picked the unfortunate rodent up by the tail and marched into the living room where they both homed in on Chloe's microwave.

* * *

Kratol insisted on supervising the transmission of the message ever since Domr'k stupidly sent it off to the wrong planet by mistake. Ironically, he was now supervising the transmission to the 'right' planet that was originally the 'wrong' planet. Isn't fate funny?

'Isn't fate funny?' Kratol said.

'In what way, Your Excellency?'

'Well, here we are transmitting the message to Earth, when only two planets ago we thought it was the wrong planet.'

'But Excellency, two planets ago it was the wrong planet.'

'Yes, but now it's the right planet. And that's funny. It makes it all worthwhile when you can have fun doing your job, don't you agree?'

'I wouldn't know, Excellency.'

'Believe me, Domr'k, it really does. Do you know, I don't remember it being this enjoyable on the last occasion we terminated Project Earth.'

'The last occasion, Excellency? I don't remember visiting Earth before.'

'Of course you do. It was one of our first jobs. Don't you remember? It was those giant lizard things with the funny long names - "Tyrannosauro-thingummy-jigs" and "Diplo-doo-dahs"'

'We've done so many; I can't remember them individually. Except Gweelox 4, of course.'

'I don't think we'll ever forget that one. It was a nasty business, wasn't it?'

'Yes, Excellency.'

'Right then, Domr'k. I think we're ready to send the message.'

'I was just wondering, Excellency.'

'About what, Domr'k?'

'It's the message.'

'What could be possibly wrong with it now? I can't shorten it any more or it wouldn't be worth sending it in the first place. Is it still too long?'

'Oh no, Excellency. I think the message is the perfect length.'

'So what is wrong with it then?'

'I just thought that maybe we ought to indicate how much time the inhabitants had to make their case.'

'I thought that was the idea for shortening the message.'

'Yes, Excellency. But still the recipients of the message do not know how long it will be between receiving the first message and when we arrive in our mighty StarDestroyer. If they had that information they might be able to think rationally about their response to our message. It might give them time to save their lives.'

'Do you know, Domr'k, I think you're turning soft. You're always trying to save these ridiculous creatures who refuse to evolve properly, aren't you?'

'No, Excellency.'

'Alright! I'll let the people of Earth know how long they've got, if it makes you happy. I'll just make the adjustment to the message and then you can send it - if you've got the heart to.'

That last verbal exchange between our two star-hopping Braakl'gians is quite an eye-opener, don't you think? It answers quite a huge question in the Earth's evolution. It has always been a matter of great speculation how, all of a sudden, dinosaurs became extinct. Was it some mysterious plague? Did an asteroid hit the Earth? Could there have been massive volcanic activity that threw clouds of dust up into the atmosphere, blocking out sunlight for many years? No. Now, at last, we know the truth. At the time of Kratol's last visit to Earth the dominant species was the dinosaur. They were endangering the project in some way and were dealt with accordingly. Now, I know that some purists among you are probably arguing that all life on Earth didn't die out with the extinction of dinosaurs, but if you'd been paying attention, you would have heard Kratol explaining that this was one of his first jobs. And, as we now all might know, in those days he wasn't required to eliminate all planetary life associated with a project, only the dominant species. Maybe that's why he didn't quite enjoy it so much in the early days.

* * *

Isn't fate funny? Not if your name is Gavin Woosner and fate is playing a nasty game with your career prospects. Out on the street with nothing to show for his university education - apart from a cleverly-folded paper rhinoceros on his bedside table. All he ever wanted to do in life was be a part of NASA. Sure, he would really have preferred to be a part of the space programme, but that didn't really matter too much. Well actually it did, but it was no good brooding about things that were out of his reach. Mr Rheingold's bombshell meant that Gavin would have to say goodbye to NASA. He would have to turn his back on his dream of making contact with intelligent alien life-forms, unless those intelligent alien life-forms made contact with him before the end of the week.

As a boy Gavin would sprawl out on the back lawn of his home late at night and look at the thousands of stars twinkling in the heavens and say to himself, 'Space is big.' Then he would imagine himself at the controls of a spaceship as it journeyed from star to star. He swore to himself that one day he would be out there as an astronaut, travelling to strange new worlds and encountering alien civilisations. But his wheezy chest put paid to any ambitions he had of becoming an astronaut. However, undeterred he had succeeded in joining NASA's SETI programme to try, at least, to fulfil part of his childhood dreams. Dreams, of course, are made to be shattered and if Gavin Woosner had been the sort of person to indulge in self-pity, he would be feeling very sorry for himself indeed now. Instead, he just sat at his desk, put his head in his hands and wept uncontrollably for fifteen minutes.

* * *

The dead mouse went hurtling through the air in a kind of macabre fly-past as Frogmorton reacted with shock to the apparition in Chloe's microwave. This time there was no mistaking it. Chloe showed her displeasure by arching her back, spitting over Frogmorton's foot and making a mad dash for it to the relative safety of the chimney, and within five seconds she had made it to the roof. That cat ought to be in the Olympics.

Frogmorton got down on all fours and peered into the microwave, staring open-mouthed at the four-inch-tall humanoid figure, bathed in a purple glow, that stood inside it. It appeared to be saying something, so he began to open the door to hear what it had to say. He only hoped that it wasn't another ploy to see if he'd been mis-sold payment protection insurance.

* * *

Gavin Woosner would probably have wept for at least another fifteen minutes if he hadn't have had the strong feeling that something was happening. He dried his eyes and glanced at his monitor. Yes, something was happening. He was picking up strong microwave activity, and it didn't originate anywhere on Planet Earth. 'That's marvellous!' he said to his monitor. 'You have to wait until I'm fired before you make contact. Why couldn't you have done this last week?' He was getting angry now. 'All these years you could have called me up and said "Hi!", but you have to wait until I'm history. I'm here cleaning my desk out and you decide to drop in for a little chat. Well it's too late. Didn't you hear Rheingold say to me that if you guys didn't phone up by the end of the week it's "goodbye NASA"? So, go ahead. Chatter all you like, but don't expect me to ....'

At this point, Gavin began to realise what was really happening. This was it - the big one. He checked the print-outs to verify the data on the monitor. It checked out. He tapped a few commands into the computer to establish the source and destination of the transmission. Facts and figures started to dance before his eyes as the computer went about its work. The first thing that it was able to establish was the transmission's destination - somewhere in England and finally, after what seemed like an eternity, it revealed the source of the transmission as being extra-terrestrial. Bingo!

* * *

Squadron Leader Fligg was right to exercise caution, for it seemed that no sooner had the mighty StarDestroyer slowed down to below light speed than it sped up again.

'See, Elite One,' he said triumphantly, 'I was right. They are trying to shake us off.' And in an act of supreme defiance he clung on to the alien invaders' ship like a piece of doggy-doo does to the sole of your shoe.

* * *

Frogmorton opened the door of the microwave oven very gingerly. It was an amazing sight. The tiny figure inside was not quite human; yet it was not quite anything else. He tried to touch the creature, but his hand passed right through it as though it wasn't there, and he thought, perhaps, that it was a ghost. Maybe Chloe's microwave was haunted, but that was a ridiculous idea. Almost as ridiculous as there being a four-inch-tall humanoid figure, bathed in a purple glow, in there warning him that all life on Earth was going to be terminated in three days.

Kratol's hologram said, 'This is a short, but very important message. We are on our way to wipe out all life on your planet. If you can come up with a pretty good reason, in the next three days, why we shouldn't, please leave a message after the tone.....beep..... This is a short, but very important message. We are on our way to wipe out all life on your planet. If you can come up with a pretty good reason, in the next three days, why we shouldn't, please leave a message after the tone.....beep..... This is a short, but very important message. We are on our way... etc., etc., etc.' (Much like those people who put up signs in shop windows that say things like 'BACK IN 20 MINUTES', Kratol hadn't allowed for the fact that his message would still be saying 'in the next three days' in two days' time, when it then ought to be saying at that point 'in one day's time', like the shop sign ought to be saying 'BACK IN 1 MINUTE' at which point the proprietor has been away for 19 minutes, whereas it still says 'BACK IN 20 MINUTES'. But no matter, at the time at which Frogmorton first heard the message it was still current in terms of its 'three days' information.)

'This must be some kind of joke,' Frogmorton said in a vain attempt to reassure himself. 'Mother!'

His mother sauntered into the room carrying a rasher of bacon in one hand and a brillo pad in the other. 'What is it?' she asked whilst wiping her nose with the back of the hand carrying the bacon.

'Have you been fooling about with Chloe's microwave?'

'I wouldn't mess about in there,' she said rubbing the piece of bacon with the brillo pad. 'It's not hygienic.'

'Well something's wrong with it. Come and have a look.'

Frogmorton's mother wrapped the brillo pad in the bacon and tossed it onto the sofa. She bent down to peer into the microwave. 'Ooh!' she exclaimed. 'Tuned it into Channel 5, have you? There's a clever boy then. Just like your father.'

'Mother,' Frogmorton said, 'this isn't the television; it's Chloe's microwave.'

'Yes, I know dear. I'm not completely stupid, you know. I can tell the difference between a microwave and a telly. Mind you, some of the rubbish they put on these days, we'd be better off watching the microwave.'

'But how did it get in there?'

'I don't know. Perhaps it leaked out of the telly and fell in there. You're the one with the fancy education. You work it out.'

'Well there are only two possibilities. Either it's a very clever and probably very technologically advanced joke, or …'

'Or what?'

'Or it's a very clever and probably very technologically advanced reality.'

'You mean that's a real man in the microwave?' She looked in at the hologram again. 'He isn't very big is he?'

'It's a hologram, Mother. It's not a real being. It's a sort of photograph, if you like.'

'I've never seen a photograph talking before.'

'No, it's more like a movie. That's it. A three-dimensional movie.'

'Does that mean we'll need those funny little red and green glasses? I think I've got a pair in the top drawer in the kitchen; I'll go and get them.'

'You don't need them. In fact, you won't be needing very much at all in the near future. Listen to what he's saying.'

Frogmorton's mother did listen, but, like a lot of people, she didn't hear. 'Bit of a boring script to this movie. He keeps saying the same thing over and over. Is it one of those modern arty films?'

'I think it's real. I don't think it's a movie at all.'

Frogmorton's mother was starting to lose interest. She retrieved the bacon-wrapped brillo pad and headed back to the kitchen. 'I suppose we'll have to put up with no end of this sort of rubbish now that you're an artist. Don't be all night in there. I'm just putting this bacon on for your supper after I've finished cleaning it.'

Frogmorton continued to watch Kratol's hologram and listened intently to its message. What was he going to do? He had to let somebody in authority know about this threat to the planet. He was deep in thought wondering where this threat was coming from when the doorbell made him jump. His surprise was compounded when he answered the door to find Elaine Markham standing on his doorstep.

'Hello,' she said. 'I hope you don't mind me calling on you unannounced, but I thought I owed you an apology for the way Daddy acted today.'

'Never mind that!' he said, grabbing her by the hand and leading her into the living room. 'I've got something I very much want you to see.'

Frogmorton's mother watched her son march Elaine swiftly away, and said to herself, 'Just like his father. Randy old devil, he was,' and then she ate the bacon sandwich she had prepared for Frogmorton, not noticing the bits of brillo pad that lodged between her teeth.

* * *

Gavin Woosner burst into Rheingold's office without bothering to knock, which was a bit of a shock for Rheingold as he was standing directly in front of the closed door before it was flung open, and was consequently sent hurtling forward by the impact and ended up spread-eagled across his desk.

'It's happening!' cried Gavin, barely able to contain his excitement.

Mr Rheingold was a little less enthusiastic and, spitting out paper clips and drawing pins as he spoke, said, 'What's happening?' without really caring about the reply.

'I've got a positive contact. We're getting a message from out there,' explained Gavin whilst indicating the direction from which the message was coming with a quivering right index finger, nearly inserting it into Rheingold's left nostril as he did so.

Rheingold, quite wisely, crossed to the other side of his desk and sat in his chair to avoid any further accidents that Gavin may, or may not, have planned for him.

'Now hold on,' Rheingold said with some scepticism, 'what are you trying to say here, Gerry?'

'Gavin!'

'Are you trying to tell me that, after all the years of fruitless searching of the Cosmos for signs of intelligent life, you are getting a message from out there?' Rheingold pointed his own quivering index finger in roughly the same direction that Gavin had selected, but steering clear of his own nose.

'Yes, sir! Loud and clear.'

'Call me a cynic if you want, Greg.'

'Gavin!'

'But don't you think it just a tad coincidental that you have heard zip from those guys all the time you've worked here, and all of a sudden, less than twenty minutes after being told you're canned, they think it's high time they gave you a call?'

'I know! It's a goddam miracle!'

'Well I call it more than a goddam miracle, Glenn.'

'Gavin!'

'What I call it is a pretty feeble attempt at keeping your job.'

'But, sir ...'

'Look, I know how you must feel. I know how you love this job. But you can't go around making up your own aliens to try and impress us.'

'I'm not making it up, sir. Come and check my computer readouts; they're going crazy.'

'Okay, Kenny.'

'GAVIN!'

'I'm ready to give you the benefit of the doubt. Maybe you have got a message out there from one of ET's buddies, but I gotta level with you, kid. Quite frankly I don't give a damn.'

'What?'

'Well, that's not strictly true. I will have to act on it, but probably not in the way that you imagine.' Rheingold reached into the top drawer of his desk and pulled out a folder.

'What are you talking about?'

'Who do you work for, son?'

'NASA - until the end of the week at any rate.'

'And what does NASA do?'

'Where's all this leading to?'

'Just bear with me and answer the question.'

'Well, here at Ames we listen out for extra-terrestrial signals.'

'A sideline, Kevin.'

'Gavin!'

'What does NASA really do?'

'Space exploration.'

'There! You hit the nail on the head.'

'So what's your point?'

'The point is that NASA exists to explore space. That's what we do. That's what we're good at. And one day we are not only going to be able to explore our own solar system, but we're also going to be able to reach out beyond that. Hell, we've already done it with the Voyager program back in the seventies. But what I'm really getting at is that we want men to do it. Not just men, but Americans.'

'So where does the SETI program fit in to all this?'

'It's a red herring, David.'

'Gavin.'

'SETI is purely there as a precaution.'

'A precaution?'

'Sure.'

'I don't follow you, sir.'

'What do you think would happen if we received a signal from some extra-terrestrial intelligence?'

'I don't like to push the point, sir, but we are receiving a signal ...'

'Okay. Let's say you're right, kid. What do we do next?'

'Inform the President?'

'Don't worry about the President. He's got far better things to worry about. What's our next course of action?'

'Try to communicate.'

'Right. But we don't.'

'What?'

'We don't communicate.'

'Why not?'

'Jeez, Lenny. Do I have to spell it out?'

'National security?'

'To hell with national security. We don't communicate,

because if we did they'd probably come over for a visit.'

'And you're worried that they might want to invade our planet?'

'To hell with the planet.'

Gavin was getting confused. 'So what is it that you're afraid of?' he enquired.

'If we communicated with extra-terrestrials it would bring about the collapse of NASA itself.'

'Huh?'

'NASA exists for the space program. We're pouring billions of dollars into it. If we acknowledge the existence of extra-terrestrials, it's bound to leak out. The press would go bananas for it. If the people thought that aliens would eventually wind up visiting us they'd start questioning the need for the space program. They'd say, "Why bother going out there to look for them, let the sonsabitches come here and look for us. It would save the tax payers a fortune." Now, if we don't tell them that the extra-terrestrials exist, NASA's future is guaranteed. That's why I'm going to have to put your readings down to equipment malfunction.'

'Equipment malfunction?'

'That's what I said.'

'But don't you realise the significance of it all?'

'Sure. If you're right and some alien intelligence is breathing heavy down your phone line, I've got a lot of paperwork to do. We've got to deny its very existence.'

'Even if you do hush my discovery up, there are dozens more SETI programs all over the world that are nothing to do with NASA. What happens when they let the cat out of the bag?'

'That's the beauty of being NASA, the world's foremost experts on space and things extra-terrestrial. If we say it don't exist - it don't exist. If we debunk these signals, no self-respecting space research facility is going to go against us.'

'But if these signals are genuine, I get my job back, right?'

'I wish that was the case, Casey.'

'Gavin!'

'But the fact of the matter is that you can't have your job back.'

'How come?'

'If the signals are just junk, you can't have your job, right? Because I told you that you had to receive a genuine message.'

'This is genuine, sir.'

'Okay. Let's say it is. I'll check it out in a minute. But even if it is what you say it is, I'm afraid the reality is that you still can't have your job back.'

'Why not?'

'Because if it is genuine, I'm going to have to say it's not. It's NASA policy to deny that incoming extra-terrestrial signals are genuine for the reasons I gave earlier, and if I gave you your job back, I'd be showing that I believe the signals are genuine and that would go against NASA policy. Do I make myself clear?'

'So I can't win. Is that what you're telling me?'

'Looks that way.'

'So what's the point? What good has all the time I've spent here done?'

'None. Shut the door on your way out. I'll be out to check your readouts when I've dug out the appropriate forms.' Rheingold fumbled through the papers that were in a folder on his desk.

Gavin left Rheingold's office feeling deflated. The breakthrough of the century turned out to be a damp squib. Well, not if Gavin Woosner had anything to do with it. He strode over to his desk and started sorting through the readouts. If Rheingold was going to hush all this up, it was up to him to shout it to the world. It was no good doing it here, though. He would have to find somewhere where he could voice his opinions. Somewhere that still valued freedom of speech. He tore off the readout that showed the signal's destination. That was it. He would go to England. He could speak freely there, even if they did all speak with a peculiar accent. (They all sounded like Dick Van Dyke in *Mary Poppins*, didn't they?) And he might just be able to discover what the extra-terrestrial message had to say. Gavin Woosner gathered together all the data he needed and put it in his briefcase, and left the office early. Five hours later he was on a flight to London, England.

It is a commonly held belief that air travel is one of the safest means of transport there is. You will probably have noticed that whenever anyone displays the slightest sign of nerves before taking a flight, that some bright spark always passes on that belief in order to try and calm their nerves. If this belief has any foundation whatsoever in reality, why do the airline staff devote so much time drilling you on what to do in case of an emergency? That sort of action tends to lead me to believe that the cabin crew have very little faith in that particular belief. I must say that I have travelled extensively on many forms of transport, such as taxis, buses and trains which, if air travel is the safest means of transport, present the traveller with a much greater risk to life and limb. Yet I cannot remember at any time receiving advice on what action to take in the event of having to ditch into the sea from a London cabby.

CHAPTER ELEVEN

Three Days to Save the World

Frogmorton led Elaine to Chloe's microwave, where Kratol's hologram tirelessly repeated its message.

'What is it?' Elaine quite reasonably asked.

'I'm not sure,' Frogmorton quite reasonably answered. 'It's been doing that for about fifteen minutes and it hasn't paused to catch a breath once.'

'It looks like some kind of holographic projection. But where's it coming from?'

'My mother thinks that it leaked out of the television.'

'This is crazy. It sounds like it's threatening to destroy the Earth.'

'As if we're not capable of doing that ourselves,' Frogmorton mused.

'We've got to do something about it.'

'I was trying to, before your father closed my project down.'

'I mean about this thing in here. If this is genuine we're in a whole heap of trouble.'

'I think it is real. I couldn't have rigged this up. This looks a lot more technologically advanced than we are right now.'

'I don't know. I know a couple of guys up at Cambridge that could manage something like this. But I don't see what would motivate them to transmit it to your microwave oven.'

Though it was hardly reasonable of him to feel that way, Frogmorton seemed a little put out that Elaine knew 'a couple of guys up at Cambridge' and he tried to draw the conversation away from them by saying, 'We've got to notify the authorities. This is too big for us to handle.'

'Yes but who do we notify? The police or the Ministry of Defence?'

'The police I think. They're more readily accessible, and if they think the ministry ought to be brought in on it, they'll get in touch with them.' The decision having been made, Frogmorton hurried to the telephone, lifted the receiver off the hook and dialled the emergency services. Something he had always wanted to do. He listened intently for the operator to ask him which service he required, but there was nothing.

'There's something the matter with the phone. It's dead,' he said, quite disappointed at not being able to make that emergency call.

Elaine said, 'Maybe the hologram is interfering with it. We'll have to go down to the police station and report it ourselves.'

'I'd better take the microwave. It's pretty convincing evidence,' said Frogmorton, and he unplugged the appliance and picked it up. Of course, Kratol's hologram stayed where it was in time and space. It was, after all, only an illusion that it was coming from inside the microwave oven. In fact, had the hologram been projected only a few feet away, it would have appeared to be emanating from an ornamental coalscuttle. In their haste to get the evidence to the police, Frogmorton and Elaine hadn't noticed that they had left the really important evidence behind on the carpet. When they got to the car, Elaine did remark on the absence of the purple glow inside the microwave, but Frogmorton put that down to the fact that he had been forced to unplug it, and assumed that it would return again when he plugged it in at the police station.

* * *

Once the message had been sent and the mighty StarDestroyer Blagn'k was forging its way through the endless void to deliver the final blow to whatever forms of life had evolved in a way which displeased The Source, life on board for StarFleet Admiral Kratol and SpaceTrooper (Fourth Class) Domr'k was a little tedious. For some strange reason, that probably only Albert Einstein could figure out, it always took three days from the time the message was sent to the time the StarDestroyer arrived at its destination, regardless of the distance travelled. It seemed that the ship's drive system always compensated for the distance to make sure it never took any longer or, indeed, that the journey was never any shorter. Consequently, there were a lot of three day periods for the Braakl'gians to fill. As there was nothing to do on the StarDestroyer as far as maintenance was concerned and the astro-navigation computer was continuing to correct for the change in the ship's mass by itself, the time was being spent pursuing leisure interests.

Kratol spent his time perfecting his driving techniques in his runabout, thereby making it a very busy time for the service droids and, potentially, a very dangerous time for the StarDestroyer. If some major problem developed and if, because of Kratol's improved driving skills, all the service droids were scattered in pieces or occupied repairing each other, the safety implications didn't bear thinking about.

Domr'k, on the other hand, spent his time in the pursuit of knowledge and greater understanding of the Cosmos. He used the mighty StarDestroyer's vast computer databases to learn about all the diversity of the Universe. He studied all the information that had been accumulated on the species that he and Kratol had wiped from existence and, indeed, all those that they were yet to destroy. Domr'k's heart was not in his work. After reading all about the struggle for evolution that had taken place for all those species that he had helped annihilate, he couldn't help feeling that what they were doing was wrong, but hey - it was a job and with inter-galactic unemployment running at an all-time high of twenty-five percent, he counted himself lucky to be one of the workers.

Domr'k was particularly affected by the information he was studying about the dominant species on Planet Earth - Homo Sapiens, not least, because they had evolved in a very similar way to Braakl'gians and, apart from some minor cosmetic differences, were quite similar in appearance. He had never studied very hard back home on Braakl'g, mainly because of a lack of time, but here on the StarDestroyer, time was one of his more abundant commodities. This habit of studying was leading to the more profound habit of thinking, and that could not be healthy for a SpaceTrooper (Fourth Class). Indeed, it had already led him to question his superior officer on more than one occasion, and if he was not careful, such behaviour might be considered as being a mutinous act. If he wanted to see retirement from the Braakl'gian Space Navy rather than sucking on the void after a preliminary court martial, he was going to have to watch what he said in future. Then again, he was beginning to doubt the validity of the job they were doing, and he just might not be able to help himself if he one day got pushed beyond the limits of his endurance. But that was a problem for another day.

* * *

Saffron Road Police Station was manned by a fine body of men and women - who were unfailing in their duty. Since its opening a matter of twelve months ago, their percentage of crimes solved was a staggering seventy-five percent. Or, to be more precise, three out of the four cases they had handled. Their success, I'm afraid, was not due to superior detecting skills, but more to the inferior quality of crime in this part of the country. However, let's not take away all the credit due to them. Even if they had only dealt with four real crimes, solving three of them was no mean achievement. Admittedly, a certain amount of luck had assisted them in arriving at the crime-solving rate they enjoyed. Like the time when PC Prime, whilst out on patrol, lost control of his squad car when he spilled a cup of coffee in his lap, and ended up running into an oncoming vehicle which just happened to have been stolen less than five minutes earlier. The owner was reunited with his car in less than an hour, but would probably have been a little bit more excited about the event, had his car not been a total write-off.

And then there was the time when the post office had been held up and the robber had inadvertently written the hold-up note on a piece of his personal headed notepaper. That helped the investigating officer wrap up the case in record time - after the cleaner pointed the headed notepaper out to him. Still, quite a lot of crime solving relies on a little bit of luck. However, it was hard work and persistence that led to the solving of the third crime.

Police staked out the neighbourhood in unmarked cars for three weeks. They noted the comings and goings of the main suspects until a pattern emerged. They isolated the culprit by process of elimination, and pounced in a well-coordinated raid that caught the guilty party in the act of perpetrating the crime. After they were through with him, they made sure that young Liam the paperboy would never steal another milk bottle off a doorstep again.

The only crime that remained unsolved was the disappearance of Sindy Cartwright, a model of dubious reputation who had last been seen three months earlier by the Assistant Commissioner, although it had never been made quite clear in what capacity he had made contact with her. He swore that it was in the line of duty, but witnesses at the time said that they did not realise that a black leather mini-dress, thigh-high PVC boots and a studded dog collar were standard issue for a male member of the police force - not even the plain clothes branch. At the main desk,

Sergeant Mills was dealing with a member of the press on that very point when Frogmorton and Elaine burst through the doors carrying the precious microwave.

'Quick! Where can I plug this in?' Frogmorton shouted at anyone who might be interested in helping him.

'Excuse me, sir,' protested Sergeant Mills, 'but you can't come in here and demand somewhere to plug your microwave oven in. This is a police station, not Joe's Cafe. And I don't think Joe would let you use your own microwave in any case. He much prefers his own frying pans.'

'You don't understand, Sergeant,' explained Frogmorton whilst frantically looking around for the elusive plug socket. 'This is a matter of life and death. I've got to plug this appliance in and you'll be able to see for yourself.'

'What are you talking about?' said a bemused Sergeant Mills.

Elaine decided to chip in with, 'Planet Earth is under threat.'

'I see, madam,' said Sergeant Mills feeling duty-bound to take control of the situation. 'And you feel sure, do you, that by plugging in your microwave oven in my police station that you will be able to avert this catastrophe?'

'Yes, she does!' exclaimed Frogmorton. 'Or at least she hopes you can.' Frogmorton finally found a socket and he plugged in the microwave. He and Elaine stooped down to peer into the appliance, but they saw nothing. They were soon joined by Sergeant Mills and the member of the press that had been interviewing him prior to the arrival of the microwave oven, Susan Likely.

'Waiting for it to warm up are we, sir?' asked Sergeant Mills.

'He's not there!' Frogmorton said, and he instinctively searched behind the oven to look for him.

'Who's not there, sir?' asked Sergeant Mills.

'There was a man in this microwave,' Frogmorton explained.

'Of course there was, sir. A bit on the small side, wasn't he?'

'Well, I'd say he was about four inches tall.'

'Any distinguishing features that you can remember, sir?'

'He was bathed in a purple glow and looked different to any man I've ever seen before. I think he was an alien.'

'What makes you think that, sir?'

'Because he was warning me that if I couldn't come up with a pretty good reason for stopping him, he was going to destroy all life on our planet in three days' time.'

'So,' said Sergeant Mills, 'let me get this straight. You're telling me that a four-inch purple alien has beamed into your microwave oven to tell you that the world is going to end in three days' time. Is that the sum and substance of it, sir?'

'Yes!'

'Well, actually,' said Elaine, 'the alien didn't beam down into the microwave oven and he's probably considerably bigger than four inches. What we saw was a holographic projection of the alien.'

'Oh, I'm sorry if I'm a bit confused about this,' said Sergeant Mills, enjoying the opportunity to put his advanced skills in sarcasm to good use, 'but we get so many people in here with aliens in their domestic appliances that I get them all mixed up. Is this your microwave oven, madam?'

'No, it's not hers,' said Frogmorton helpfully, 'it belongs to my cat.'

'I hope your cat has given you permission to take its property, sir. Otherwise you would be committing a statutory offence. We take a pretty dim view of people who commit statutory offences.'

'Look, I'm not here to discuss the rights and wrongs of removing the property of my own cat from my own house. Are you going to do something about this alien threat or not?'

'Look, sir, a joke's a joke, but I think this one has gone far enough. That microwave oven poses no threat that I can see, to the human race - apart from the muck they sell these days for you to cook in it. So, I suggest that you unplug it and take it back to your sweet little pussy cat before I lock you up for wasting valuable police time.'

'But I'm telling you, Sergeant, the threat is very real. You've got to take me seriously.' Even as he said it, Frogmorton realised that he was not going to be able to convince the policeman. It was, after all, a pretty wild claim. Especially as there was no sign of the alien concerned. Maybe it had fallen out in the car on the way over from his house, but he didn't think that even hard evidence would convince Sergeant Mills. He was one cynical copper. Resigned to the fact that they weren't going to get any help from the police, Frogmorton unplugged the microwave and led Elaine out to the car.

Just as they were about to drive off, Susan Likely, the reporter, came running up to their car from the police station.

'Hey!' she shouted, waving at them to further attract their attention - a manoeuvre that succeeded. She went up to Frogmorton's window, which he wound down to better facilitate a conversation. 'What the hell was all that about?' she asked.

Elaine said, 'Who are you?'

'Susan Likely from *The Chronicle*. I'm interested in your story.'

'Jump in,' Frogmorton said, which she did, thus ignoring all the advice her mother had given her on the dangers of accepting lifts from strangers.

* * *

'I don't think I can maintain tractor beam acquisition much longer,' announced the persistent pilot in Squadron Leader Fligg's headset.

'What seems to be the problem, Elite One?' Fligg seemed more than usually annoyed at the interruption. He had been enjoying a very pleasant deep sleep of the kind he hadn't enjoyed since he witnessed the destruction of his planet a matter of only a few days ago.

'I'm experiencing an intermittent variation in the flux grid, which is causing phasing of my tractor beam. I'm trying to compensate for this by re-routing non-essential power from other systems' grids and shutting down unnecessary background programs on the ship's computer.'

'That is very resourceful of you, Elite One. Thank you for sharing that with me.'

'I just hope that I can make it, Squadron Leader. Our ships were not designed to travel at these speeds. I don't know how much longer the infrastructure will be able to withstand the enormous stresses.'

'My infrastructure is coping perfectly well. Have you been servicing your ship correctly? Are you sure you've been following the correct procedures in your maintenance book?'

'Yes, sir.'

'Well make sure you do. You know the penalty for incorrect maintenance of Space Defence Corps Asteroid Class Deep Space Medium Armoured Interceptors. Loss of two months' pay.'

'Yes, sir.'

'Right. Now keep on top of your problem and let me know if there is any development.' Squadron Leader Fligg tried to slip back into his peaceful slumber, but the memory of how badly he used to maintain his own ship played heavily on his mind, and so he kept a wary, watchful eye on the readout of his own flux grid.

* * *

Susan Likely listened to Frogmorton's story intently on the journey from the police station to his house. Elaine had said that the hologram was probably still in the house where the microwave oven had been, and that's why they couldn't see it at

127

the police station. She was clever like that. Frogmorton screeched to a halt outside his house and, forgetting the microwave in the heat of the moment, took Elaine by one hand and Susan by the other, and quickly led them through the front door, past his mother and into the living room to where the microwave used to stand.

'By God!' his mother said as she witnessed her son dragging two willing females behind him. 'I was wrong. He's worse than his bloody father.'

Kratol's hologram was still there on the floor where they had left it, and it was still delivering its fateful message.

'How do you do that?' asked Susan, clearly impressed with what she was seeing.

'Do what?' Frogmorton asked in return.

'I've seen holograms done like that on the telly. You know, Star Trek and Babylon 5 and all that stuff. But how do you do it in here?'

'He's not doing it,' Elaine said. 'It just appeared here from nowhere and started churning out that message. Listen to what it's saying.'

Susan did listen to what it was saying and felt a little unnerved by it.

'Are you telling me that that thing's for real?'

'Yes,' said Frogmorton. 'And if we don't get someone in authority to do something in the next three days it will be too late to do anything.'

Susan started to believe. 'We've got to tell the police.'

Elaine was amused at that reaction. 'Where do you think we just came from?' she said.

'Oh, yes. I'd forgotten. The Sergeant wasn't too convinced, was he?'

'No,' said Frogmorton. 'And, thinking about it, it's not really surprising, is it? I mean, what kind of idiot would believe you if you told them about this.'

'I believe it,' said Susan.

'Yes,' Elaine said, 'but you've seen it. How can we convince somebody in authority to come and look at it? They'd give the same reaction the police sergeant did. They'd think we were having them on, or had too much to drink or something.'

'Can you help us Susan?' Frogmorton asked. 'Can you write about it in the paper? Somebody might take notice of us then.'

Elaine looked sceptical. 'They might just think we're UFO freaks or something. They'll just ignore it.'

'It's worth a try, though,' Frogmorton said. He looked at Susan hopefully. 'Will you be able to get it in the morning edition. Time isn't a thing we've got an excessive amount of.'

'I can try,' said Susan. 'I'll get a photograph of it. That's bound to get the editor interested. But I can't guarantee what form the article will take. I'll submit it for what it is, but the editor has the final say on how we slant the story.'

'Just get it in there. We'll worry about all the rest of it when it happens,' said Frogmorton.

Susan took more than a dozen pictures of Kratol's hologram and recorded his message on her digital voice recorder, and then left at breakneck speed to get the scoop back to the office. Frogmorton had kindly loaned her his car. As she was driving back to the office, Susan Likely knew that the story she was about to run would either earn her Journalist of the Year or one hell of a heap of ridicule.

Frogmorton and Elaine sat in complete silence for a while just staring at the hologram until Frogmorton finally said, 'I suppose I'd better ring for a taxi for you.'

'Are you kidding?' Elaine said. 'If you think I'm leaving now, you must be crazy.'

'I can't believe this is happening. A short while ago I was worried about saving the planet from greenhouse gases and the hole in the ozone layer. I never dreamed it would end like this.'

'Who says it's going to end?'

'He does,' said Frogmorton pointing at Kratol's image.

'But listen to him. He says if you can come up with a pretty good reason, we're safe.'

'Well I'm all out of "pretty good reasons" right now, I'm afraid,' Frogmorton said, displaying a certain amount of frustration and anger in his voice.

'Are you?' Elaine said and kissed him on the cheek.

Frogmorton looked at this beautiful woman sitting next to him and realised that she was "pretty good reason" enough.

It was raining in London when Gavin Woosner checked into his hotel. He realised that taking all the data he needed and some of the software from NASA's SETI installation at Ames Research Center near Palo Alto, California was not strictly legal, and decided it might be better if he registered under a different name in case anybody came looking for him. He didn't want anything to spoil his chances of confirming that the signal he had witnessed was the real thing. He decided on the name Gary Goldrhein, for some reason he wasn't himself clear on. Once inside the relative safety of his room, he unpacked his things and plugged in his laptop to analyse some of the data that he had brought with him, and placed his cleverly-folded paper rhinoceros on his bedside table. Gavin had no way of picking up the signal from his laptop unless he had access to a satellite dish, and so he made certain that the hotel received satellite television before he booked in. The desk clerk had told him that they did indeed have satellite television, but there seemed to be a problem with it at the moment, because there was a small amount of interference spoiling the reception. That interested Gavin. He was almost sure that he knew what was causing that interference, and wasted no time in hooking his laptop up to the satellite connection. Unfortunately, the signal that he was receiving was inconclusive, and he decided that he would have to realign the dish. There didn't seem to be any way of reaching the roof from inside the hotel, so it was clear that he would have to climb up to the satellite dish on the outside. He was glad he had booked a room on the top floor. Climbing up onto the roof, however, was a very sobering thought. Gavin had never been too keen on heights. His friends always used to tease him on that point, calling him 'yellow', because he was afraid of falling. Actually, he wasn't afraid of falling at all. It was landing on the ground afterwards that used to scare him silly.

He was just getting out of the window when there was a knock on his door and a waiter entered saying, 'A nightcap with the manager's compliments.' The waiter stopped in his tracks on seeing Gavin halfway out of the window.

'I'm - er - just popping out for a while,' Gavin explained.

His accent was enough to satisfy the waiter. 'Ah, you're an American,' he said, and he placed the drink on the bedside table next to the cleverly-folded paper rhinoceros, and left the room without further comment.

Outside the window the rain lashed against Gavin as he tried to make his way to the roof. There were a great many handholds on the outside wall of the hotel that he could use, which made the task of climbing to the top a little less daunting, and which made the burglar fraternity of London very grateful to the hotel's architect on more than one occasion during the year. Apart from a tricky moment when his foot slipped on something a pigeon had left behind, the climb to the top was uneventful. All that Gavin had to do now was realign the dish to the point in the night sky where the signal had originated from. His knowledge of astronomy made the task simple, but the inferior quality of the materials used in the construction of the satellite dish proved an obstacle. He could get the dish to tilt up and down easily enough, but try as he might, he couldn't budge it from side to side and that was a critical adjustment to make. Putting all his strength into the effort, Gavin finally felt the dish start to give, and then it gave way completely as it broke free of its housing and sent Gavin plummeting off the roof gripping tightly to the dish, hoping that it would, somehow, take on the form of a parachute and save him. Luckily, the cable attached to the dish was a lot stronger than the housing, and it stopped Gavin's downward momentum. He was left swinging from side to side, upside down on the outside wall of the hotel like some grotesque pendulum. The rain was further compounding Gavin's situation, driving into his face, and also making the dish slippery, putting him in danger of losing his grip and crashing to the ground. After a gargantuan struggle against the forces of nature and the force of gravity, Gavin managed to climb back through his bedroom window. He pulled the dish in behind him, and rigged it to the back of a chair that he had dragged to the window, using his entire supply of neckties to fasten it in place. He made final, minute adjustments to the angle of the dish until he was satisfied that he was locked on to the point in space where the extra-terrestrial signal was coming from, and a glance at his laptop computer confirmed that he had got it right. It was one hell of a strong signal. More to the point, it was constant, as if it were relaying a very long message or set of instructions. The very consistency of the signal ruled out the possibility that it was anything but genuine. Gavin's problem now was finding out what the message said. His readouts only confirmed the existence of a carrier wave. If he were going to try to communicate with this alien intelligence, he must first find out what they were trying to say. Gavin tapped a few keys on his computer and, with the marvels of modern technology and NASA's superior software at his fingertips, was able to pinpoint the precise location that the extra-terrestrial signal was being beamed at. He disconnected his laptop from the satellite, and left his hotel room in search of alien intelligence, and as he closed his bedroom door behind him the draught sent his cleverly-folded paper rhinoceros floating out of the open window and into the rain drenched night.

Back at NASA's SETI installation at Ames Research Center near Palo Alto, California, Mr Rheingold finally saw fit to look into Gavin Woosner's claim that he had made contact, and was a little put out when he found out that he had. Part of him wanted to jump up and down and tell the world that 'we are not alone', but the part of him that was committed to NASA's future told him to suppress it. The trouble was that suppressing it involved a hell of a lot of paperwork, especially as it wouldn't take long for other SETI programs to latch on to it if their dishes were pointing at the same bit of sky that NASA's were. Rheingold asked his secretary to send Woosner in so that he could verify the dish alignment.

'Mr Woosner left,' he informed him.

'Left? He's not due to leave until the end of the week.'

'I know, sir, but he's gone already. And he's left his workstation in a terrible mess. That's not like Mr Woosner.'

Rheingold didn't like it. Woosner was usually a methodical kind of guy and tidy with it. The fact that he had left his job before he was due to and that he'd left his workstation in a terrible mess added up to something serious. Woosner might be considering going public, and that could have serious implications for NASA, America in general and, more specifically, Rheingold's career. He had to be found. Rheingold picked up his phone and dialled a number.

'Get me Security,' he said.

CHAPTER TWELVE
Two Days to Save the World

The front page banner headline in *The Chronicle* read 'INDUSTRY TO SHED MORE JOBS'. Susan Likely had brought a copy straight from the press for Frogmorton to look through.

'Why didn't we make the front page?' he asked, genuinely puzzled by the editor's apparent lack of interest in the future of his own planet.

'It's even worse than that,' Susan said. 'The editor thought it was a great story, but he's convinced that you're a fruit-cake.'

'Here it is,' Elaine said turning the last few pages before the sports section. She read out the headline, 'ALIENS DELIVER FAST FOOD TO LOCAL MAN'.

'What?' said Frogmorton. 'Let me see that.' He picked up the newspaper and read the article out aloud. '"Local scientist, Frogbarton Coalscuttle..." - they didn't even get my name right - "has found the ultimate answer in fast food home delivery in the shape of miniature alien beings who beam right into his microwave oven with his pizza order."' Frogmorton lowered the newspaper and looked at Susan for an explanation.

'I told you that I didn't know what slant the editor would put on the story,' Susan said with a shrug of her shoulders.

'Did you write this?' asked Elaine.

Susan said, 'Of course not. I said that I would write it how it is and I did. The editor thought that you were nuts, though. Come to that, he thought that I was crazy for being taken in by you, and said that he wouldn't approve any payment I might have made for the story.'

Frogmorton was quite upset and worried by the editor's

attitude. The whole planet was going to hell in a handcart and he thought it was all a big joke. 'How on Earth are we going to resolve this if nobody is going to take the threat seriously?'

'Frogmorton,' Elaine said, 'maybe the government already know about it. They're probably receiving this message as well.'

'But what if they're not? What if they're completely ignorant of the fact that this world has only got three days left?'

'I don't want to worry you unduly,' Susan chipped in, 'but there's only two days left.' Isn't it funny how time flies when you're enjoying yourself?

* * *

Time does have a habit of either going by peculiarly swiftly or annoyingly slowly, doesn't it? Oh, I know that I have said that in reality time doesn't really exist and is a man-made invention, but as I live in a world dominated by man-made invention, I might as well accept its existence and be done with it. However, I am right in my observation of the irregularity of the speed of time. Holidays are a prime example. You must have noticed that when you have booked a week's holiday from your place of employment, in the week prior to the holiday the days just drag by. But when that holiday week finally arrives you have no sooner unpacked your case than you are ready to start packing it again, because the days have just flown by. Time is also a very elusive commodity. People that I know are always telling me that they can't find any - especially if I've asked them to spare some to do me a favour. I wonder where it all goes to?

* * *

The NASA Security team did a thorough job at Gavin Woosner's home. They left no stone unturned as they ransacked his apartment. They spent several hours sifting through his belongings and, finally, telephoned Mr Rheingold and announced, 'He isn't here.'

'I had already gathered that, you moron!' Rheingold said rather unfairly. 'I don't want you to tell me where he isn't! I want you to tell me where he is!'

'Well, as he is no longer on NASA property, sir, it's no longer under my jurisdiction,' the man from the security team said.

'So who's gonna goddam find the son-of-a-bitch?' Rheingold demanded.

'I suggest you contact the FBI in the first instance, sir,' said the very helpful security guard in the face of growing abuse from Rheingold.

Rheingold flung the receiver down in anger. The situation was starting to get complicated and he was not very keen on complications. They tended to be rather - well, complicated. Woosner could be anywhere by now, telling anybody who wanted to listen everything he knew. The longer he was out there spreading the news of his discovery, the more difficult the job of covering it all up would become. The trouble was that people in general were starting to take the whole question of extra-terrestrials far too seriously. Things weren't too bad in the early days, when UFO spotters could be ridiculed as some kind of lunatic fringe, but now a lot more people believed in them. The Roswell Incident had made it terribly difficult for the authorities to suppress information about aliens. That leaked information was the thorn in the side of every fact manipulator in the employ of the US Government, because it had captured the public's imagination - which was always a dangerous thing.

Rheingold picked up the receiver again and said, 'Get me the FBI.'

* * *

Gavin Woosner stepped out of the taxi outside Frogmorton's house and found it rather surprising that the signal he had traced from the Cosmos had decided to choose British suburbia as a place to beam to. He stepped up to the front door and rang the bell. It was time to see if his calculations had been accurate and, more importantly, to find out what the alien intelligence had to say for itself.

The door was eventually opened by what Gavin presumed to be a woman, adorned with curlers in her hair and the stub end of a badly-rolled cigarette drooping from the corner of her mouth, which moved almost hypnotically when she spoke.

'Good morning, ma'am,' he said. 'Are you receiving a message from the heavens?'

'God all-bloody-mighty!' said Frogmorton's mother. 'Not you bloody Mormons again? I thought I told you last time that I can't remember where I put your book. I'd offer to pay for it if I thought you'd leave me alone.'

'No, ma'am, you don't seem to understand,' Gavin tried to explain.

'Oh yes I do,' Frogmorton's mother assured him. 'Look dear, if you want to believe Jesus was married to a Red Indian woman, that's up to you, but our vicar has never mentioned it. And he's supposed to know about that sort of thing, you know. Mind you, he's not married himself.'

'But, ma'am ...'

'Did I tell you that my boy isn't married either? But he's not a vicar. I've told him that he ought to get himself a wife. It's not healthy being unmarried at his age - a boy of nearly thirty-three. I expect you're married to a Red Indian woman as well, are you? Two or three I expect, because you lot are like that, aren't you? My husband would have liked to join your lot, you know. A randy old devil he was. Always after it.'

'You have a son, ma'am?' Gavin said, sensing that it might be more productive if he could talk to somebody else.

'I thought I'd told you that, already.'

'Could I speak to your son, perhaps?'

'Well he's a bit busy right now,' said Frogmorton's mother, and she leant towards Gavin as if what she was about to say was some dark secret. 'He's got two women in there you know. One of them stopped all night and the other one couldn't wait to get back here this morning. She charged in here this morning all out of breath and panting. Just like his father you know. Randy old devil.'

'I wouldn't take up much of his time,' Gavin said hopefully.

'You'll have to come back later,' Frogmorton's mother said, breaking wind at the same time. 'Now you'll have to excuse me, I've got to go and yank out a few nasal hairs.' And with that she shut the door, leaving Gavin dazed and confused. He wandered off down the road in search of a café or bar where he could hang out until he felt strong enough to try again.

Frogmorton's mother wondered if she ought to tell her son about the Mormon, but decided that he wouldn't welcome being disturbed whilst entertaining his two lady friends. He might have been a late starter, she thought to herself, but he's certainly making up for lost time.

As she passed by the living room, she leant her ear against the door to see if she could hear what was going on. The door was not shut properly and it opened, catching her off balance and sending her gambolling across the floor, ending up laying prostrate beside Kratol's hologram. Everyone in the room turned to look at her following her exquisite entrance.

'That's a long film,' she said, indicating the hologram. 'Why is there only one actor in it?'

'It would take far too long to explain, Mother,' Frogmorton said as he picked her up and ushered her out of the room, partly to avoid a lengthy and pointless explanation and partly to avoid the embarrassment of having her present.

'You're going to have to deal with this, Frogmorton,' Elaine said when Frogmorton came back into the room.

'Me?' he asked, hoping that Elaine was not serious. 'Why me?'

'Because you must figure in the equation here,' she said. 'These aliens must have selected you as Earth's representative.'

'That's crazy!' Frogmorton exclaimed. 'There are about six billion people on the entire planet. Why should they select me?'

'I don't know why,' she admitted, 'but you can't deny the fact that they did select you. There's the proof of that statement right there on the floor.' Elaine pointed at Kratol's hologram to indicate the proof of that statement, but Frogmorton was ahead of her.

'Just because they send me their message of doom, doesn't automatically qualify me as their choice of representative.'

Susan, feeling left out of the conversation at this point, decided to say, 'So why send their message here at all, then? Why didn't they send it to 10 Downing Street, or the White House or the Kremlin?'

Frogmorton shook his head to show that he couldn't answer the questions.

'Because,' Susan continued, 'they chose you. You are the Earth's only hope against this threat.'

'But what can I do to save the Earth? I can't jump into my space ship and blast them out of existence, can I?'

'The answer is in the message,' Elaine said. 'We've got to try and reason with them.'

'Why should they listen to anything I tell them?'

'Because they chose you. They'll listen to you,' said Susan. 'The Earth is relying on you to save it.'

This was a great responsibility on Frogmorton's shoulders. He had never had anyone rely on him before for anything - except Chloe, of course. The thought both frightened and excited him at the same time. What if he could pull it off? Never mind the Nobel Prize for saving the Earth from destruction by mankind, they'd have to invent a new honour to bestow upon him for saving the Earth from aliens. He would be a global hero. He would have a holiday named after him. He would be able to marry Elaine; she would be unable to resist him. Yes, he could do it. He and he alone had the power to avert the cataclysmic catastrophe that threatened the planet. Frogmorton Culpepper - Saviour of the Earth! Doesn't this boy get carried away?

Then a thought crossed Frogmorton's mind that worried him slightly. 'How?' he asked, as if the two women might have the definitive answer between them.

'You've got to get a message back to them,' Elaine offered helpfully.

'How can I do that? They haven't left their telephone number,' Frogmorton said.

'I think I might be able to help there,' Susan said, and at that Frogmorton half-expected her to get her mobile out and search through her list of telephone numbers. Instead, she continued speaking. 'I don't know if there's anything in it, but a while ago I did an interview with a woman who said she had been abducted by aliens.'

'What's your point?' Elaine asked.

'If she's on the level, she might know something about them. She might be able to make contact with them.'

'Well what are we waiting for?' asked Frogmorton, already making for the door. 'Let's go and see her.'

'There's one minor problem,' Susan confessed.

'And what would that be?' It was Elaine's turn to be inquisitive.

Susan looked a little uncomfortable and shifted about nervously.

'Well?' said Frogmorton, pressing the point.

'She's in a psychiatric hospital,' said Susan.

'Well, let's still go and see her,' insisted Frogmorton.

Susan still looked uncomfortable, and said, 'It's a high-security psychiatric hospital.'

'You mean, like as in Broadmoor?' asked Elaine.

'Sort of,' Susan said.

'How nuts is she, then?' Frogmorton asked.

'She tried to kill her husband and two daughters. She told the police that the aliens had told her to do it.'

'Do you still want to go and see her?' Elaine asked Frogmorton.

'She's the only lead we've got,' said Frogmorton. 'Let's go.'

As they left the room, they bumped into Frogmorton's mother, who was a little taken aback at the apparent urgency they were displaying.

'Where are you off in such an all-fired hurry?' she asked her son.

'We're going after a woman. At Moorhampton hospital. We won't be long,' Frogmorton said, and the three of them piled into Frogmorton's car, and drove off in search of the mad alien abductee.

Frogmorton's mother watched them disappear. Although she was pleased at her son's new found appetite for the fairer sex, she wasn't sure that he should be indulging himself quite as much as he seemed to be. After all, she had heard of threesomes before, but couldn't quite grasp the concept of a foursome, especially as one of the participants resided in a mental institution.

CHAPTER THIRTEEN
The FBI Agent

Alexander Korinyakov was an unusual name for an FBI agent. In the past, he had spent a lot of time explaining to people how he had started working for the FBI, but now he just tells them to mind their own business. After all, the cold war was over now, communism had toppled, and the FBI were free to headhunt for top operatives anywhere in the world. Alright, I admit that they do tend to prefer to recruit American citizens, but they were also able to fast-track suitable candidates through the immigration procedures, and have them humming the 'Star Spangled Banner' before the ink was dry on their entry visas.

Alexander Korinyakov was very good at his job, and was not averse to bending the rules slightly if it made his work easier. Bending the rules slightly had enabled him to get a lead on the runaway NASA ex-employee, Gavin Woosner.

Mr Woosner had lived with an elderly aunt and, through patient interrogation techniques and liberal use of pistol whipping, Korinyakov had found out from this elderly relative that her nephew had booked a flight to London, England shortly before she lost consciousness - that is to say, she imparted the information before she lost consciousness, not that Gavin had booked a flight to London, England before she lost consciousness. Alexander Korinyakov was not totally devoid of feelings and called 911 to arrange for an ambulance before he left for the airport.

The FBI agent was no stranger to the United Kingdom, having worked there on numerous occasions in the past for his previous employer - the KGB. With his network of informants and connections with the underworld, finding Gavin Woosner would be a piece of cake. Within minutes of his plane touching down at Heathrow, a shadowy figure slipped a carefully-folded piece of paper into Alexander Korinyakov's hand. He stopped and looked at the paper, on it was scrawled the name of a hotel in red ink. It was the hotel where Gavin Woosner had stayed the previous night. Korinyakov made a mental note of the address, took a cigarette lighter out of his coat pocket and then set fire to the paper. He thought that it was a very cleverly-folded paper rhinoceros indeed. He hailed a taxi and told the driver to take him to Gavin Woosner's hotel. Well, actually, he didn't say, 'Take me to Gavin Woosner's hotel.' Instead, he told the driver to take him to the hotel whose name had been scrawled on the cleverly-folded paper rhinoceros.

On arrival at the hotel, a cleverly-folded twenty-pound note slipped into the desk clerk's top pocket enabled Alexander Korinyakov to gain access to Gavin Woosner's room. He noticed the satellite dish lashed to the chair by the window, and started to put two and two together. He soon made four. It looked like his NASA runaway was trying to track down the incoming signal. He hoped that meant that Gavin Woosner had intended not to talk about it before he had been able to confirm its existence. The FBI agent searched the room for any clues that might lead him to Gavin, but couldn't find anything of any relevance, and so he went back down to the reception area to question the desk clerk, who was quite put out because he was in the middle of reading his newspaper during the slack period.

'Hey, buddy,' he said to the desk clerk, 'did the American make any telephone calls from the hotel?'

'Not that I know of, sir,' the desk clerk said without looking up from his copy of *The Chronicle*.

Alexander Korinyakov didn't like the answer and he snatched the newspaper from the desk clerk's hands and said, 'Are you quite sure about that?'

The desk clerk was quite shaken, but not wishing to be intimidated by a foreigner kept his composure and said, 'Quite sure, sir. Guests rarely use the phones in their rooms. I think they suppose we will charge them outrageously, if they do so. Most people have the sense to use their mobiles. Now, may I please have my paper?'

Alexander Korinyakov could see that this line of questioning was going to get him nowhere, and so he shoved the paper back at the desk clerk. It was then that the headline caught his eye - 'ALIENS DELIVER FAST FOOD TO LOCAL MAN'. That had to be more than just a coincidence. Much to the annoyance of the desk clerk, Alexander Korinyakov tore out the page containing the article and left the hotel intent on paying the recipient of the alien fast food delivery a visit.

* * *

The trouble with hurtling through space at speeds beyond our comprehension was that there was never anything of interest to see out of the window, and that annoyed StarFleet Admiral Kratol. It was all very well visiting all the far-flung quadrants of the Universe, but there was never any time for sight-seeing. It was always work, work, work. Destroy all the life forms on one planet, set the coordinates for the next. Boring routine. Sometimes he felt more like an inter-galactic janitor than an Admiral of the Braakl'gian Space Navy. It was almost criminal that the wonders of the Cosmos were denied to him just because of his work schedule. And running down the service droids in his little runabout was getting tedious as well.

Kratol flicked the switch on the intercom and said, 'Any response to the message yet?'

'No, Excellency. Do you think there will be?'

'I sincerely hope so, Domr'k. It might give us time to have a look around down there on the planet before we have to wipe them all out.'

'Do you think that the inhabitants of Earth will be able to save themselves, Excellency?'

'I shouldn't think so. Nobody has ever been able to save their planet before; why should things change now?'

'They might have a valid reason for survival.'

'Yes - well let's not get into that argument again, Domr'k. I only really called you up because I was bored. Not to discuss the rights and wrongs of what we are doing.'

'Ah! So you think it's wrong too, do you, Excellency?'

'I never said that! It's not my place to decide what is right or wrong. It's my duty to follow out the instructions of The Source - without question. Now back to your work. And don't forget to call me if we do get a response.'

Kratol wished that there would be a response. He could then take time to explore the planet and take in its beauty - unless, of course, the response was of the same type offered to him by the inhabitants of Gweelox 4. He soon got tired of wondering what visual delights awaited him on Planet Earth and climbed into his runabout in search of service droids.

* * *

Moorhampton Hospital was one of the newer facilities built by the British Government to house the ever-increasing numbers of the criminally insane. The place was full of Harley Street consultants and ex-government ministers. The staff, on the other hand, generally came up through the ranks of the nursing and medical professions.

The hospital was set in its own wooded grounds and, on the basis that the inmates were completely mad and therefore unlikely to want to escape, security in this high-security facility was in actual fact exceedingly low. There had been one attempted breakout, but he only got as far as the ornamental pond before he had to stop a member of the nursing staff and ask for directions to the main gate. Fortunately, the inmate got confused with the directions he was given and ended up back inside his own room, where he promptly turned on the television and forgot all about the escape attempt altogether.

Rhona Willett was housed on the first floor of 'A' wing, where she constantly gazed out of the window, scouring the heavens for the aliens who had abducted her, telling anyone who would care to listen, 'They're coming back for me.'

Rhona very rarely had any visitors. Not surprising really, because the only family that she had were all nearly slaughtered by her own hand. They were all too busy trying to recover from their horrible injuries to even consider dropping by for an idle chat. In any case, what would they talk about? Rhona didn't even know who any of them were. Mind you, even if she could remember them, she wouldn't be able to recognise them. It's remarkable what a lump hammer in the face can do to disguise what a person really looks like. It's not that Rhona was violent, you understand. And she certainly didn't hate her family. But when the aliens took her away, they did something to her that removed any sense of family values that she might have had, and she felt duty bound to get rid of the people who were infesting her house - her husband and two daughters, as it turned out.

It was with some surprise, then, that Rhona greeted her three visitors. They were not aliens. Rhona could see that as soon as they entered the room. Aliens don't use doors. However, neither were they humans she recognised. A man and two girls, though - that struck a chord deep in the recesses of her sub-conscious. She had known a man and two girls once. She couldn't quite get a handle on it right now, but the thoughts started to hurt her. She wasn't sure if she wanted these visitors if they were going to hurt her by being memories she couldn't quite remember. But it was impolite to turn visitors away and, anyway, there was always the hammer somewhere if they started to get into her mind too clearly.

'Mrs Willett?' one of the girls said to her. It was Susan Likely. Incidentally, although we know who Susan Likely is, you must remember that Rhona Willett is quite mad and has only seen Susan once before. So don't be surprised if she doesn't recognise her.

'Who are you?' Rhona said abruptly. You see. She didn't recognise her.

'I'm Susan Likely - from *The Chronicle*. We met once before.'

'The Chronicle?' Rhona said. 'What planet is that?'

'It's not a planet, Mrs Willett. It's a newspaper.' Susan explained.

'It might only be a newspaper now, my dear,' said Rhona, 'but it won't be long before it turns into a planet, and then I can come and visit you when my friends come back in their spaceship.'

'Susan,' said Frogmorton softly in Susan's ear, 'this is a serious fruit-cake we have here. Are you sure that she can help?'

'I don't know. Look, it's being in here that's sending her like this. When I interviewed her about nine months ago she was quite coherent.'

'Well, she doesn't seem all that coherent now,' Frogmorton protested.

'Frogmorton,' Susan said, 'she's probably our best hope at the moment. She's been in contact with these beings. She may know how we can get a message to them.'

'God help humanity!' Frogmorton said, hoping that perhaps God might.

Elaine gripped Frogmorton's arm and said, 'We've got to give her a chance.'

Susan tried to make contact with Rhona again. 'Mrs Willett,' she said, 'we need your help. It's of the utmost importance. A matter of life and death.'

'There's a lot of that about,' Rhona said, as if it had any relevance to the conversation. Quite frankly, making contact with Rhona was probably only infinitesimally easier than making contact with the aliens themselves.

Frogmorton decided that he would try to get through to her. After all, he was the chosen one. 'Mrs Willett,' he said, 'your aliens are in contact with us, and we need to send them a message. Can you tell us how we can do that?'

Susan turned to face Frogmorton and said, 'Oh, the direct approach. That's good. No point in wasting time trying to gain her confidence and try to make her feel comfortable with talking about the thing that made her mad and nearly drove her to kill her entire family.'

'We don't have time for all the little niceties of life, Susan,' he explained. 'We are on a bit of a tight schedule.'

Elaine joined in with, 'Don't argue about it, you two. That won't get us anywhere. Frogmorton, let Susan deal with this. She knows Mrs Willett.'

Rhona was oblivious to the argument. She had heard part of what Frogmorton had said, and was busy collecting her things together and looking all around the room for something that was obviously eluding her.

'What are you looking for, Mrs Willett?' Susan asked.

Frogmorton feared she was going to reply, 'My hammer.' Happily, instead she answered, 'My suitcase,' adding, 'I knew they were coming back for me. I told everyone that they were coming back for me.'

'But you can't leave, Mrs Willett,' said Susan.

'Why not?'

'Because you did a very bad thing and the doctors need you to stay here so that they can make you better.'

'But they've come back for me. They said they would. They're going to take me all around the galaxy. In space. It's very big, you know - space. I wonder if I'll be able to see my house from up there.' Rhona crouched down to look under her bed for her suitcase in case it had decided to go back there since she last looked for it twelve seconds earlier.

Frogmorton was getting nervous. The clock was ticking away and they were trying to reason with a madwoman. 'Mrs Willett,' he said, 'do you know how we can get in touch with the aliens?'

Rhona stopped searching for her suitcase, and stood up to face Frogmorton. 'What did you say, young man?'

'I said, "Do you know how we can get in touch with the aliens?", Mrs Willett?'

'Of course I do,' she replied.

Frogmorton, Elaine and Susan stared with open mouths at Rhona for what seemed an eternity, waiting for her to impart the details of extra-terrestrial communication, until Frogmorton finally said, 'How?'

Rhona started to acquire a kind of sharpness in her manner that seemed to be missing before. Without appearing to ramble, she said, 'If you think that I'm going to tell you the answer to that in here, you must think I'm mad.'

Frogmorton didn't really want to disappoint the woman by telling her that he did think she was mad, a fact which was reinforced by her internment in a mental institution, so he said, 'What are you suggesting?'

'Get me out of here,' came the definite reply from Rhona.

'You are mad!' Frogmorton concluded.

'Only when I need to be. Alright! I admit that I may have done something slightly illegal.'

'Oh, yes,' Frogmorton agreed, 'trying to kill your husband and kids is still slightly illegal in this country.'

'They only said I did that to get me locked away,' Rhona confided. 'It's all a government conspiracy, you see. A cover up.'

'A "cover up"?' Frogmorton said.

'They don't want people knowing about the aliens.'

'But I saw your family,' Susan said. 'When it happened, I covered the story and saw them in the hospital. They were unrecognisable.'

'So how do you know it was my family then, if you couldn't recognise them?' Rhona said, believing that she had gained the upper hand in that argument. She turned back to Frogmorton, feeling that he was less of a threat, and said, 'You don't really need to be all that strong to make a reasonable impression with a lump hammer.'

'Who were they then?' Frogmorton asked.

'Who knows? I came back from the alien mother ship to find these people infesting my house. Oh, they tried to tell me that they were my husband and two daughters, but I wasn't taken in. I would have remembered having a husband and two daughters, wouldn't I? In fact, I might have had a husband and two daughters in the past, but I don't think I have now.'

Susan said, 'We can't take you out of here. They wouldn't let us.'

'They wouldn't know,' Rhona informed them, 'if you didn't tell them.'

Elaine started to get agitated. 'Hang on a minute,' she said, 'what you're suggesting here is a criminal offence. We could all end up going to jail.'

'We've got no choice, Elaine,' Frogmorton said. 'If she's the only chance we've got, we've got to do what she says. I'd rather risk a few years in jail to save the planet, than sit in a room somewhere just waiting for the end to happen.'

'He's right, Elaine,' Susan chipped in. 'We're caught between a rock and a hard place.'

'So,' Rhona said with a smile of self-satisfaction, 'you're going to spring me?'

Gavin Woosner finished his third cup of coffee and wondered if it would be safe to go back and talk to the man who was receiving his signal from space. Maybe that creature who had answered the door, posing as his mother, would be gone. He could only hope. He started off down the road towards Frogmorton's house, determined not to be intimidated if the old woman did answer the door. As he turned the corner into Frogmorton's road, he stopped in his tracks as a taxi pulled up outside the house he was heading for and a large man who walked with a Russian accent piled out of it. It could be the man he had come to see. But didn't the woman who answered the door say that her son was inside with two women? This man had just arrived in a taxi and was knocking on the front door. Surely the woman's son would have a key? Gavin thought that it would probably be better if he stayed out of sight for a while, until the large man who walked with a Russian accent had concluded his business. He might just be a door-to-door salesman, but he couldn't afford to take any chances. Gavin knew that Rheingold would probably have someone out looking for him. It wasn't the done thing to walk out of NASA with a whole bunch of top secret software and not expect someone to come looking for you. Gavin hadn't expected to be found quite so quickly, though, and was grateful that he had ordered that third coffee. Without that little over-indulgence, he might very well have been caught. For the time being he ducked down an alleyway until the coast was clear.

* * *

It wasn't difficult to track down the man in the newspaper article, and Alexander Korinyakov told the taxi driver to put his foot down if he wanted a hefty tip. Ten minutes later the taxi screeched to a halt outside Frogmorton's house.

'Do you want me to wait for you, squire?' the cabby asked in his friendliest cockney accent, hoping to receive a similar tip on the return journey.

Korinyakov said, 'No, thank you,' and handed the taxi driver the required fare and a fifty-pence coin as a 'hefty' tip.

The taxi driver looked at the huge tip with disgust and, as he drove off, shouted, 'I hope your bollocks drop off!' in his friendliest cockney accent.

Korinyakov strode up to Frogmorton's front door and knocked hard. After several minutes Frogmorton's mother opened the door, a portrait of loveliness, the curlers removed from her hair and her teeth removed from her mouth. The badly-rolled cigarette was still in place.

'Good day, madam,' Korinyakov said with a smile. 'May I say that you look enchanting.' Korinyakov had strange taste in women.

'You may,' Frogmorton's mother said, 'unless you're wanting to sell me something.'

'No, not at all,' Korinyakov assured her as he took out the wallet containing his ID card to show her. He flicked it in her face in that annoying way that US law enforcement officers are inclined to do in the movies, 'I'm from the FBI.'

'Oh, are you?' Frogmorton's mother said. 'Well, I'm glad you called. I bought some of your furniture about twelve months ago and, quite frankly, I'm not altogether satisfied with it.'

'Sorry, ma'am?' said the baffled FBI agent.

'And so you should be. I know I bought it in one of your closing down sales, but I would have thought that I would have had a bit more wear and tear out of it.'

'I'm afraid I don't understand ...'

'Nor do I,' Frogmorton's mother said. 'You always seem to be having closing down sales, but you never actually seem to close down, do you?'

'But ...' Korinyakov tried to interject, but Frogmorton's mother grabbed him by the collar and lead him into the house.

'Now,' she said, 'I don't mind if you want to replace it or if you would rather repair it.'

'I'm afraid I don't know what you are talking about,' Korinyakov said to Frogmorton's mother.

'Oh, yes!' she said, leading the way into the living room. 'You try and squirm out of it now. You high-pressure salesmen are all the same, aren't you? Get rid of the goods and if they don't quite come up to scratch plead ignorance. You soon changed your tune, didn't you? You couldn't apologise enough until I asked for a repair or a replacement. Then you deny all knowledge.' By this time she had thrust Korinyakov into the living room. 'Just look at the state of that table,' she continued.

'It's very nice,' Korinyakov said, trying to play along with her.

'Very nice? Very bloody nice? It's a disgrace; that's what that is. I've only had that table twelve months and just look at it.'

Korinyakov didn't look at it. His attention had been grabbed by something going on in another part of the room. There seemed to be some sort of purple glow coming from around the back of the television. 'What's that?' he asked Frogmorton's mother.

'Never mind that. What are you going to do about my table?'

Realising that he had lost the great furniture debate, Korinyakov said, 'We'll send you a new one. Now tell me, what's going on behind your television?'

'Oh, nothing much. It's just one of those arty films. It fell out of the back of the telly the other day. It's not very interesting. Would you like a cup of tea?'

Korinyakov went round the back of the television and gazed in wonder at Kratol's hologram. He didn't know whether or not it had fallen out of the television, but he was sure that Woosner wouldn't be far away from this. 'No. No tea, thank you,' he said. He pulled out a photograph of Gavin Woosner and showed it to Frogmorton's mother. 'Have you seen this man?'

'You're not one of those religious types as well, are you?' Frogmorton's mother said, instantly recognising that Mormon chap who called earlier.

'Religious?'

'You know. Got fifteen wives and reckon the disciples were the entire Apache nation?'

'I'm afraid I don't fully understand the British sense of humour. All I need to know is whether or not you have seen the gentleman in this photo?'

'Do you know,' Frogmorton's mother said, 'you're rather inquisitive for a furniture salesman. Are you sure you don't work for some foreign government agency or something?'

'I thought I already told you that I did.'

'Ah!' Frogmorton's mother said. 'So you're working undercover as a furniture salesman. I understand now. But does that mean that you won't be sending me a new table after all?'

'I'm afraid not.'

'Oh, that's a bit of a shame.'

'Now, perhaps you could answer my question?'

There was a slight pause whilst Frogmorton's mother thought about that. 'What question was that, then?' she asked.

'Have you seen this man?' Korinyakov said, poking the portrait with his finger so that there would be no doubt about whom he was referring to.

'Yes. He was here earlier on, trying to convert me to the faith.'

'Convert you to the faith?'

'Yes. He wanted to know if I was receiving a message from the heavens.'

'So, he has been here?'

'Yes. Like I said - earlier on.'

'And did you show him this?' Korinyakov said, indicating Kratol's hologram.

Frogmorton's mother looked at the hologram, not understanding why everyone found it so interesting. Not only was the film singularly boring, it went on for far too long. 'No,' she replied. 'He never even came into the house. And in any case, my son was entertaining his two lady friends in here, and I didn't want to disturb him. He's getting just like his father. Randy old devil.'

'Yes, well I don't need to disturb you any longer,' Korinyakov said. 'But if you see this man again, would you give me a call on this number.' He handed her his card and headed for the front door. So, he thought, Gavin Woosner had not seen the hologram yet. It would only be a matter of time. Frogmorton's mother saw the FBI agent out, and said that she would ring him if she saw anything. She really enjoyed all this cloak and dagger stuff.

Alexander Korinyakov hailed a taxi, not knowing that he was being watched by Gavin Woosner from a distance of only twenty yards.

* * *

I suppose that you are probably wondering what the two Muridaens are doing at this point in the story. I know how some people worry about characters when they are hanging about in the wings unseen waiting for their scene to be seen, if you know what I mean. Well, let's go and have a look at what's happening to them.

Squadron Leader Fligg and Elite One bravely maintained tractor beam acquisition on the alien ship and fearlessly kept a watchful eye on their flux grids for any sign of malfunction.

There. I hope you feel better for that. As you can see, life is pretty boring when you are being towed through space at speeds beyond our comprehension.

CHAPTER FOURTEEN
The Ornamental Coalscuttle Comes in Handy

Frogmorton, Elaine and Susan had a lengthy discussion exploring the possible ways of spiriting Rhona Willett out of Moorhampton Hospital for the Criminally Insane. These included hiding her in a laundry basket - an idea Susan got from the film *Annie*; knocking out a few members of the medical staff, stealing their uniforms and hijacking an ambulance - the imaginative approach that Elaine took; and Frogmorton's plan to wait and sneak her out under the cover of darkness. The argument was starting to get a little heated when Rhona came up with a suggestion of her own.

'I could pretend to go out to the shops and forget to return,' she announced.

'What?' said Elaine.

'I often go out to the shops. They don't mind, because I always come back.'

Frogmorton was a little taken aback by this revelation. 'You mean to tell me that they let you go out to the shops?' he said.

'Not just me. Everyone does it.'

'Oh, this is great!' Frogmorton said. 'We pay our taxes to keep these raving loonies locked up where they can't be a danger to the public and they let them out whenever they please to go and do a bit of shopping.'

Susan didn't like the idea of Frogmorton upsetting Rhona and said, 'Look, don't antagonise her. We need her help.' She turned back towards Rhona and smiled a friendly smile at her. 'Alright, Mrs Willett,' she said reassuringly, 'we'll go and wait in the car and in about ten minutes time you can pretend to go shopping and then we'll take you away with us.'

'Alright, my dear,' Rhona said and she sat on the bed and started reading a book.

'Come on,' Susan said to the other two, 'let's go and wait for her.'

Once they'd got into the car, Frogmorton drove it around the corner just out of sight of the main entrance, and there they waited.

'Do you think we're doing the right thing?' Elaine asked.

'Do you mean saving the planet,' Frogmorton replied, 'or sitting in a car waiting for a homicidal lunatic?'

Nobody answered Frogmorton's question.

* * *

Mr Rheingold answered the telephone that was buzzing on his desk at NASA's SETI installation at Ames Research Center near Palo Alto, California. It was the special line that he had told Alexander Korinyakov to reach him on, and he hoped it was good news.

'Good news I hope,' he said into the receiver.

'Some good, some bad,' reported Korinyakov.

'I would have much preferred you to have told me there was no bad news, Kalishnakov,' Rheingold snarled.

'It's Korinyakov.'

'What is?'

'My name. My name is Korinyakov.'

'Well, that can hardly be classed as bad news.'

'My name is not bad news,' Korinyakov said.

'Well, that's your opinion,' Rheingold said, barely hiding his own dislike of the FBI agent's name. 'Now get to the point. Have you found and apprehended Woosner?'

'Ah! Now, that is the good and bad news.'

'I do hope that you are going to tell me that the good news is that you've found Woosner and the bad news is that you had to kill him because he tried to escape.'

'Not exactly.'

'And what does, "Not exactly" mean?'

'It means that I haven't found Woosner.'

'Then why in God's name are you calling me on this number, Krunchov?'

'It's Korinyakov! And I'm calling you to tell you that I am closing in. I have found the signal from space that you mentioned, and I'm staking the place out. Woosner is bound to show.'

'When he does, you grab him. I don't want any of this "signal from space" nonsense to get out. Do you understand, Mr Jerkov?'

'It's Korinyakov! Why can't you get it right? It's Korinyakov!'

'Like I said,' Rheingold said, 'that's your opinion,' and he replaced the receiver.

Rheingold wasn't too happy about the FBI assigning an ex-KGB man to this case. It was un-American. He decided that he couldn't be trusted. Even if this Khrushchev, or whatever he was called, did track Woosner down, there was no guarantee that the goddam Russian wouldn't sell out to the highest bidder. Once a communist, always a communist. What the hell was Uncle Sam doing employing a goddam communist in the FBI? There was only one course of action left open to Rheingold. He picked up the phone again and said, 'Get me the CIA.'

* * *

Gavin Woosner waited until the taxi that the man who walked with a Russian accent got into had disappeared from sight, and then he knocked on Frogmorton's front door. When it opened, he pushed his way inside and closed it behind him, then lifted up the flap of the letterbox and surveyed as much of the street outside that he could see. When he was sure that the taxi was not going to return, he stood up straight and said to Frogmorton's mother, 'Who was that man who was here just now?'

'I don't know if they do things differently in your country, but I've always found the best way of finding out who somebody is, is to go up to them and ask them.'

'What did he want?'

'I can't believe that you travelled three thousand miles across the Atlantic to meet some bloke at my house. Haven't you got anywhere to meet people in the United States? Or can't you Mormons do that sort of thing? Too busy with all them Red Indian women, I suppose.'

'Listen woman!' Gavin said with something approaching authority in his voice, 'Who was that man and what did he want?'

'He was a furniture salesman or something. Working for the government. And he wanted you.'

'A furniture salesman?'

'Yes. He worked for that firm that's always holding those closing down sales but they never do. You know, FBI.'

'FBI?'

'Yes. He left me his card and told me to ring him if I saw you again. What did you do? Try to cancel your order?'

'God! If the FBI are on to me already I've got to move fast. Can I talk to your son?'

'I'm afraid he's gone out. On the lookout for more women, I suppose. Randy old devil.'

'Do you know if he has any sophisticated radio equipment or anything?'

'Well, he's got his little Sony Walkman. I bought him that for his last birthday.' (Frogmorton's mother was particularly proud of the said purchase, as it had followed a very successful piece of haggling at the local car boot sale, where she got the price for the item down from the originally suggested three pounds to just one pound.)

'Has he not got anything capable of receiving transmissions from outer space?'

'We've got satellite television in the living room. Did you want to watch some?'

'Not at present, thank you,' said Gavin, feeling perhaps that he was on a fool's errand.

'It's probably just as well. I think it might be broken. One of those arty films has fallen out of the back of it. Funny little purple actor it is, going on and on about the same old thing. He doesn't quite look human either.'

'What are you talking about?'

'There's a little purple bloke on our living room floor, churning out some repetitive message or something. Fell out the back of the telly, he did.'

This new piece of information interested Gavin. 'Can you show me this little purple guy, ma'am?'

'I suppose so,' said Frogmorton's mother. 'I don't know what everybody gets so excited about. It's the most boring film I've ever seen in my life,' and she ushered him in to the living room where he beheld the thing he had travelled all the way from the United States of America to see. A message from an alien intelligence. He circled round the hologram once or twice, and reached out to it with his hand, which passed right through it. After taking in the wonder of its visual properties, Gavin started to listen to what it was saying.

'Oh, my God!' was all he could think of to say.

The short taxi ride from Frogmorton's house was merely a ploy to let Woosner think that the coast was clear, should he be watching the house from some vantage point that the FBI agent couldn't see. Korinyakov was convinced that the ex-NASA employee would return. He got out of the taxi just round the corner, and called Rheingold from his cell phone (or mobile to us Brits). After he had finished the call, he walked back to the corner of Frogmorton's street to see if Woosner would return. He waited for about fifteen minutes until, finally, his patience paid off. Gavin Woosner looked exactly the same as his photograph, which was probably more than a mere coincidence. Korinyakov watched as the fugitive pushed past the enchanting creature he had met earlier and disappeared into the house. He decided to make his move. He knew that once Woosner could confirm the presence of the extra-terrestrial signal he would go public with it, and that was one scenario that he couldn't allow.

The ex-Russian, ex-KGB man, now turned fast-track American National and FBI agent, walked quickly and purposefully, yet with a Russian accent, towards Frogmorton's house, his fingers lovingly caressing the barrel of the weapon that he kept tucked in his trousers for safe keeping. He stopped momentarily as a woman emerged from the house next door to Frogmorton's. It was Mrs Douglas, the lady who was having morning coffee with Frogmorton's mother when Frogmorton came running into the kitchen stark naked waving his credentials about. She took one look at the big man running his hand up and down something long and hard tucked inside his trousers and decided to go back indoors.

Korinyakov started walking again. He went up the short garden path to Frogmorton's front door, which he knocked loudly. The woman answered the door, but Korinyakov had no time to spare for pleasantries this time. 'Where is he?' he asked through gritted teeth, and he pushed past Frogmorton's mother and strode towards the living room, releasing his mighty weapon from his trousers as he did so.

Frogmorton's mother had seen enough Bruce Willis films to

realise what was going on.

'Here!' she cried out. 'You can't come in here waving that thing about. You'll do somebody a mischief with that.'

Korinyakov ignored her and flung the living room door open to find Gavin Woosner crouched down beside Kratol's hologram, looking at it with the reverence of a child after opening its first Christmas present.

'The game's up Woosner!' he yelled, levelling his gun at Gavin's head.

'You can say that again, brother!' said Gavin with a voice tinged with irony as he gazed at Kratol's message of doom. 'In more ways than you can imagine.' He stood up and turned to face Korinyakov. 'Who are you, anyway? You're not an American.'

'I am an American citizen. Granted, I didn't used to be. I used to be a Russian, but now I work for the FBI.'

'That figures,' said Gavin.

'You've got something that doesn't belong to you, bud. And Mr Rheingold would like it back.'

With her usual aplomb, Frogmorton's mother completely misread the situation. 'Don't you think that you're taking this furniture repossession business a bit too far?' she asked Korinyakov.

'You keep out of this lady!' Korinyakov advised her.

'If you wanted me to keep out of it, why did you come to my house to settle your business?' she asked undaunted. 'We've got courts in this country to deal with these kinds of dispute, you know. You don't have to resort to violence.'

'What?' said a confused Korinyakov.

'All I'm saying is that there's no need to spill any blood just because this gentleman wants to cancel his furniture order.'

'Will you shut up about furniture? Are you crazy?' Korinyakov yelled at her. He turned his attention towards Gavin

Woosner. 'Have you told anybody about this?' he asked, indicating the hologram.

'No,' he said. 'What's the point? They'll all know soon enough.'

'Good,' said Korinyakov. 'So it's just you two that I need to worry about.' He pulled a silencer from his pocket and started screwing it to the barrel of his gun.

'Is this because he's one of those Mormons, then?' Frogmorton's mother asked, still unable to grasp the gravity of the situation.

'What?' asked Korinyakov, who was unable to follow the woman's logic if, indeed, she employed any.

'Well, if it's not about furniture, it must be about religion. You foreigners are funny about religion, aren't you?'

'Lady,' Korinyakov stated, 'I think I'm going to have to waste you first. You're driving me nuts!' He aimed the gun between Frogmorton's mother's eyes and tensed his finger on the trigger. He would have killed her too, if Chloe hadn't chosen that precise moment to fall down the chimney with a squeal that made the hairs on the back of your neck stand up and dance around. The noise and clouds of soot that the cat disturbed on its way down were enough to distract Korinyakov and, sensing that she should do something decisive in order to avoid being 'wasted' (something she understood from those Bruce Willis films), Frogmorton's mother picked up the ornamental coalscuttle and hit Korinyakov on the back of the head with it as hard as she could. The noise of coalscuttle against cranium was reminiscent of the start of a Rank movie and Korinyakov was rendered unconscious.

Gavin Woosner helped Frogmorton's mother to tie Korinyakov to a chair, and then made his excuses to depart. He said he had some calculations to check out and he gave her a piece of paper with his cell phone number written on it. She looked at the piece of paper as Gavin left, and thought to herself that it was a very cleverly-folded paper rhinoceros indeed.

* * *

Frogmorton drove as fast as he could, hoping that the police would follow him and be forced to come inside his house where he could show them the hologram, but he didn't see a single patrol car on his way home. He screeched to a halt, almost knocking over a man who seemed to be running away from his house. He and the three women piled out of the car and ran up to the front door that had been left open. As they entered the living room, they were greeted with the sight of Frogmorton's mother pointing a gun at the head of an unconscious man that she had tied to a chair.

After getting over the initial shock, Frogmorton said, 'Mother! What the hell is going on here and who was that man we just saw running out of the house?'

'It's a long story, Son,' she quite rightly said.

'Try me.'

'Well,' she started, 'that man who just left in a hurry was one of those Mormon fellows. You know the sort - got five or six Red Indian wives. Now, he ordered some furniture from this bloke I've got tied to this chair, but he wanted to cancel. Then this bloke here got upset about it and pulled out a gun and threatened to 'waste' the pair of us. So, I hit him on the head with the ornamental coalscuttle. We tied him to this chair, and the Mormon chappy ran off to do some calculations. Probably working out the repayment figures if he decides to go ahead with the furniture order, I suppose.'

Frogmorton, of course, was totally confused by his mother's description of events. 'I'm sorry I had to ask you now,' he said quite candidly.

'And they reckoned that I was mad,' said Rhona.

'Is that a real gun?' asked Elaine with some concern.

'I don't know,' said Frogmorton, 'but I don't think we ought to take any chances with it. Do you want to put that gun down now, Mother? I think you're quite safe. You've tied him up tight enough.'

'Yes,' she said. 'It was getting a bit heavy anyway.'

'Are you sure this man was a furniture salesman, Mrs Culpepper?' Susan asked, so that she could get the details right for the newspaper.

'He said so himself,' Frogmorton's mother insisted. 'Mind you, he did say he used to be a Russian or something.'

'A Russian?' said Elaine, who was quite impressed.

'But why would an armed Russian furniture salesman be threatening to kill a Mormon in our house?' asked Frogmorton, who felt that an explanation was in order.

'Search me,' was his mother's reply.

'Look,' interjected Elaine, 'it doesn't really matter why they were here. What are we going to do about him?'

Rhona said, 'You should ring for the police.'

'Good idea,' said Frogmorton, forgetting momentarily that he was taking advice from a homicidal lunatic. He reached for the phone and dialled the number for Saffron Road Police Station.

* * *

Vanessa O'Mara was a beautiful, flame-haired, green-eyed, twenty-eight-year-old, third generation colleen, skilled in the martial and marital arts and one of the CIA's top operatives - code-named Banshee because her appearance usually preceded someone's death. She was the agency's first choice when tracking down male quarries. The men she pursued could never resist her beauty and she could never resist killing them. In any other walk of life Vanessa O'Mara would be branded a psychopathic killer, but as an agent of the CIA, she was a heroine. Although she was third generation Irish, she realised that the lyrical lilt of her ancestors' native accent was a most alluring asset, and so she spoke with a voice that sounded like the dew falling on the Kerry mountains where their wooded slopes rise abruptly from the shores of the Lakes of Killarney. She enjoyed assignments in the British Isles, but would have preferred them to be in the Irish Republic. Still, after she had tidied up the Woosner affair she had decided that she would visit the home of her forefathers. Vanessa's insatiable appetite for killing men was matched by her equally insatiable desire to make love to them. And when she was very lucky she got to do both.

Her arrival in England was uneventful and she immediately went to the hotel that Korinyakov was supposed to be booked into to get an update on the case. The receptionist told her that the ex-Russian, ex-KGB FBI agent had not arrived. This made the case more interesting. Maybe Gavin Woosner would be more of a challenge than she imagined. Perhaps he had got the better of Korinyakov. Well, she knew he would never get the better of her. Many men had tried and many men had died. She flashed the receptionist a cold, heartless smile, and left the building to pick up Korinyakov's trail and ultimately track down and kill Woosner - and anyone else who got in her way. Vanessa loved her job.

* * *

It had been a long day for Sergeant Mills. A day of endless paperwork. The trouble with being a Police Sergeant was the endless amount of paperwork. Hardly any crime at all, but still a mountain of paperwork. And telephone answering. An endless amount of paperwork and telephone answering. Sergeant Mills was just reflecting on all the telephone answering when the telephone rang.

'Saffron Road Police Station,' he announced into the mouthpiece, 'Sergeant Mills speaking. How may I help you?'

'Ah, Sergeant,' Frogmorton said, 'I'd like you to send a patrol car...'

'Now, hold on a moment, sir,' interrupted the Sergeant, 'before we go to all the trouble of despatching a patrol car, may I enquire as to what your name is?'

'Er, Frogmorton Culpepper.'

Sergeant Mills slowly repeated the information as he took note of it, 'Frogmorton Cul ...' he stopped mid-sentence realising that he knew the name from somewhere. 'Excuse me, sir,' he enquired, 'but didn't we speak yesterday?'

'Yes. That's right.'

'He's come back then, has he?'

'Who?'

'That four-inch purple alien in your domestic appliance.'

'No! No, Sergeant, it's nothing like that.'

'I must say, I'm very pleased to hear it. So, what seems to be the problem?'

'We've apprehended a man in our house.'

'May I be permitted to ask if he is taller than four inches, sir?'

'Yes, of course. He's a normal size man.'

'You say you've apprehended him, sir?'

'Yes. My mother has him tied to a chair. But I've taken the gun away from her.'

'Your mother has got a gun?' Sergeant Mills said nervously.

'Oh, it's not her gun. It belonged to the man.'

'Who exactly is this man, sir?'

'My mother said that he was a Russian furniture salesman.'

'A Russian furniture salesman?'

'Yes.'

'And what was he doing at your house with a gun?'

'Apparently he was after the Mormon that I nearly ran over

when he ran out in front of me when I arrived home.'

'And may I be so bold as to ask what the Mormon was doing?'

'I'm afraid I don't really know.'

'I see,' said Sergeant Mills. 'You do seem to have had quite an eventful couple of days, sir, if you don't mind me saying so.'

'So will you be sending a car round, Sergeant?'

'We are rather busy at the moment, sir. As soon as one is free, I'll send it round,' said Sergeant Mills, tactfully trying to humour the madman on the other end of the telephone.

'What should we do in the meantime?'

'Oh - erm, just keep him under surveillance, sir.'

'Right, sergeant. Thank you,' said Frogmorton, and then he cradled the phone.

Sergeant Mills put the telephone down, and stared at his computer screen for a few moments, wondering how he was going to write up that call without looking like a candidate for early retirement.

CHAPTER FIFTEEN

No Time for Tea and Biscuits –
We've Got to Save the World!

Things were not going too well for Elaine's father, Professor Markham - Head of the Environmental Technology Department at Dawson University and Frogmorton's soon-to-be-ex-employer. No matter how hard he tried, he could not quite duplicate Frogmorton's experiment and was, therefore, unable to produce the masses of diamonds he had hoped for. Oh, he was able to reproduce all the whizzes and bangs, and managed quite easily to singe his hair when the experiment frequently blew up in his face, but he was not yet ready to trade on the international diamond market. What upset Markham nearly as much as not being able to get rich quick was the idea that an idiot like Frogmorton Culpepper was able to stumble across the process in the first place. Markham had had 30 years of research behind him and nothing much to show for it. Oh, he had received accolades in the past, but always for someone else's work that he had managed to steal. The trouble was that he wasn't a very good scientist at all. He had no natural flair for it. It was just as well that he had a natural flair for plagiarism; otherwise he would still be a lab assistant.

It finally dawned on him that there must be something in Frogmorton's notes that would throw some light on the problem. He had read and re-read all the notes that Frogmorton had left behind, and came up with nothing. Markham realised that the missing link must be in any notes that Frogmorton may have at his house. Now a new problem presented itself. How was he going to get his hands on those notes? He couldn't try to get hold of them himself. After all he was a respected member of the community. He toyed with the idea of hiring a common criminal to break in and steal the notes, but decided that was a bad idea, because the burglar would have no idea what he was looking for and had as much chance of coming back with Frogmorton's shopping list as he had of bringing back the important missing documents.

What Markham needed was a scientist. Preferably an environmental technology scientist at that. Someone who could gain Frogmorton's confidence. Someone Frogmorton would feel at ease with and whom he would probably willingly show the notes to. But where would he find such a person? Then he remembered. Didn't he have a daughter who fitted that bill?

Gavin Woosner checked the calculations in front of him with something approaching concern. He had hoped that maybe the signal had been some kind of elaborate hoax being bounced off various satellites to give the impression that it was coming from deep space. But the proof was indisputable. The signal was coming from out there. And that meant that the Earth was heading for big trouble. Or, more to the point, big trouble was heading for the Earth. He piled all his notes and figures into his briefcase and headed back to where he had seen the alien hologram. The message it was delivering was quite clear, and the only thing left to do was to communicate with the aliens and persuade them to call off their attack.

Communication. Now there's another peculiar concept. We all know what communication is, but we're all pretty bad at it. The trouble is that communication is a two-way process, and if one party isn't tuned in to the other, it just doesn't take place. I think this is because there are many different levels of communication. If the two parties concerned are not on the same level, the communication process fails. For example, parents and teenagers are on such different levels of communication that one will never get through to the other, no matter how hard they try. Not unless one or other takes the bold step to cross over to the other's level, so that a parent knows how it feels to try to communicate as a teenager and a teenager knows how it feels to try to communicate as a parent. I know I often feel like a teenager ... but at my age I'm not likely to get one.

The greatest extra-terrestrial event in mankind's history had passed the British SETI seekers by - not through incompetence, but due to a series of government cutbacks. Radio telescope time had been drastically cut. In fact, similar financial pressures on a global scale had ensured that Gavin Woosner's discovery had not been made by any of his colleagues in other countries and on other continents. This was a bonus for Rheingold, because it meant that he had a real chance of keeping the whole affair under wraps - as soon as it was possible to silence Gavin, Kevin ... whatever that damned Woosner chap was called, once and for all. Being an employee of a US government agency meant that he had no faith whatsoever in US government agencies and, therefore, didn't trust the FBI or the CIA to get the job done. There was only one course of action left open to him, and so he picked up the telephone and dialled a number. After waiting long enough for the person on the other end to lift the receiver, Rheingold said, 'Don Salvatore, I have a little contract for you ....'

In the bigness of space, the mighty StarDestroyer Blagn'k hurtled on towards its destiny with Planet Earth, the inhabitants of which - for the most part - were oblivious to its very existence. This information would have disappointed Kratol. He had this grand vision that his message was received with awe and foreboding, that the entire planetary population was trembling at the power which he alone wielded. It made him feel really big and clever ... let's not disillusion him.

Isn't power a wonderful thing? It is nice to be in control ... I would imagine. What a marvellous feeling it would be to know that destiny was to be what you wanted it to be. Mind you, it wouldn't really be destiny then, would it? After all, if destiny is predetermined, you would hardly be able to shape it to your own desires, no matter how powerful you are. That sort of thing is best left to the powers-that-be - whoever they are. And who, I wonder, predetermined the destiny of the powers-that-be who predetermine our destiny? I wonder who sat around a table in the first place and decided what destiny would turn out like? And why couldn't they have made it a little bit more interesting? And what happened before they decided to invent destiny? It doesn't bear thinking too hard about, does it?

Frogmorton cradled the telephone and walked across behind the chair to which the unconscious ex-Russian was securely tied. 'It doesn't sound as if the police believed me,' he informed his friends and family. 'They just told me to keep this chap under surveillance.'

'We don't have time to be babysitters to him,' said Susan. 'There are more pressing things that we should be attending to.'

She indicated Kratol's hologram in case any of them had forgotten what the 'more pressing things' were.

'I've never trusted those high-pressure salesmen,' Frogmorton's mother confided, feeling that she ought to contribute something to the conversation. 'They're all mouth and trousers. Could sell a one-armed bloke a pair of gloves they could. Mind you, I've never seen them resort to this sort of violence before.'

'Who is this?' Rhona asked.

'An armed Russian furniture salesman,' replied Frogmorton.

'No, not him. This little fellow on the floor.' It was the first time that Rhona had set eyes on the alien since our trio sprung her from Moorhampton Hospital for the Criminally Insane.

They all gathered round Kratol's hologram, crouching down to get a better look. The hologram continued relaying its message of doom, and Rhona bent down so close that her nose was only about an inch away from it. 'Who is he?' she asked.

'He's the reason we brought you here, Mrs Willett,' Elaine said. She tried a smile, but found she couldn't manage one.

Frogmorton's mother watched her son and his three lady friends getting more and more immersed in that awful arty film that had fallen out of the back of the television, and decided that they were all mad and left them to it. 'Now he's an artist I suppose this sort of thing is going to be happening more often. Ought to get a real job. And a wife,' she muttered to herself as she vacated the room, taking care of a particularly persistent itch on her backside as she left.

* * *

Understandably, the people at MI5 tend to take more than a passing interest when foreign secret service agents enter the country. Especially when they belong to a friendly power and arrive unannounced. Particularly when two agents arrive within hours of one another. It generally means that something is going on and, if it's 'going on' on British soil, it's only fair that MI5 are in on it. Within hours of Vanessa O'Mara touching down, one of MI5's top men, Arthur Stubbins, was summoned to the Director General of the Security Service's office. Arthur's immediate thought was that something big was going down.

Arthur Stubbins strode purposefully into the Director General's office and said, 'You sent for me, sir?'

'Yes, come in, Stubbins,' the Director General said.

'I am in, sir.'

'Ah, so you are. Well, Stubbins, what can you tell me about Vanessa O'Mara the beautiful, flame-haired, green-eyed, twenty-eight-year-old, third generation colleen, skilled in the martial and marital arts and one of the CIA's top operatives - code-named Banshee because her appearance usually precedes someone's death. Educated at Oxford University, she gained an honours degree in modern political history. The only daughter of Seamus O'Mara, self-styled leader of the right wing religious sect known as 'Leprechauns of Jesus', married at 23 - widowed at 24 by a stray bullet at her father's wake. Arrested for the murder of her husband's killer after strangling him with her bare hands whilst making love to the man. Recruited by the CIA as a result of that murder, and an active operative with them ever since - responsible for the assassination of dozens of international figures whose interests clash with those of the United States of America, and who flew into the United Kingdom this morning?'

Arthur Stubbins looked his boss squarely in the eye and said, 'Never heard of her.'

The Director General cleared his throat and continued, 'Alright then, what do you know about Alexander Nikolayevich Korinyakov? One time KGB agent and now fast-track American citizen and FBI agent who walks with a pronounced Russian accent. Decorated three times with the Order of Lenin for services to his motherland, Russia, and a Congressional Medal of Honor nominee who only missed out on the big gong because he used to be a Russian. Unlike all the FBI agents we see on the television or at the movies, he prefers to work alone, which suits his colleagues because he is very unpopular with them, due to the fact that he used to be a Russian. Has a particular penchant for large, muscular and ugly women, and who is also presently operating on English soil, despite the fact that the FBI are only supposed to be interested in internal matters of national security in the United States?'

'Can't say I know him either, sir,' was Arthur Stubbins' response.

'We also have it on good authority that an ex-NASA employee named Gavin Woosner has entered the country, and is the main reason for the aforementioned agents being here. I don't suppose you know anything about him either.'

'Do you mean the same Gavin Woosner who attended the California Institute of Technology until 1994 when he joined NASA's SETI installation at Ames Research Center near Palo Alto, California after graduating in astrophysics and advanced origami, specialising in cleverly-folded paper rhinoceroses?' Arthur asked smugly.

'I haven't the foggiest idea,' said the Director General with a shrug of his shoulders. 'Why do you think I'm asking you about him?'

'Good point, sir'

'There is something big going on here, Stubbins, and I want you to get to the bottom of it. These American types think they can come over here and do what the hell they like. And to be perfectly honest with, you they usually do. But I'm getting pretty fed up with it. We're always playing second fiddle to those damned Yanks.'

'So where do I come in?'

'Through that door behind you usually.'

'No, sir, I mean where do I come in regarding this particular scenario with the Americans?'

'Ah! I'm glad you asked me that, Stubbins. I want you to find out what the blighters are up to and, if you think there's any points to be scored off them, I want you to do whatever it is that they are going to do before they get a chance to do it.'

'I'll do my best, sir.'

'I hope you're going to do considerably more than that, Stubbins. You have to come out on top here. I mean, it's not so bad when these Yanks take all the credit elsewhere. But on British soil we have to be the ones who get the job done.'

'You can leave it with me, sir. I won't let the side down,' said Arthur Stubbins with patriotism fuelling the fire within him.

'You'd better not let the side down. Your pension is riding on this one. Get it right, Stubbins, and you can retire in style. Screw up and you'll be living on fish fingers for the rest of your natural days.'

'Yes, sir,' Stubbins said and then made his way to the door.

'Oh, Stubbins,' the Director General said as an afterthought.

Arthur swung round and faced the Director General expectantly.

'As our American friends say, in a most irritating fashion - "have a nice day".' The Director General smiled ineffectually at Stubbins and then returned to his *Times* crossword.

Arthur left the office.

* * *

Okay, I know what you're saying. Arthur Stubbins is a pretty stupid name for a secret agent. I must say, I take exception to that. Why shouldn't he have an ordinary sort of name? The world is full of people with less than spectacular names, but it doesn't make them dull or uninteresting. Look at James Brown. Alright, so he wasn't a spy, but his life was far from dull and uninteresting. I'll bet if Ian Fleming had called his spy Arthur Stubbins you'd have just accepted it. Well, I'm not changing it now in any case ... it might upset his mother.

It didn't take Vanessa O'Mara long to pick up Korinyakov's trail. A man who walks with a Russian accent is easy to trace. Well, in England at any rate. It might prove more difficult in Russia. The trail led to Gavin Woosner's hotel, and if she had arrived there ten minutes earlier, she would have had the pleasure of interrogating the ex-NASA employee. The room was more or less how Korinyakov had found it, and Vanessa started sifting through Woosner's belongings to look for a clue to this case. The CIA bosses had been peculiarly sketchy on the details, telling Vanessa that the less she knew about the background the better. Just suffice it to say that Woosner was a dangerous man and had to be silenced at all costs. They were unsure too about Korinyakov's convictions, and thought it desirable that he should share the same fate as Woosner - after all, he used to be a Russian.

Vanessa was sorting through the contents of a drawer when the hotel manager chanced to pass by the open door. He couldn't resist challenging her, reasoning, quite rightly, that she really had no business rummaging through one of his guest's personal belongings without the permission of that guest. Being British, he knocked on the door politely before starting his interrogation.

'Er, excuse me, miss. Can I help you?' he asked.

'Yes,' she replied. 'You can ransack the bathroom, whilst I

finish in here.'

That wasn't exactly what the hotel manager had in mind, so he decided to rephrase the question.

'Are you supposed to be in here?' he tried.

'Not really, pal. Now will you either poke your toffee nose into the bathroom or take a hike.'

'Madam, I cannot permit you to carry out purloinious activities on the premises of this establishment,' the hotel manager said in his most official tone.

'Purloinious?' queried Vanessa. 'Are you sure that's a real word?'

'Whether the word is correct or not, madam, I cannot allow you to continue the activity in which you are engaged without summoning the assistance of the local constabulary to prevent you with the utmost expediency.'

Vanessa was getting tired of this small talk. Well actually in the case of the hotel manager, the talk was far from small. She had never heard so many syllables used to so little purpose in one sentence before, which both impressed and annoyed her. Sensing that the hotel manager was not going to disappear, she decided to take action. She went up real close to him and adopted a seductive pose, which generally rendered men incapable of speech or deed. Had the hotel manager not been so attracted to men she might have succeeded.

'It's no good looking at me in that fashion, madam. You are not my type,' he announced with a wry smile.

Vanessa reached down between his legs and grasped his manhood and accompanying hardware with a vice-like grip. The smile on the hotel manager's face rapidly changed to a worried frown.

'Now then,' she said as she tightened her grip. 'We don't want to do anything that will upset me, do we?'

'No,' squeaked the hotel manager with uncharacteristic

brevity. Beads of sweat formed on his forehead, which made it look as though his wig was starting to cry.

'Where can I find the guy who booked into this room?'

'I don't know. Mr Goldrhein left the hotel just over ten minutes ago. In quite a hurry, as I remember.'

'Goldrhein?' she queried.

'That's the name he booked in with. Odd sort of chap. But then - he is American.'

'Another man came here looking for Mr er ... Goldrhein. Can you tell me what happened to him?'

'He's gone too. Very rude gentleman. Destroyed a member of staff's newspaper before he left. He went looking for a local man who claims to be having pizzas delivered by tiny aliens.'

'Right. Thank you for that piece of information. I'll forget how rude you were to me before.'

'Thank you so much,' the hotel manager said. After a couple of minutes he added, 'Do you think perhaps you could let go of my ... er ...'

'Oh, yes!' Vanessa said with a sweet apologetic voice, 'I nearly forgot I was still holding them.' And she let go - after pulling and twisting hard to the right first.

As she left the room, the hotel manager said from his foetal position on the floor, 'So kind.' The voice had the edge of a boy soprano.

'Don't mention it,' Vanessa said as she disappeared from sight. Then from a distance she added, 'Have a nice day.'

The hotel manager didn't.

* * *

Frogmorton and his three lady friends were still marvelling at Kratol's hologram when his mother burst through the door.

'That Mormon chap is back,' she announced.

At that precise moment Alexander Korinyakov regained consciousness. Without even looking and with one motion, Frogmorton's mother hooked the ornamental coalscuttle with her foot, sent it somersaulting into the air, caught it with her left hand, passed it to her right hand and connected it with Korinyakov's skull in less than three seconds. The result of such a spectacular display of skilful footwork and hand and eye coordination was that Korinyakov slipped back into a comatose state where he would be unable to trouble anyone.

Gavin pushed past Frogmorton's mother with the minimum of ceremony. 'Hi, I'm Gavin Woosner, formerly of NASA, and I gotta tell you that what you have there in front of you is the genuine article.'

Frogmorton felt that introductions were in order and said, 'Hello Mr Woosner. I'm Frogmorton Culpepper and these ladies are Elaine Markham from the Environmental Technology Laboratory at Dawson University, Susan Likely a reporter from the *Chronicle* and this is Mrs Rhona Willett a patient... er... a patient woman from the... er... from around here.'

'They said they were coming back for me,' Rhona confided in Gavin Woosner. 'They've shrunk a bit since I last saw them, though.'

'Who's in charge here?' Gavin asked.

Elaine said, 'Frogmorton here is the one they chose to contact; so I guess he is.'

'Right,' Gavin said, 'there's not a moment to lose. We have to get a message to these aliens.'

'We'd already worked that one out for ourselves,' Frogmorton said. 'Only they didn't leave their phone number.'

'Oh yes they did,' Gavin said, waving his calculations about impressively. 'I've got all the information I need right here. All we have to do is tune in and send our reply.'

Susan Likely regarded the Mormon chap who claimed to be

from NASA for a moment, and said, 'What if we can't get the reply to them in time?'

'No problem. Radio waves travel at the speed of light and, presumably, these guys are headed towards the Earth at near-to-light or even faster-than-light speeds so our transmission is bound to collide with them before they reach Earth.'

'Faster-than-light speeds?' Elaine enquired.

'Their technology must be vastly superior than ours to have developed inter-stellar or even inter-galactic manned flight, so we must assume that faster-than-light speeds are attainable to them.'

Frogmorton said, 'You mean to say that they can travel at velocities that we can only dream of?'

'More than a probability,' came Gavin's reply. 'But I've got to be honest with you, I'm more worried about getting the message sent in the first place, than whether it gets to them or not.'

'What do you mean?' asked Elaine.

'They're after me,' said Gavin.

'Who? The Aliens?' Frogmorton asked.

'Worse than that. The United States Government.'

Frogmorton's mother was feeling decidedly left out of the conversation. 'Would someone mind telling me what's going on?' she quite reasonably asked.

'It's a long story, Mother,' Frogmorton offered. And, of course, it was. (Heck, we're already on page 182.)

'That's it,' Frogmorton's mother mumbled, 'leave your poor mother in the dark. I'm not important. You carry on with your new-found friends and your arty films that fall out the back of your television set. You just go ahead and ignore me.' She left the room and Frogmorton did just as he was told - he ignored her completely.

'Why is your government after you?' Susan asked.

'I discovered this signal at the NASA SETI installation at Ames Research Center near Palo Alto, California, and I've been in hot water ever since.'

'Why?' asked Frogmorton. 'I thought the whole point of SETI was discovering signals like this.'

'So did I,' replied Gavin. 'The trouble is that the whole thing has turned political. Budgets are at stake. The discovery of intelligent life out there seems to be threatening the very fabric of NASA's existence, and so they don't want to admit that all this is happening. That guy over there that we got tied to the chair, he's FBI. I'll bet the CIA aren't far behind and believe me, those guys don't use kid gloves.'

'We've got to go to the authorities with this,' Elaine said.

'No,' Gavin said. 'We can't afford to do that.'

'But surely you don't fear the British Government,' said Susan.

'It's not that,' Gavin said defensively. 'It's just that we'll get lost in red tape. We don't have time for any delays. We are the only ones who can do this. Are you with me?'

'Of course we are,' said Frogmorton, just as his mother returned carrying a tray with tea and biscuits on it.

'I've brought you some refreshments,' she announced as she placed the tray on the table. 'Don't worry about the biscuits. I dropped them on the kitchen floor, but I wiped them over with my hanky.' This she said whilst extracting something from her left nostril with the aforementioned hanky.

'Mother,' said Frogmorton, the only one in the room qualified to call her that, 'we don't have time for tea and biscuits right now. We've got to save the world.'

'Well you can't expect to do something as important as all that without having a cup of tea,' she said. 'This country won the last world war on cups of tea.'

They all ignored her. There was an uneasy silence, all except for the drone of Kratol's voice as his hologram churned out its deadly message. That was until Frogmorton's mother broke the silence with an almighty belch. 'Excuse me,' she said in the most polite way she could. 'Had eggs again for breakfast.'

They all tried very hard to ignore her.

'How are we going to do it, then? Send the message I mean?' asked Frogmorton.

'We need to get to a radio telescope. Jodrell Bank would be the best bet,' said Gavin.

'I thought that was there to receive radio emissions, not to transmit,' said Elaine.

'I can take care of that,' said Gavin. 'Just get me in there and leave the rest to me.'

'That might not be easy,' said Susan. 'I expect they've got security guards there.'

'Susan's got a point,' said Frogmorton.

'But we've got to try,' said Elaine.

'I know how to contact the aliens,' said Rhona.

Frogmorton turned to Rhona and said, 'Look Rhona, no offence, but we've got a real space expert here now - not a homicidal maniac who thinks she got kidnapped by little green men just because she wanted an excuse to smash her family's faces in. You were great when you were our only hope, but now, well, I think you might be surplus to requirements. We might as well drop you off at Moorhampton Hospital for the Criminally Insane on our way. What do you say to that?'

'Suit yourself,' said Rhona, 'only I think I could still be of some use to you?'

'And how do you work that one out?' Frogmorton asked.

'Well, I've got a cousin in Cheshire,' she said.

'Your point being?' asked Frogmorton.

'Hey! Cheshire? That's where Jodrell Bank is. Right?' said Gavin Woosner enthusiastically.

'That's right,' said Rhona. 'And that's where my cousin works - at Jodrell Bank with all those radio telescope things.'

They all looked at Rhona, not sure whether to laugh or cry knowing that the future of civilisation lay in the hands of a madwoman again.

CHAPTER SIXTEEN
The M1 Northbound

Elite One was starting to have serious doubts about the chain of command. Understandable really, as the chain of command only had one link in it. Not only one link, but a link that was responsible for the destruction of one of his own squadron members. This 'water skiing' through the Cosmos attached by tractor beam to the alien invaders' ship might have been fun when it first started, but the novelty was beginning to wear off. Where was it all going to end? Even if they did manage to hold on long enough to track down the alien invaders' home planet, even if they were able to destroy their home-world with only four Armageddon missiles, what would they do then? It was clear to the pilot of Elite One that Squadron Leader Fligg's obsession with revenge was clouding his judgement. This mission meant certain death for the only two remaining Muridaens in the Universe. A prospect that he felt was unfair. After all, he only joined the Muridaen Space Defence Corps for the uniform, generous pay and as many females as he could lay his hands on; death was never an attraction.

The sound of a voice over the intercom disturbed Squadron Leader Fligg from a dreamless sleep.

'Elite One to Squadron Leader Fligg, come in please, sir,' it said.

'Fligg here. What do you want? Have you traced the alien invaders' home-world?'

'No sir. It's just that I've been thinking.'

'Haven't we all Elite One.'

'I think we are wasting our time, sir.'

'You do, do you?' Squadron Leader Fligg wondered where

this conversation was leading.

Elite One showed him exactly where it was leading by saying, 'I think we should break off this attack and try and find a planet that will support life. Try and settle down.'

'I must say, I'm flattered Elite One, but I don't think I'm ready to settle down right now and, in any case, you're not my type.'

'I'm just saying sir, that what we are doing is futile. We can't make a difference. Our beloved Muridae has gone. We must find somewhere to go to live the rest of our lives. This mission is suicide.'

'Is this mutiny Elite One?' Squadron Leader Fligg asked, just in case he was mistaken.

'No sir, just common sense.'

'It might be common sense to you to run off with your tail between your legs, Elite One. But Muridae meant something to me. When they destroyed our planet, they didn't just blow up a chunk of rock, they blew up millions of our species; they blew up our cultures; they blew up our heritage. And you want me to turn a blind eye to all that and let the alien invader get away with that?'

There was a moment's silence. Squadron Leader Fligg was just about to congratulate himself on the quality of his speech when Elite One said, 'Yes. I think it's best if we don't pursue this.' And then Elite One switched off his tractor beam and was lost in the void. The Elite Squadron now consisted of one Asteroid Class Deep Space Medium Armoured Interceptor piloted by the best of the Muridaen Space Defence Corps.

Fligg sensed that things were not going well. After all, his planet and everything on it had been totally wiped out, his squadron had slowly diminished to the grand total of one, and he was the only Muridaen left to seek out the alien invaders' home-world and destroy it in an act of glorious retribution - armed with only two Armageddon missiles.

Squadron Leader Fligg thought hard about the situation and said, 'Shit!'

Domr'k was disturbed from his study of Planet Earth when the alarm sounded on the navigation computer. Although he knew that the computer was programmed to compensate for the change in mass that they had experienced, he felt he ought to just see that everything was going smoothly. He checked all the figures on the readout and saw that the ship's mass had changed again, ever so slightly. It was a good job, he thought, that he had programmed the computer to allow for mass change, otherwise they would probably miss the Earth completely; and that would never do. He had a good feeling about the Earth. He felt a kind of bond with the dominant species - man. He thought that if ever a planet was going to survive their inter-galactic janitorial duties, the Earth would be it. Mind you, he had the same feeling about Gweelox 4 and look what happened there.

Frogmorton, Gavin and the three women all piled into Frogmorton's car, and set off for Cheshire leaving Frogmorton's mother behind to make sure that the FBI agent would be safely out of the way and not on their trail. Frogmorton drove and Elaine sat beside him in the front passenger seat with his road atlas. Frogmorton wished he had bought that sat nav he had once promised himself. (All that had stopped him buying it was his mother saying she would get him one for his birthday, and instead all she got him was a rather tired and ancient second-hand Sony Walkman that looked like she'd bought it from a car boot sale for a pound.) Susan, Gavin and Rhona sat in the back.

Susan started jotting things down in her reporter's notebook as Frogmorton drove. She was going to have one hell of a story to write if they ever got through the next couple of days - and she was damned if she was going to let the editor mess with it this time. After a while, the movement of Gavin Woosner's hands caught Susan's attention. They were deftly crafting something out of a scrap of paper. She watched enthralled as he turned the sheet of paper this way and that, turning corners in, folding sides over and tucking flaps in here and there. When he had finished she could hardly believe her eyes, and thought to herself that it was a very cleverly-folded paper rhinoceros indeed. Rhona just sat in her corner and smiled the smile of someone that knew something and wasn't going to tell anyone else what it was she knew.

So much had happened over the last forty-eight hours, and Frogmorton knew that so much more needed to happen in the next twenty-four if Planet Earth was going to stand a chance of survival. It played heavily on his mind that nobody in authority was likely to believe him about the alien in the microwave. I mean, what's the point of them being in authority if they're not going to listen to anyone? Frogmorton was getting so deeply involved with his thoughts that he nearly missed the turning to take the motorway. Elaine's elbow gently brought him back to reality as it wedged between his ribs when she shouted, 'Take this turning here for the M1!'

Frogmorton obliged with a swift turn of the steering wheel that sent Gavin Woosner's very cleverly-folded paper rhinoceros hurtling out of Rhona Willet's window as the ex-NASA employee flew across Susan Likely's lap so that his nose ended up about an eighth of an inch away from Rhona's nose.

Without batting an eyelid, Rhona said to Gavin, 'They told me they were coming back for me, you know?' and then she drew back within herself and re-adopted her mysterious smile.

Gavin struggled back to his side of the car, apologising to Susan for the intrusion. Susan just smiled at him and said, 'That's alright.'

Gavin looked into her eyes for a brief moment, saw how they sparkled and glowed and how there was a trace of something very special that emanated from deep within. Then he tore another sheet of paper from his notebook and started on another very cleverly-folded paper rhinoceros.

Frogmorton glanced across at Elaine. 'Thanks,' he said with a grateful smile. 'I nearly missed it. Got a lot on my mind.'

Elaine patted his hand and said, 'Don't worry. You're not alone.' The smile she gave him would have melted him, but he missed it as he turned away to check for traffic as he joined the M1 motorway for the long trek north via it and the M6 towards Cheshire.

Markham was getting pretty angry. He had devised a foolproof plan to get at Frogmorton Culpepper's notes. but his daughter, who figured prominently in that plot, was nowhere to be found. She could be so inconsiderate at times. He remembered that she was even inconsiderate at birth. Why on Earth did she have to be a girl when he really wanted a son? Life can be so unfair. He also didn't like the unhealthy way she was siding with Frogmorton, and he reasoned that she was probably with the moron right now. He hoped to goodness that she wasn't falling in love with him - that would be just too much to bear. So, he continued to reason, if his daughter was at Frogmorton's house, it would be perfectly reasonable for him to call and see if his daughter wanted a ride home, giving him the opportunity to ask to use the bathroom and then find Frogmorton's room and steal the missing notes. Once he had all the answers and had finally perfected the diamond manufacturing process, he didn't intend sharing the knowledge with the scientific community. This was definitely one invention he didn't want the credit for ... he just wanted the diamonds. With the thought of untold wealth running around in his mind, Markham decided that he would call at Frogmorton's house in search of his daughter and, at the earliest available opportunity, he would excuse himself and go and search for the missing notes. After all, he was the one who knew what to look for and the fewer people who knew about his diamond mine the better. He left for Frogmorton's house with a wry smile on his face. The one he always reserved for when he was being a complete bastard.

It was not difficult for Vanessa O'Mara to track down Alexander Korinyakov. After all, she would be a very poor secret agent if she could not fulfil a simple task like tracking down a man who walked with a Russian accent in England - even if he was an American citizen now. His last known whereabouts was a house in suburbia, information she had extracted from the taxi driver who took him there and who was now driving her to the same destination.

'He was a bit of a mean bugger if I remember rightly,' the taxi driver informed her. 'Didn't leave much in the way of a tip, if you know what I mean, love.' The cabby gave her a meaningful wink and smiled a warm smile, feeling that he was winning over the gorgeous redhead.

'Cut the crap and drive,' she said with a smile of her own that would have curdled cream. She thought that it was a pity that the taxi driver wasn't her target, because he was beginning to annoy her.

The taxi driver was a bit put out by the woman's attitude and came to the conclusion - quite rightly as it happens - that she was no big tipper either, and so decided to go the long way to make up for it.

* * *

The traffic was particularly heavy on the M1 and it was bumper to bumper for miles ahead. Frogmorton felt that this was not a good day to get held up on the roads. It was a pity that they couldn't fly to Cheshire; it would have been a lot quicker and, of course, time was ticking away. The endless waiting in the traffic jams was beginning to show in the others. Rhona had taken to singing nursery rhymes in the back seat, whilst Gavin and Susan were playing endless games of noughts and crosses without one of them ever winning a game. This left Frogmorton and Elaine free to chat in the front.

'How long have you been working on your Project Earth, Frogmorton?' she asked with genuine interest.

'It seems like forever,' he answered honestly, because time seemed unimportant to him compared to the enormity of the task he was undertaking, 'and I thought I had it all worked out too.'

'Don't give up, Frogmorton. Every great scientist has had to overcome setbacks before they find the solution to their problems.' She smiled at him and this time he saw it. He felt his face redden.

'Oh!' said Elaine. 'I've embarrassed you now.' And she gave out a little giggle. Frogmorton looked at her and knew that he had fallen in love.

'I'm sure you're not really interested in me,' he said, curiously dreading an affirmative response to that statement. 'I expect there are much more interesting scientists about. Anyway, I'm not a real scientist.'

'You are to me,' Elaine said and this time not only did she pat the back of his hand, but she also lifted it up and placed it in her hand. They sat there without speaking for a while, looking at each other occasionally and knowing that a special bond was beginning to form between them and all the while trying to blot out Rhona's out-of-tune version of 'Baa Baa Black Sheep' that she sang as she rocked back and forth on the back seat.

* * *

Meanwhile back in the United States of America, Salvatore Rabatti was mourning his dead cousin Alessandro 'Lashes' Mascara. It was a very sad occasion for him for several reasons. Firstly, because Alessandro was family. Secondly, Salvatore had been given a contract by that nice man at NASA, Mr Rheingold, that he would have difficulty fulfilling. And thirdly, because it was he, Salvatore Rabatti, who iced Alessandro in the first place. It was regrettable that he had to kill his favourite cousin, but then it would never do to let sentiment get in the way of business. Besides, Italians knew how to have a good funeral.

Salvatore knew that he wouldn't be able to get away to England to take care of the Gavin Woosner affair for that nice man at NASA, Mr Rheingold, and so he decided to make a telephone call to his sister in England. She wasn't a true Rabatti. She didn't have that killer instinct and, what's more, she was married to a boring restaurateur. Where was the passion in that? Salvatore knew that she was not the ideal choice to take on the contract, but she was still family and that obligated her. He picked up the telephone and dialled her number.

'Hello, seven double nine four six eight,' she said into the mouthpiece of her telephone several thousand miles away. By the way, I don't mean to say that the mouthpiece was several thousand miles away from her mouth, but that she and, indeed, her telephone were several thousand miles away from Salvatore.

'Mimi!' Salvatore declared. 'It's your brother Salvatore!'

'Salvatore?' Mimi said, her voice tinged with surprise and annoyance. 'What the bloody hell do you want?'

Isn't it strange how members of your own family instinctively know when you want them to do you a favour? Particularly when, like Salvatore, that's the only time you ever bother to speak to them. But then again, isn't that what families are for, to help one another?

I think it's a shame, though, when families drift apart. Mine's like that, I'm afraid. I have dozens of great-nephews and great-nieces that I hardly ever see. Except at weddings, christenings and funerals, of course. In fact, I'm sure they think that I'm their rich great-uncle. After all, they only ever see me dressed in a suit. When families are very close, people say that they live in each other's pockets. Perhaps my own family is close, then, after all. I've always got my hand in my pocket for them for something.

'You want me to do what?' Mimi Sarchetti shouted into the telephone.

'Now, calm down, Mimi,' Salvatore said reassuringly. 'I would do it myself, you know that, but out of respect for poor Alessandro I must stay here and comfort his widow.'

'But I can't kill a man in cold blood. I'm a nursery school teacher, for goodness sake,' Mimi pleaded.

'There is no other way, my little sister,' Salvatore persisted to insist to his sister. 'We are family. You have your obligations.'

'No, Salvatore!' insisted his persistent sister. 'I categorically refuse to do it.'

'It's worth $200,000,' Salvatore announced.

Mimi Sacchetti went silent for a few seconds and then said, 'Where will I find the creep you want wasted?'

'That's my girl,' said Salvatore smugly. He really loved the mercenary side to his persistently insistent sister. 'I will make a few calls to my contacts over there and I will call you back.' He cradled the phone and went back to mourning his recently deceased cousin. Because the family was so close, Salvatore resolved that 25% of the money he was to receive for killing his cousin Alessandro would be given to Alessandro's widow. See - he wasn't completely heartless, after all.

CHAPTER SEVENTEEN
The M6 Northbound

Markham arrived in Frogmorton's street at roughly the same time as Vanessa O'Mara, and noticed that the flame-haired beauty was heading for Frogmorton's house. He had armed himself with a hefty crowbar in case the notes he wanted were locked away in a filing cabinet or something and, for safe keeping, had hidden it down the front of his trousers. Discretion being the better part of valour, Markham decided not to call at Frogmorton's house whilst the woman was there; he didn't want there to be too many witnesses to the crime he was about to commit. So, he decided to call at the house next door on some pretext or other until the coast was clear. The crowbar felt heavy in his trousers, and so he held onto it in order that it didn't fall out on the floor and reveal his true intentions. He knocked on the door with his free hand, and watched the redhead at Frogmorton's door from the corner of his eye. The crowbar started to slip and he held onto it with both hands. It was then that Mrs Douglas opened the door to be confronted with the sight of a middle-aged man eyeing up a pretty young woman whilst clutching something long and hard down his trousers with both hands.

To say that Mrs Douglas was shocked at this apparition on her doorstep would be an understatement. Admittedly, in the last forty-eight hours she had been subjected to more confrontations with certain parts of the male anatomy than she had ever had to deal with in her entire life before. What worried her most, though, was that she was starting to enjoy it.

'Can I help you?' she said as she eyed up the curious bulge in Markham's trousers.

'Er… yes,' said Markham caught slightly off guard, 'I'm doing a survey and I wondered if you could answer a few questions.'

Mrs Douglas's new found interest in male appendages was getting the better of her. She couldn't help being impressed by the fact that Markham had to hold the protuberance with both hands, and felt her breathing start to become erratic. Desires started to well up inside her that she hadn't experienced before. She started to feel passion and lust.

'Won't you come in?' she asked, in a manner that should have worried Markham, had he been taking any notice. He watched the redhead disappear inside Frogmorton's house, and then followed Mrs Douglas into her sitting room. He could keep an eye on the street from there.

Vanessa O'Mara took note of the man with the crowbar down his trousers visiting the house next door. Carrying crowbars down one's trousers was a little bit too eccentric, even for an Englishman, she thought. She would have to check that guy out after she had dealt with Woosner. She knocked on the door again, and this time it was opened and she pushed her way in.

'I'd like to know what the hell is going on. Why do people keep barging in here?' demanded Frogmorton's mother.

'Where is he?' demanded Vanessa O'Mara.

'Who are you?' demanded Frogmorton's mother. It looked like it was going to be a demanding conversation.

'I'm CIA,' was the short but accurate reply.

'I don't know what the world is coming to,' said Frogmorton's mother, shaking her head. 'I never shop at C&A because they rarely do my size and now they're sending shop staff round my house.'

'Just be quiet and answer my question. Where is Woosner?'

said the CIA agent.

'They don't seem to teach you shop assistants any manners these days. You'll never sell a pair of knickers with that attitude, young lady,' said Frogmorton's mother, disgusted at the falling standards of service offered in modern retail establishments and, of course, completely unaware of the fact that C&A had closed the last of its retail stores in the UK years ago.

Vanessa O'Mara was getting tired of being nice to this obnoxious woman, so she grabbed her by the arm and twisted it behind her back. 'I'm not playing games, bitch!'

'I hate these high-pressure sales techniques. Do you take Barclaycard?' said Frogmorton's mother, hoping that making a purchase might make this rude sales girl leave her house.

'Now for the last time... where is Woosner?' Vanessa O'Mara said in a way that indicated her lack of patience.

'I'm not sure which one Woosner is,' explained Frogmorton's mother. 'Is he the furniture salesman gentleman I've got tied to a chair in the other room?'

'Let's take a look shall we?' Vanessa O'Mara said with the closest thing resembling a smile that had ever crossed her lips.

Frogmorton's mother led Vanessa O'Mara into the other room, where the bound and comatose Korinyakov was trying to regain consciousness.

'That's not Woosner! It's the goddam Russian FBI man – Korinyakov,' said Vanessa O'Mara. She turned her attention back to Frogmorton's mother and said, 'So... you are in on the conspiracy too, are you? What happened here and where is Gavin Woosner?'

'Well... if it's not this furniture salesman you're after, you must want that Mormon chap. He's gone off with my son and his three fancy women. He's getting worse than his father you know. Randy devil he was.'

'Where did they go?'

'I'm not sure. There's been a lot of coming and going round here today. That man with the Red Indian wives cleared off earlier on to check his figures, then dashed back here and they all took off in my son's car.'

Vanessa O'Mara was growing impatient, and decided to speed the explanation up by twisting Frogmorton's mother's arm a little harder. 'But where did they take off to in your son's car?'

'I don't know what you're trying to achieve, you know. I can scratch the top of my head with my arm behind my back.' And Frogmorton's mother illustrated that point by reaching her arm further up her back and scratching the top of her head. Then she added, 'I think they went to the bank.'

'The bank?' asked the CIA agent.

'Yes. Probably to arrange a loan for that Mormon chap's furniture order off this gentleman,' Frogmorton's mother said pointing at Korinyakov.

'Ohhh! What happened to my head?' asked Korinyakov with a genuine interest in the cause of his horrendous headache.

'Do you know which bank?' quizzed the flame-haired beauty.

'They did say. But I'd never heard of it before. Jodhpurs or something. Can't say I've ever seen that one down the High Street,' said Frogmorton's mother.

Hearing that Woosner and his friends had gone to a bank worried Korinyakov. Maybe they'd sold out already. It was up to him now to eliminate Woosner before he caused any more trouble. And his friends too – they obviously knew too much. And he needed to find out who Woosner had sold out to and eliminate them. But first he needed to untie himself and find out who the aggressive redhead was who was attacking the lovely creature that rendered him unconscious earlier, before he'd had the chance to waste her.

'What's going on here?' Korinyakov asked with genuine interest.

'You're hardly in a position to be asking questions, Korinyakov,' said Vanessa O'Mara, 'but if you must know, my name is Vanessa O'Mara of the Central Intelligence Agency and you're off the Woosner case.'

'The hell I am!' exclaimed Korinyakov. Note the subtle use of an exclamation mark to denote Korinyakov's exclamation.

Any further argument on the subject was negated by the resounding clang of the ornamental coalscuttle as it made contact once more with the back of Korinyakov's skull. The force of the impact sent him flying face first onto the floor where, on landing, the wooden chair he was tied to decided that enough was enough and it split into several pieces.

'We bought that chair from him too, you know,' said Frogmorton's mother. 'It's no wonder they're always closing down with the lack of quality of the goods they sell.'

Vanessa O'Mara was tired of small talk. She started to push Frogmorton's mother towards the door.

'Where are we going?' asked Frogmorton's mother.

'To the bank to find Woosner,' came the reply, 'and you're coming along for insurance.'

'I think I'm fully covered, actually,' said Frogmorton's mother, misunderstanding the situation more than usual.

* * *

Mrs Douglas was finding it hard to keep control. After acquiring her new-found acquaintance with what men had to offer, she realised that she had been missing out all these years, and was determined not to waste another minute. She wondered what it would have been like if she hadn't kept refusing Frogmorton's father - he was a randy devil after all. With carnal thoughts racing through her mind, she adopted her most seductive voice and said to Markham, 'Can I get you a cup of tea?'

Not understanding the obvious innuendo in the question, Markham said, 'Yes please.'

'Well, make yourself at home,' she continued. 'I'll go and put the kettle on and slip into something a little more comfortable.' Her eyes remained transfixed on the bulge in Markham's trousers as she left the room. Markham's eyes remained transfixed on Frogmorton's house. He hoped it wouldn't be too long before the redhead left and he could try and con his way in there by pretending to be a furniture salesman or something.

Mrs Douglas closed the kitchen door behind her and leant against it, breathless with excitement. That nice man with the bulging trousers had said yes to a cup of tea! She could hardly contain herself as she started to feel a hot flush wash all over her. She put the kettle on and seductively placed a tea bag into a chipped mug. Then a pang of overwhelming apprehension surged through her body. Was she going mad? How could she possibly have let this happen? What was she going to do about it? She started to breathe deeply to try and control the panic attack, and determined that she would have to go back in to the other room and face him. She checked the mirror to make sure her face hadn't reddened, and then bravely went back in to the other room.

'You'll probably think I'm foolish,' she said to Markham, noticing that nothing had changed within his trousers, 'but there is something I should have said.'

'What's that?' enquired Markham, not looking away from the window.

'Do you take sugar?' Mrs Douglas blurted out, feeling her face start to glow as she blushed at her own boldness.

Markham was just about to respond when he saw the redhead emerge from Frogmorton's house. Better still, he saw that another woman was going with her - presumably Frogmorton's mother. He watched as he saw the redhead hail a cab, and was pleased to see both women get in. He allowed himself a wry smile when he saw the taxi speed off.

'Er... I'm afraid I won't be able to stop for tea now, Mrs ...er...' Markham tried to explain, 'something's just cropped up that I have to attend to.' Markham moved towards the door and Mrs Douglas flung herself across it barring his exit.

'You can't leave now; I've got the kettle on,' she explained.

'Some other time, perhaps,' offered Markham almost apologetically. He wondered if he'd have to use the crowbar secreted within his trousers to pry this strange woman from the doorway, but Mrs Douglas knew that she had blown it and moved away dejectedly.

As Markham left she said to herself, 'Bloody men! They get you all worked up and then just at the last minute they let you down.' Mrs Douglas was very quickly getting disillusioned with men.

Satisfied that the taxi was long out of sight, Markham walked up to Frogmorton's front door, and was delighted to see that the two women were in so much of a hurry to leave that they had left it open. He looked up and down the street to make sure no one was looking before he pushed the front door open and went inside. He couldn't help thinking that things were going a little too smoothly, but blessed his luck in any case. All he had to do now was find the missing notes in Frogmorton's room and he could soon retire in luxury. What a fool Frogmorton had been not noticing the true potential of his experiment, thought Markham. The production of diamonds was far more interesting than solving the problem of the greenhouse effect and fixing the hole in the ozone layer.

Markham was so busy thinking about the diamonds that he nearly tripped over the cat that was curled up on the stairs. Chloe was a little put out about nearly being trodden on. In fact, she was a little put out about a great number of things that were going on just lately. She thought that the house was turning into an asylum with all the comings and goings of the last couple of days. She was glad that she was only a cat and didn't have to worry about those kinds of things.

It didn't take Markham long to find Frogmorton's room. This was mainly because there was a plaque on the door that read, 'Frogmorton's Room'. He slowly opened the door, peering through as he did to make sure it was empty. It was. Everything was going well. He went over to Frogmorton's computer and turned it on; hoping that he would be just as lucky and the missing notes would be stored on there. He had a USB drive with him ready to copy the files onto. He was met with the requirement to enter a password, but, as it happened, this wasn't much of an obstacle as Frogmorton kept a notebook with all his passwords on his desk, clearly labelled 'Passwords' on its cover. Frogmorton diligently used a different password for each requirement he came across for one, always making sure each was a strong password replete with special characters, numbers and random use of upper case characters. Less diligently, such varied complex passwords were obviously difficult to remember, so he kept a careful record of them in his 'Passwords' notebook.

Markham was searching for likely files on Frogmorton's computer when he felt something cold and metallic being gently pushed into his neck at the back, just below the skull.

'Don't move,' commanded a voice with a strange mixture of American and Russian accents, 'or I'll spray your brains all over that computer.' Thus becoming aware that the cold metallic object being pressed against his neck was the barrel of a gun, and being anxious to keep his brains and the computer monitor from being introduced, Markham didn't move.

'Who are you?' asked Korinyakov.

'My name's Markham,' Markham replied truthfully and somewhat nervously.

'What has Woosner told you? Who do you work for?'

'Woosner?' quizzed Markham quizzically.

'Don't try and be smart with me,' said Korinyakov. 'What did he tell you and who do you work for?'

'I don't know any "Woosner",' said Markham, 'and I work at Dawson University. I'm Head of the Environmental Technology Department.'

Korinyakov pushed the barrel of the gun a little harder into the back of Markham's neck, leant over to whisper in his ear and was about to say, 'Stop playing games with me,' when he was prevented from doing so by the resounding clunk of Markham's crowbar on his skull.

* * *

The advantage to space being big is that there are very few traffic jams up there. Unlike the situation on the M1 motorway that had seen Frogmorton and his merry band held up for the best part of six hours. So, it was with some relief that Frogmorton was able to pick up a little speed just past the Watford Gap services.

'You need to turn off at the junction with the M6,' Elaine said. 'It's the one after the turn for Rugby.' Actually, Elaine never mentioned the turn off for Rugby. I put that there because it looks nice seeing the town I was born in being mentioned in a book.

'How much longer will it take?' asked Gavin Woosner, who was cleverly folding his twenty-third paper rhinoceros.

'Only a couple of hours now,' said Frogmorton as he turned onto the M6, 'providing the traffic keeps moving.' And then, as if through some grand master plan of cosmic proportions, the traffic stopped moving.

'What's the hold up?' asked Susan Likely.

'I think it's just the sheer volume of traffic,' said Elaine and

Frogmorton turned and smiled at her.

'Well I think we ought to formulate a plan of action,' continued Susan Likely. 'It's all very well rushing off to Jodrell Bank, but we really ought to know what we're going to do when we get there.'

'I'd hardly call this rushing,' said Gavin Woosner, sticking his head out of the window to get a better view of the traffic. Seeing the stationary line of vehicles stretching for as far as the eye could see was of little comfort to him.

'They said they'd be back,' chanted Rhona Willett in between choruses of 'Humpty Dumpty'.

'All the same,' said Susan, 'we need to work out a gameplan.'

'It's quite straightforward really,' said Gavin Woosner. 'All we have to do is get inside the control room, realign the dishes to the coordinates in space that I've calculated and transmit our message to the aliens.'

'What if we can't get inside?' asked Elaine.

'That's why we've brought the madwoman,' explained Frogmorton. 'Her cousin works there.'

'I know,' said Elaine, 'but is her cousin likely to want to help her. After what she did and where they sent her?'

'Well, we'll have to cross that bridge when we come to it,' replied Frogmorton. The traffic edged forward another ten yards. At this rate the Earth would be destroyed before they even reached the Corley service area.

* * *

Squadron Leader Fligg of the very much diminished Elite Squadron concentrated very hard on maintaining tractor beam acquisition on the alien invaders' ship and kept a watchful eye on his flux grid. He alone carried the hopes of the Muridaens. He alone was going to deliver the fatal blow that would destroy the alien invaders' home planet and deliver retribution in the shape of two Armageddon missiles. Admittedly it would be more difficult to destroy a planet with only two Armageddon missiles, but preliminary calculations on his ship's computer showed that all things are possible.

It was a great testament to his tremendous bravery that he never once considered his mission to be impossible, or that he might be vaporised at any moment by the alien invader, or that he had absolutely nowhere to go if he did actually succeed in his mission - well, a great testament to either his tremendous bravery or his tremendous stupidity.

Arthur Stubbins had sold twenty-four choc ices, forty-two cones and thirteen assorted ice lollies - a testament to how good his cover was as an ice cream vendor as he maintained surveillance on Frogmorton Culpepper's house. He had parked his ice cream van a little further down the street after trailing Korinyakov to that address. It was a bonus that he had also seen Vanessa O'Mara and Gavin Woosner at the same address. The thing that puzzled him most, though, was that Korinyakov hadn't come out yet, despite everyone else coming and going at an alarming rate. In fact, Arthur had noticed that there was a lot of urgency about all the others that made him wonder what might be going on in that house. Maybe the others had killed Korinyakov, and were all in on some huge conspiracy that might have implications for Her Majesty's Government. In fact, there might be things going on in that house that had implications on a global scale. Arthur sensed that the time had come to make a move – after all, he had almost completely sold out of ice creams. There only appeared to be two people left in the house, Korinyakov and the unknown man with a curious bulge down the front of his trousers, and Arthur felt that he would be more than a match for them both, especially if, as he suspected, Korinyakov had indeed been murdered.

Arthur Stubbins stepped out of the ice cream van and carefully locked it up, skilfully ignoring the pleas of children hungry for the taste of his wares, and noticed that the man with the curious bulge down the front of his trousers had emerged from the house and was making a speedy departure from the scene of the crime - if indeed Frogmorton's house was the scene of the crime. There was still no sign of Korinyakov, though, and that seemed to indicate that the man who walked with a Russian accent was in fact dead. This being the case, there was no hurry, and so Arthur decided to serve the annoying little brats who were hounding him for ice cream before he continued with his investigation. Besides, with the salary he got from the British Government he needed to supplement his income in any way he could.

Markham was running scared. How on Earth had the Russians got to Frogmorton's house ahead of him? Maybe Frogmorton wasn't as stupid as he first imagined and had gone to the Russians in case he couldn't get anywhere at the university. Markham could only hope that Frogmorton hadn't yet demonstrated his experiment to them. If they hadn't witnessed the spectacular phenomenon of instant diamonds, there might still be a chance that he, Markham, could be incredibly rich. He didn't like the idea of the Russians being involved and he also didn't like the idea of guns being involved. Events had definitely taken an unexpected turn. After a lot of thought, Markham decided that, for the sake of safety, he would have to cut Frogmorton in on the diamonds. He was sure that he could negotiate a very favourable partnership of say 80-20, the 80%

going to Markham, of course. Once he was completely resolved to the idea of such a partnership being the only sensible option, Markham turned around and headed back to Frogmorton's house to see if he could find a clue that would enable him to discover his former employee's whereabouts. He shouldn't have any trouble from the Russian. It's wonderful how effective a crowbar on the cranium can be in dissuading someone from remaining conscious.

Mimi Sarchetti checked the mechanism of the semi-automatic pistol she had obtained from her uncle Alberto who kept a rather well-stocked arsenal in the back room of his little restaurant in North London.

'Mimi,' he said to his favourite and only niece, 'your uncle Alberto is so proud that you are taking care of family business at last.'

Up until this point in time, Mimi had been a bit of a disappointment to her relatives. She had shown absolutely no criminal tendencies, which led many to believe that she may have been adopted. But the killer instinct had been passed down through her genes and so, now that she had been called upon, she was ready to fulfil her destiny and honour her first contract. Holding the gun in her hand, she felt very powerful and realised that only one thing stood in the way of the $200,000 she had been promised for the 'hit'. Nobody had told her who the target was. Sensing that this may have been a slight oversight, Mimi resolved to phone her brother in America in order to clarify that small detail.

Even though the feel of the gun in her hand made her feel good, she knew that she was expected to kill someone and that felt a little uncomfortable. It might get her into trouble. She remembered how she got into trouble at the nursery school where she worked when she gave little Ethan Carter a tap on the leg for pulling little Sophie Brown's hair. And she imagined that she might get in slightly more trouble than that for killing someone. Of course, if she didn't want to get into trouble for killing people, she should have got a job with a government agency that encourages that sort of thing.

Although Arthur Stubbins worked for such an agency, he had never killed anyone. The necessity had never arisen. There had been occasions when he came close to it, but he had never had to go through with it. Arthur was just serving ice cream to the last of his customers when he spotted the man with the curious bulge down the front of his trousers returning to the house that Korinyakov had failed to emerge from. The thing that concerned Arthur was that the man with the curious bulge down the front of his trousers wasn't known to him, and it was obvious from the way that he was acting that the house that Korinyakov had failed to emerge from was not his. Arthur also wondered what connection the woman from the house next door had to the situation. The man with the curious bulge down the front of his trousers had spent quite some time in there prior to going into the house that Korinyakov had failed to emerge from. Arthur realised that he wasn't going to get any answers until he stopped selling ice cream and started investigating. So that is what he did.

Being bludgeoned about the cranium was not Alexander Korinyakov's favourite pastime. Apart from anything else - it hurt. One of the major side effects of being struck on the head was unconsciousness — the result of which was the fact that

Korinyakov didn't notice Markham when he came back inside Frogmorton's house. Another (minor) side effect was delirium, which meant that when Markham kicked the comatose Korinyakov and asked, 'Where did Frogmorton go?' the man who walked with a Russian accent couldn't resist mumbling, 'Jodrell Bank.' Markham couldn't understand the relevance of Jodrell Bank to Frogmorton's experiment, and assumed that he had gone there with his daughter for an outing to take his mind off his dismissal. He decided that he ought to go and find Frogmorton without delay, because he couldn't risk the Russians getting to him first. He would sweeten the deal he was going to make with Frogmorton by offering him a research post in the Environmental Technology Department. That way Markham wouldn't have to waste time looking for the missing notes or risk blowing himself up whilst conducting dangerous experiments. And with a bit of luck Frogmorton might just perfect the diamond making process and blow himself up at the same time.

* * *

The traffic on the M6 motorway started to move faster. Soon Frogmorton was able to put his foot down and move into the outside lane and make up for lost time. His car might have been a little old and in need of a good clean, but he was able to reach speeds of 110mph. Because time was of the essence, Frogmorton was driving a little more erratically than was comfortable for his passengers, weaving in and out of the traffic in an attempt to save the world.

'Do you have to drive quite so fast?' enquired Gavin Woosner.

The traffic policeman who stopped Frogmorton asked the same question and added, 'Anybody would think you are weaving in and out of the traffic because you are on a desperate mission to save the world.'

All the occupants of the car wanted to tell the policeman that that was exactly what Frogmorton was trying to do, but felt it might compound the problem and land Frogmorton with more trouble than the fine and penalty points that were already heading his way.

Rhona Willett, who was less concerned about such things as the others, confided in the policeman by saying, 'Spaceships travel a lot faster than this you know.'

'Not if they're travelling on my stretch of the M6, madam,' was the policeman's stern reply.

The policeman did a quick check of Frogmorton's car to satisfy himself that it was roadworthy, and eventually told Frogmorton that he could continue with his journey. This little inconvenience had cost them almost an hour. The policeman followed Frogmorton for nearly twenty miles before turning off the motorway and heading back down the southbound carriageway in search of new victims, which were always in plentiful supply.

'Good,' said Frogmorton when he saw the policeman disappear, 'now we can get up to speed and get on with what we've got to do.' He pushed his foot to the metal and the car accelerated again to over 100mph. They would have just made Cheshire by mid-afternoon if the engine hadn't decided to break down on them at that point.

CHAPTER EIGHTEEN
The Fuse Burns

A thorough search of the town proved the non-existence of any financial establishment trading under the name of 'Jodhpurs Bank'. Vanessa O'Mara was not well known for her patience, and turned to Frogmorton's mother with fire in her eyes and said, 'Listen lady, you better not be screwing with me. Where's this Jodhpurs Bank?'

'I've already told you,' said Frogmorton's mother, who had already told her, 'I've never heard of that one before. Maybe you should ask someone.'

Feeling that, at last, the woman had come up with a good idea, Vanessa O'Mara did in fact ask someone.

'Never heard of it,' was the genuine reply of the first person she asked. In fact, it was the genuine reply of the next six people she asked.

'Are all you British people stupid?' she asked Frogmorton's mother, 'For all the good it's doing me, I might as well ask this passing child!' she said, indicating a passing child.

The passing child in question heard the outburst and said, 'Ask this passing child what, missus?'

Vanessa regarded the passing child for a moment and then said to him, 'Okay smartass. Can you tell me where I can find Jodhpurs Bank?'

'Smartass yourself!' exclaimed the passing child, 'There's no such place. You probably mean Jodrell Bank.'

'Jodrell Bank?' Vanessa repeated.

'Oh yes,' said Frogmorton's mother, 'that's the place. I remember now.'

'So where is this Jodrell Bank and why isn't there a branch in this godforsaken hole?' enquired Vanessa further of the passing child.

'Branch?' enquired the passing child further of Vanessa. 'It isn't one of those kinds of bank. It's where they keep the radio telescope dishes. Up north somewhere I think.'

Suddenly everything made perfect sense to the CIA agent. Woosner was some kind of boffin at NASA, so it wasn't unreasonable that he would be interested in radio telescopes. Radio telescopes are useful if you want to look at things in space and after all, didn't NASA have something to do with space?

A search on her smart phone for 'Jodrell Bank' revealed more useful information to Vanessa O'Mara than the smart-phone search for 'Jodhpurs Bank' had done. (The latter revealed only information about banks in Jodhpur, India, by the way, in case you're interested.) The Jodrell Bank Observatory was in Cheshire in the North West of England.

Vanessa O'Mara decided that the best way to get there was to fly by helicopter, and she further decided, with some reluctance, that she would have to take Frogmorton's mother along, thinking her somehow important to the case. If they made good time, they might even catch up with Woosner on the way.

Frogmorton's mother became very excited at the prospect of flying. 'I've never flown before,' she informed the flame-haired Irish beauty.

'No shit!' was Vanessa's only comment.

Markham had long gone before Arthur Stubbins ventured into the house that Korinyakov had failed to emerge from, but not before the MI5 agent had taken his photograph. Arthur decided that while he waited for information from Central Processing on the photograph he would go and recover Korinyakov's body. He hoped that there might be some kind of lead he could follow secreted about the ex-KGB man's corpse. Maybe he should have tried following some of the other people who had emerged from the house that Korinyakov had failed to emerge from, but he thought that Korinyakov was probably the key to it all.

Arthur moved deftly through the house that Korinyakov had failed to emerge from until he came across the prostrate form of the man who would have walked with a Russian accent had he been in a position to do any walking. The MI5 agent searched through the ex-KGB man's jacket pockets, but found nothing of interest other than a cleverly-folded paper rhinoceros. As he started to examine the contents of Korinyakov's trouser pockets with his probing fingers, he felt the same cold metal in the back of his neck that Markham had experienced earlier. The voice that accompanied the sensation said, 'I hope you are trying to rob me, because if I thought that what you are doing was sexual, I would be inclined to blow your brains out.'

'Ah, Mr Korinyakov. You're not dead after all,' said the remarkably observant Arthur Stubbins.

Korinyakov was slightly taken aback that the stranger knew who he was and asked, quite reasonably, 'Who the hell are you?'

'Arthur Stubbins – British Intelligence.'

'The words "British" and "intelligence" seem a far-fetched combination.'

'Even so, that's who I am. Now perhaps you could holster your weapon and answer a few simple questions for me.'

'It's a general rule Mr Stubbins that the person with the weapon does all the asking.'

'Yes, well I know you American-cum-Russian types like to play by those rules, but I'm afraid over here we like to do things in a more civilised manner. Now kindly put your weapon away or I will be forced to arrest you in the name of Her Majesty's Government.'

'What the hell has Her Majesty's Government got to do with all this?' Korinyakov asked angrily. He was quite surly when he had a sore head.

'Well, it may have escaped your attention Mr Korinyakov, but you are actually on British soil which, as a general rule, means it has everything to do with Her Majesty's Government.'

'I don't give a damn whose soil I'm on; this is none of your goddam business. The United States Government is quite capable of sorting this problem out without you amateur British spies interfering.'

'Could I point out at this stage Mr Korinyakov that, as an operative for the Federal Bureau of Investigation, you are outside your jurisdiction here in England and if, as you say, the United States Government is quite capable of sorting this problem out without us amateur British spies interfering, what part of your superior investigating technique called for you to be in a state of unconsciousness when I found you here?'

'All the time people keep hitting me on the head,' explained Korinyakov.

'Well, that's a good way of being rendered unconscious,' admitted Arthur Stubbins, 'but I'm afraid I can't allow you to continue your activities here. We don't like people running around brandishing guns over here, you know.'

'I have to finish my job Mr Stubbins. The security of the United States of America and maybe the whole world is at stake.'

'Well if the stakes are that high, you'll need help. I'm willing to assist you with your enquiries.'

'I work alone,' hissed Korinyakov, making it sound as if he had a puncture.

'It's alright, Korinyakov. You can work with me – I'm British. I don't hate you for being Russian. We British aren't that petty. We hate all foreigners.'

The ex-Russian, ex-KGB, fast-track American citizen gave

the matter a little thought and, sensing that there may be an advantage to be gained by teaming up with the British spy, said, 'Do you know how to get to Jodrell Bank?'

'I certainly do. And, what's more, I have a vehicle outside.'

'Let's go then,' said Korinyakov adding, 'partner.'

Arthur Stubbins and Korinyakov emerged from the house that Korinyakov had failed to emerge from and piled into the ice cream van ignoring the shouts of hungry children as they sped off with the strains of 'Greensleeves' jingling from the van's loudspeakers.

*   *   *

Frogmorton wished that he had kept up his membership of the RAC. The cost of being towed off the motorway was astronomical. He was still moaning to himself about the huge bill when Elaine brought him back to Earth by reminding him that if they didn't get hold of another car and get to Jodrell Bank, he wouldn't need to worry about the cost of being towed off the motorway.

Frogmorton had never been to Wolverhampton before and was determined that, if they successfully completed their mission, he would never go there again. Obviously unimpressed with the beauty of the Black Country, Frogmorton quickly hired a car and they resumed their trek north towards Jodrell Bank, heartened by the news that their destination was less than sixty miles away. The volume of traffic was less than heartening news and their progress northwards was restricted to only fifty miles per hour.

*   *   *

Frogmorton's mother was not enjoying her first helicopter ride as much as she thought she would, but then the pilot, who was being forced to fly north at gunpoint, was not having a

216

particularly good time of it either. Vanessa, on the other hand, was enjoying it immensely. Using the vast resources of the CIA, she had fed Frogmorton's licence plate number into her laptop computer and was currently receiving satellite pictures of its whereabouts.

'It looks like Woosner is on to us,' she informed whoever wanted to listen. 'They've dumped the car they were in and swapped vehicles. However, lady, your son was dumb enough to hire a car in his own name and I'm getting a GPS fix on him right now.'

'GSP?' asked Frogmorton's mother, 'Isn't that where you get premonitions and portents of doom and such like?'

'That's ESP, you dumbass!' smiled Vanessa in reply.

'I was never any good at spelling,' muttered Frogmorton's mother, looking out of the window, and immediately wishing she hadn't. 'I don't think much to this flying business; are you sure it's safe?'

Vanessa O'Mara ignored Frogmorton's mother and studied the images on the screen of her laptop.

'Got them!' she said triumphantly. 'They're still headed north on the M6 motorway.'

Vanessa turned to the pilot and said, 'How long will it take you to fly us to these coordinates?' She showed the coordinates in question to the pilot.

The pilot glanced at the screen of the laptop computer. 'About an hour,' he said. Vanessa pressed the barrel of her gun into the pilot's groin and raised her right eyebrow. 'Well, maybe twenty-five minutes,' was the pilot's revised ETA.

It looked like Vanessa was going to be able to wrap this case up in less than an hour. Everything was working out much smoother than she had imagined, and she promised herself that she would pay a visit to the old country before she returned to America.

* * *

Markham was relaxing as best he could on the train to Cheshire. It had been a very tiring day so far and he wasn't used to being threatened by Russians with guns. He reflected on how fortunate he had been to have a crowbar stuffed down his trousers with which to strike his assailant about the head in order to make good his escape. The rhythm of the train was making Markham sleepy and he drifted off with thoughts of untold wealth spinning through his mind. As soon as he started to snore, the pickpocket in the seat next to him made sure that he didn't have the weight of his wallet to burden him on the remainder of his journey.

* * *

Mimi Sarchetti tracked Gavin Woosner's movements, arriving at Frogmorton's house about twenty minutes after the departure of Stubbins and Korinyakov in their turbo-charged ice cream van. There was no sign of life at the house, so Mimi called next door to see if she could find out anything from the neighbour.

Mrs Douglas reluctantly opened the door, but seeing a woman there made her feel a little more comfortable. If she had had the remotest idea what Mimi was there for she may not have felt quite so much at ease.

'Sorry to bother you,' Mimi said sweetly, 'but I was looking for a gentleman who was visiting next door.'

Mrs Douglas quickly pulled Mimi into the house and looked purposefully up and down the street to make sure no one was about. Satisfying herself that Mimi had arrived unseen, she leant forward and confided in her, 'Do you mean the one who was rubbing himself when he arrived or the one with the huge bulge down the front of his trousers?'

Naturally Mimi didn't know which one she meant and told her so.

'You can't trust men,' Mrs Douglas continued. 'They're forever leading you on and letting you down. That one with the bulge down his trousers made a right fool of me, I can tell you.'

'Do you know where he went?' asked Mimi, in case she was referring to Woosner?

'He can go to hell for all I care,' said Mrs Douglas remembering how he had left her just as she had put the kettle on to make him a cup of tea. For some reason unknown to her Mrs Douglas started to cry.

Mimi's instincts took over and she comforted the sobbing woman, telling her, 'There, there. Everything's going to be just fine. If you tell me where he went I promise you he'll never upset you again.'

'That's just it,' sobbed Mrs Douglas, 'I don't know where he went. He just walked out of that door and out of my life without so much as telling me whether he took sugar in his tea or not.' This was too much for the poor Mrs Douglas to bear and she broke down uncontrollably.

Mimi knew that there was no more information to be had here and that she would have to gain access to the house next door if she was ever going to find Woosner. There might be a clue – anything that would lead her to the runaway ex-NASA employee and the $200,000 she had been promised for the 'hit'. It was with some relief that she found the door had not been locked. She found nothing of interest on the ground floor apart from a sleeping cat and a clever purple hologram, so she decided to investigate the rooms upstairs. A thorough search of each room revealed nothing, but Mimi was drawn to the computer. She instinctively reached for the mouse. The lock screen required a password, but that was a simple matter as an open notebook on the desk carefully indicated that the 'PC lock screen password' was 'leTTuce$%LolliPop1'. She entered this and was met with a further stroke of luck, as prior to leaving for Jodrell Bank, Arthur

Stubbins had used Frogmorton's computer to visit theaa.com and plan a route. There on the screen for Mimi to clearly see was the destination: Jodrell Bank Observatory, Macclesfield, United Kingdom. She dashed out of Frogmorton's house and sat astride her scooter, a three-year old Vespa GTS300 which boasted a top speed of eighty miles per hour. She zoomed off in the general direction that all those before her had taken – towards Jodrell Bank, Cheshire.

In the vastness of space the mighty StarDestroyer Blagn'k also headed in the general direction of Jodrell Bank, towing behind it the sole surviving Asteroid Class Deep Space Medium Armoured Interceptor piloted by the best of the Muridaen Space Defence Corps. StarTrooper (Fourth Class) Domr'k was continuing his studies of the planet Earth, whilst StarFleet Admiral Kratol continued refining his droid destroying skills. Domr'k was acquiring an unhealthy admiration for the inhabitants of Planet Earth. He marvelled at the achievements they had made and noticed with great interest that they had achieved manned space flight. The one thing he couldn't fathom about them, though, was their insatiable desire to destroy one another and the planet on which they lived. He could hardly believe how they had let their world fall into disrepair, allowing the ozone layer to be depleted and a build up of greenhouse gases when the solution was so simple using a giant laser beam and ample quantities of soot. Domr'k felt sure that if any species could save themselves from destruction, the inhabitants of Earth were the ones to do it – providing they could convince StarFleet Admiral Kratol. Domr'k checked the communications computer to see if any messages had been received from Earth. Of course, none had been received. Well, maybe it was time for Domr'k to intervene.

Maybe if he could find a reason for life to continue on Planet Earth through the research he was doing, then maybe Kratol would see the sense in it and spare them from their fate. The difficulty was in knowing how to present the case for saving life on Planet Earth without StarFleet Admiral Kratol mistaking it for a blatant act of mutiny. Domr'k decided that there was no use worrying how to present a case when he hadn't been able to make a case in the first place, and so he continued with his studies.

Elsewhere on the mighty StarDestroyer Blagn'k, Kratol had reached a decision. Regardless of whether or not the inhabitants of Earth had replied to his message, he was going to visit the planet before he divested it of life. Of course, visions of Gweelox 4 kept springing to mind, but he dismissed them and hoped that he wouldn't have the same problem on Earth. He felt it was about time that he got to see more of the Universe, and in any case the fresh air wouldn't go amiss – presuming, of course, that the Earth had a supply of fresh air. Kratol couldn't help thinking that perhaps Domr'k's mutinous thoughts were starting to have an effect on him, and resolved that he would take serious action if his subordinate continued to think for himself. Perhaps a little excursion to the surface of Planet Earth would help bring Domr'k to his senses, especially if there was a repeat of the Gweelox 4 incident. Kratol allowed himself the luxury of an inward smile and manoeuvred his runabout so skilfully that he managed to disable three droids in one go.

* * *

Although Squadron Leader Fligg was also heading in the general direction of Jodrell Bank, he had absolutely no idea about it. As far as he was concerned, he was being towed towards the alien invaders' home planet, which he intended to destroy in glorious retribution for the destruction of his own planet. However, destroying an entire planet with only two Armageddon missiles had never been achieved in the past. In fact, it is fair to say that destroying an entire planet with any number of Armageddon missiles had never been achieved in the past. Like so many other things about the Muridaen Space Defence Corps there had never been any practical experience with the technology they possessed. Everything worked in theory, but on a practical level they were yet to find out. Ever since he had been left on his own to deal with the alien invader, he had been feeding data into his on-board computer in an effort to find a way of destroying the alien invaders' home planet with just two Armageddon missiles. Finally his computer came up with a possible scenario. The crucial factor was that he had to fire his missiles into the exact centre of a massive geological fault, so that the natural flaw in the planet's structure would assist the Armageddon missiles in their job. There was no room for errors, because a decimal point in the wrong place in his trajectory could make him miss his target by several thousand miles

The thought that it was possible to destroy the alien invaders' entire planet gave new hope to Squadron Leader Fligg, and he just prayed that there was a sufficiently faulty geological fault for his Armageddon missiles to be aimed at. There was nothing to do in the meantime but relax and try and get some sleep to make sure he was alert when he came in range of the alien invaders' home planet and so that his computer could get to work and find the weakest spot on the surface. Squadron Leader Fligg was beginning to enjoy his job again.

* * *

Alexander Korinyakov and Arthur Stubbins were making good time in the ice cream van. This was mainly due to the fact that, in true British spy tradition, the ice cream van was not what it seemed. This became clear to Korinyakov when Arthur Stubbins succeeded in avoiding a traffic jam by driving the aforementioned ice cream van into an adjacent canal. Instead of sinking, a rubber skirt inflated around the bottom of the vehicle and it transformed miraculously into a hovercraft. Without any loss of speed, the two men skimmed across the surface of the water, amazing fishermen who had never seen an ice cream van travelling at sixty miles an hour along the canal before.

CHAPTER NINETEEN
Showdown at Jodrell Bank

Back in the United States of America, Rheingold's attempts to silence Gavin Woosner had made ripples all the way to the White House and, consequently, the President had asked to see him. The thought of being interviewed by the most powerful man in the world didn't worry Rheingold at all and he showed no sign of nerves when he was led into the great man's office.

'Take a seat, Rheingold,' the President said. Rheingold did as he was told and the President said, 'Actually Rheingold, that's my seat. Do you mind sitting the other side of the desk?'

Rheingold moved to the other seat and the interview began.

The President said, 'Rheingold, it's come to my attention that you are availing yourself of various government agencies in an attempt to locate an ex-employee of yours. Is that right?'

'Well, Mr Pepsi-dent,' Rheingold began.

'It's President.'

'Sure it is – and that's why you are where you are today, because of the good citizens of this mighty nation of ours.'

'Can you cut the crap, Rheingold, and answer the question?'

'But Mr Impediment…'

'President!'

'We have to ask ourselves, "what is the question?" That is the key to all the answers. In fact, we continually burden ourselves with so many questions that it takes too much time to allocate the correct answer to each one. Surely it makes more sense to furnish ourselves with more and more answers, so that the questions become irrelevant?'

'What the hell are you talking about, Rheingold?'

'I'm talking about the future, Mr Pleasure Sent...'

'President!'

'... a future where the answers are available before the questions have even been thought of. A future for our kids to grow up in with the sound knowledge that they never need say what, where or why again.'

'Can we stick to the issue here, Rheingold? Did you or did you not engage certain government agencies to find an ex-employee of yours?'

'We both know the answer to that, Mr Decadent...'

'President!'

'... you wouldn't hold the office you do now if you didn't know the answer to a question like that.'

'Okay, okay!' the President conceded, feeling that a change in the line of questioning might prove more fruitful. 'We do all know you got the agencies involved, but we want to know why?'

'Why, Mr Plenty Bent?'

'President!'

'You want to know why?'

'Yes.'

'Well, I'll tell you why, shall I?'

'I wish you would,' said the President, wishing he would.

Rheingold paused for a moment as if in deep thought. The President, expecting something profound, bowed his head slightly towards Rheingold so that he didn't miss a word of it. Rheingold cleared his throat and said, 'Could you repeat the question?'

The President was beginning to lose his patience. 'Why did you set these government agencies on Woosner?'

'National Security.'

'National Security?' quizzed the President.

'Well, Mr Testament, since official government funding was withdrawn from the SETI program the public thought that

NASA was no longer involved in the search for extra-terrestrial intelligence. If word gets out that NASA are using unofficial government funding to carry on their research in order to debunk any genuine claim of extra-terrestrial contact to protect America's superiority in space, it could prove somewhat troublesome for your administration, especially with an election on the horizon. There could be rioting in the streets.'

'Rheingold, are you telling me that NASA are still continuing SETI research behind the government's back?'

'Yes Mr Sediment …'

'President! It's President! Can't you get that into your thick skull?' By this time the President had lost any interest he may have had in the Woosner case and said to Rheingold, 'I don't know half of what the hell you've been talking about, Mr Rheingold, but you've got forty-eight hours to find your Mr Woosner and then you're on your own. No more help from the agencies. Do you understand me?'

'Yes Mr Tenement …'

'President! You moron!' the President shouted as he banged his fist down heavily on the desk. 'Now get out of here and keep me informed. I will find out what's going on here, Rheingold, and if you're trying to cover anything up, I'll have your ass before you can sit down on it. Do I make myself clear, mister?'

'Loud and clear, Mr Effervescent,' Rheingold said as he marched out of the office, narrowly avoiding a solid gold eagle that the world's most powerful man had aimed at his head. Once outside the office, Rheingold thought to himself that he was glad he hadn't voted for such a bad-tempered President. Rheingold hoped that the Woosner problem could be resolved before the President pulled the plug on his resources. But then there was a resource that the President didn't have any control over.

He punched a few keys on his cell phone. 'Hi, Salvatore. How are you getting on with that little job I gave you?'

* * *

Mimi Sarchetti was making good progress. Riding a motor scooter had some distinct advantages over cars. Weaving in and out of busy traffic was one of those advantages, and Mimi made full use of this technique and managed to close the gap a little between her, Woosner and the $200,000. Things were certainly changing in Mimi's life. Here she was, hot on the trail of her quarry, feeling excitement pulse through her veins. Something she never got as a nursery school teacher. Mimi realised that danger was a drug - one she wished she had taken a long time ago.

The traffic was really heavy on the M6 motorway, so Mimi guessed that Woosner would be held up somewhere along the road and that she would certainly arrive at Jodrell Bank first and be able to set up a nice little surprise for him. Mimi's mobile telephone rang and she fumbled with her bag whilst riding her scooter at fifty-five miles an hour along the busy M6 motorway.

'Hello!' she shouted into the mouthpiece in an effort to be heard over the traffic.

'Mimi!' said the voice on the other end. 'It's your brother Salvatore.'

'You'll have to speak up. I'm having trouble hearing you through my crash helmet,' said Mimi having trouble hearing him through her crash helmet.

'You'll have to speak up. I'm having trouble hearing you over the noise of the traffic,' said Salvatore having trouble hearing her over the noise of the traffic.

'Who is it?' shouted Mimi.

'I still can't hear you properly, Mimi. Just tell me — how are you getting on with the Woosner affair?'

'I'm not having an affair!' cried Mimi to the mystery caller. 'Is this some sick attempt at blackmail?'

'No, Mimi. He is not a black male. He is Caucasian. And the job just got urgent. Rheingold has put up the hit money to $250,000.'

'$250,000? You can't be serious!' retorted Mimi. She would have gone on to say how extortionate such a blackmail demand was when her mobile phone slipped from her hand and was crushed by the traffic. The reason the phone slipped from her hand was that she caught sight of a passenger in the car in front as he turned to speak to a female next to him. He was showing her a cleverly-folded paper rhinoceros and looked remarkably like Gavin Woosner who was renowned for folding cleverly-folded paper rhinoceroses.

A smile came to Mimi Sarchetti's lips at her good fortune. She determined that once the Woosner job was finished, she would track down the blackmailer who had just called her and make sure he went the same way as the aforementioned ex-NASA employee.

* * *

The helicopter pilot made good his revised ETA, and all that was left for Vanessa O'Mara to do was to spot the car Woosner and friends had hired and take it out. It was a tidy package really, a chance to get rid of her target and those he was associated with all in one go. Once they had been taken care of, she would only be left with tying up the loose ends created by the obnoxious woman and the helicopter pilot.

'Where are we going then?' asked Frogmorton's mother, who was finding her first flight in a helicopter quite boring.

'Why don't you let your mouth take a break,' said Vanessa O'Mara quite unkindly.

Having more sense than Frogmorton's mother, the helicopter pilot remained silent.

'I just wondered,' said Frogmorton's mother, 'because I could really do with going to the little girls' room. Do you have one on board this aeroplane thing?'

'You're just going to have to hang on to it,' Vanessa O'Mara informed her. Discussing toilet breaks was not high up on her agenda.

Frogmorton's mother was about to press the point when Vanessa O'Mara spotted something out of the window and started to get excited.

'There they are!' she exclaimed, pointing at the hire car she had been tracking by satellite, which was being closely followed by a woman on a motor scooter. Vanessa O'Mara decided that she would put a bullet through Gavin Woosner's head and then put another through the driver's head, so that the resulting car crash would make doubly sure of the demise of the ex-NASA employee.

'Take us in lower,' Vanessa told the helicopter pilot, and she prepared her weapon for the task ahead.

'You want to be careful with that thing,' Frogmorton's mother advised. 'You might end up hurting someone with it.'

Vanessa O'Mara was too involved with what she had to do to worry about what the stupid woman beside her was saying. The helicopter pilot took his craft lower as ordered by the dangerous but gorgeous redhead. The CIA agent opened the side window next to her and started to aim at the head of Gavin Woosner and, as the helicopter closed in, her finger started to tighten on the trigger.

Mimi Sarchetti was the first one to notice the low-flying helicopter closing in, and it didn't take her long to weigh up the situation. The fact that someone was leaning out of the helicopter's window aiming a gun at the head of the man who was supposed to be her target didn't go unnoticed either.

'What the hell?' Mimi said to herself, mainly because she was alone. 'First they try to blackmail me and now they're trying to muscle in on my kill. I'm not having any of this.' And so saying she fumbled in her bag for the piece of hardware supplied to her by her uncle Alberto who kept a rather well-stocked arsenal in the back room of his little restaurant in North London.

It was at this point that Frogmorton looked into his rear view mirror and saw Mimi Sarchetti brandishing her weapon and Elaine looked out of her window to see a helicopter drawing up almost level to them with Vanessa O'Mara pointing a gun straight at them. At exactly the same time Frogmorton and Elaine turned to each other and shouted, 'There's a woman with a gun!'

'Where?' demanded Gavin Woosner, who had a little more to worry about than the other occupants of the car.

'Behind us,' said Frogmorton.

'No, out there,' said Elaine, pointing out there.

There was confusion in the car - Elaine and Frogmorton arguing about the location of the 'woman with the gun', Gavin Woosner diving for cover, Susan Likely taking photographs of everything and anything, and Rhona Willett singing 'Baa Baa Black Sheep' for the two-hundred-and-forty-third time.

Vanessa O'Mara lost sight of Woosner as he ducked and so adjusted her aim so that she would kill the driver instead. She was about to squeeze the trigger and finish the job when the helicopter suddenly lurched to one side and smoke started to spew out of the controls where Mimi Sarchetti's well-aimed bullet from the saddle of a motor scooter had embedded itself. That is to say, Mimi Sarchetti was sitting on the saddle of a motor scooter and not that the bullet came from there. The pilot fought the controls as best he could to minimise the impact when the helicopter finally crashed to the ground.

Frogmorton could hardly believe what was going on. Two women with guns and one of them had shot down a helicopter. He slowed down as he watched the aircraft spin out of control and for a moment his eyes played tricks on him. He could have sworn that he had seen his mother aboard the helicopter.

Mimi Sarchetti was so pleased that she had managed to bring down the helicopter that she hadn't noticed that Frogmorton had slowed down considerably. Mimi on the other hand, had not slowed down and the impact with the back of Frogmorton's hired car was a spectacle to behold. Mimi was catapulted from the seat of her scooter and landed on the roof of Frogmorton's hired car. The riderless scooter slid towards the hard shoulder of the motorway, and the momentum flung it up the embankment and over a fence into the field where the hapless helicopter made contact with the ground.

'Shouldn't we stop and help those people in the helicopter?' enquired Susan Likely, trying not to tread on Gavin Woosner as he cowered on the floor.

'There are two good reasons for not stopping and helping them,' said Frogmorton. 'Firstly, we can't spare the time if we want to send a message to the aliens before they destroy all life on Earth and, secondly, they were pointing a gun at our car!'

'Who were they though?' asked Elaine.

'I don't know,' said Frogmorton honestly, 'but it all has to tie in with the hologram.'

Susan Likely plucked Gavin Woosner from the floor. 'What's going on Gavin? Are those people after us because of that hologram?'

Gavin Woosner took a couple of deep breaths to help regain his composure. 'I guess so – in a way,' he offered.

'What sort of way?' asked Susan Likely.

'When I discovered the signal I informed my boss and he

didn't want to know. Kept saying that it would destroy NASA itself if word got out. I expected him to try and silence me, but I didn't think he'd go to such great lengths.'

'Well this thing is bigger than NASA now,' said Susan Likely. 'And what happened to the helicopter?'

'The other woman with the gun,' said Elaine. 'She shot it down.'

'How did they find us? This isn't even my car,' said Frogmorton.

'They can find anyone they want to,' said Gavin Woosner cynically.

'What happened to the woman with the gun on the scooter?' asked Elaine.

As if to answer the question, Mimi shifted her position on the roof of the hired car so that her head hung down in front of the windscreen so that she could get a shot inside the car. The manifestation of an upside-down woman on his windscreen pointing a gun at him was too much for Frogmorton and, in an act of extreme bravery, he turned on the windscreen wipers. Miraculously the windscreen wipers did their job and cleared the screen of Mimi Sarchetti, her gun and several squashed bugs that had accumulated there since they had left Wolverhampton.

Mimi Sarchetti picked her bruised and cut body up off the hard shoulder of the motorway as she watched Frogmorton's hired car speed off on its way to Jodrell Bank. At least she knew where they were heading and she had got rid of the opposition. Being stranded on the M6 motorway with no transport was just a minor setback. She flagged down a passing car and told the driver, 'Take me to Jodrell Bank or I'll blow your brains out.' To emphasise the point, she placed the barrel of her gun against the man's temple.

* * *

Luckily, the helicopter pilot managed a controlled crash landing before passing out. Vanessa O'Mara was thrown from the aircraft as it hit the ground and Frogmorton's mother held her hands above her head as if she was on a roller coaster and enjoyed every moment of the flight once the bullet from Mimi Sarchetti's gun had adjusted the helicopter's handling characteristics.

'Woohoo!' shouted Frogmorton's mother. 'Can we do that again?' But the helicopter pilot was in no fit state to repeat the experience. Neither was his helicopter.

Although Vanessa O'Mara was in better shape than the helicopter, the fall from the aircraft had injured her ankle and she found she couldn't get up off the ground. She could see that they were unable to resume the flight from the crumpled state of the helicopter, and she knew that she couldn't walk two paces, let alone trek all the way to Jodrell Bank. Then she spotted the motor scooter in the field just a few yards away from the wreck of the helicopter. It didn't look too badly damaged at all. She could ride that to Jodrell Bank and finish the job in the morning. She tried to get up again, but her ankle couldn't take her weight. Vanessa O'Mara realised that the only way she could get to Jodrell Bank was for Frogmorton's mother to drive the scooter whilst she rode pillion. She didn't like the idea, but it was the only solution.

'Lady!' shouted Vanessa O'Mara, trying to attract Frogmorton's mother's attention. 'Get out here; I need your help.' And with a little more shouting and some coaxing with the gun she held, she persuaded Frogmorton's mother to drive her to Jodrell Bank on the back of the scooter.

By alternating between inland waterways, the British railway system and the extensive road network, Arthur Stubbins and Alexander Korinyakov reached Jodrell Bank before any of the others were even within a ten-mile radius. They had spent the time getting to know one another better and consuming what was left of the ice cream. The ex-Russian, ex-KGB man, now turned fast-track American National and FBI agent was getting tired of this assignment, not least because of the sore head it was giving him. He decided that he might as well fill the British agent in with all the details he had on the case and maybe the two of them could resolve the problem quickly – enabling Korinyakov to return to the United States of America at his earliest possible convenience. Of course, Arthur Stubbins was very dubious at the mention of beings from another planet, but other than that he could see why NASA was anxious to retrieve all their research material.

'I'd better inform the Ministry,' Arthur Stubbins informed Alexander Korinyakov and then he proceeded to mumble something into the top of his fibre tip pen. Of course, the Ministry was very dubious at the mention of beings from another planet, but other than that they could see why NASA was anxious to retrieve all their research material.

The Ministry decided they ought to inform the Prime Minister. Of course, the Prime Minister was very dubious at the mention of beings from another planet, but other than that she could see why NASA was anxious to retrieve all their research material.

'Right,' said Arthur Stubbins, 'I've got the green light on this one. I'm to offer you any assistance you require.'

'All I need is for you to lead me to this Woosner guy – then I can take him out,' said Korinyakov.

'Take him out?'

'You know – waste him. Turn out his lights. Kill him,'

explained Korinyakov.

'Oh, no, no, no!' protested Arthur Stubbins. 'That's not how we do things over here. Gracious me, no.'

'But my instructions are to eliminate this canary before he sings.'

'Why?'

'Because NASA wants to keep this whole alien business under wraps. They can't afford for it to leak out.'

'Well it's far too late for that I'm afraid,' said Arthur Stubbins.

'What do you mean?' asked Korinyakov.

'Well I've just been in communication with Her Majesty's Government on the matter and that's not a good place for stopping leaks. It'll be in all the papers in the morning.'

'Goddam! Can't you British keep anything secret?' Korinyakov enquired.

'Oh yes,' Arthur Stubbins assured him, 'we have no difficulty keeping secrets – unless, of course, the government find out about them. Then we have the devil's own job keeping it out of the media. So, unless you're prepared to kill everyone who knows about it from me right up to the Prime Minister, you'll just have to do it the British way.'

'Well, we'll just have to cross that bridge when we come to it,' said Korinyakov enigmatically.

* * *

The train pulled into Glasgow Central station before Markham woke up. Completely disoriented from his deep slumber, the Head of the Environmental Technology Department got off the train and left the station before he realised that everyone seemed to be talking with a Scottish accent, which wasn't the native tongue of Cheshire.

In an effort to discover his whereabouts, Markham stopped a

passer-by and said, 'Whereabouts am I?'

'You're here,' said the passer-by unhelpfully in a very broad Scottish accent before disappearing from view.

Markham guessed he was north of the border and decided the best course of action was to go back to the railway station and hope that he could get on a train heading in the right direction before he missed Frogmorton altogether. It was imperative that he got to him before the Russians. There was no telling what the Russians might do if they got hold of Frogmorton's process. Markham went to purchase his train ticket, making a mental note that he was in Glasgow, only to find that his wallet was missing. He decided that the only solution was to jump on a southbound train whilst no one was looking. He delved into his trouser pockets for some loose change and bought a platform ticket and figured he must be some two hundred miles away from where he wanted to be. Markham only hoped that the Russians had fallen asleep on their train too.

Trains are marvellous things, but are terribly misunderstood. It is uncanny how nobody knows where any of them are going. You can guarantee that when a train is standing at a platform waiting to depart for Birmingham, several passengers will be running around outside like headless chickens asking anyone who cares to listen, 'Is this the train to Birmingham?' It doesn't seem to matter how many people they ask, they are never convinced and run around again in search of somebody else to ask. It makes you wonder if any of them ever arrive in Birmingham. You can just imagine the relatives of those poor lost souls as they meet train after train only to find their loved ones are not aboard. They are in railway limbo, perpetually asking the destination of a train, but never daring to climb aboard it. I have seen them board a train after seeking reassurance from a station porter only to jump off in sheer panic again as the train starts to pull away, sensing that it is heading in the wrong direction and that the station porter was part of some complicatedly elaborate scheme to get people onto the wrong trains. I think all policemen investigating missing persons should check railway stations out first. It would probably solve many of their more difficult cases.

* * *

The shooting down of the helicopter was still causing excitement and concern to the occupants of the car speeding towards Jodrell Bank.

'I think we should turn back,' said Susan Likely feeling that a news story wasn't worth getting killed for.

'There is no turning back,' Frogmorton said. 'If we turn back now there will be no point going on.'

This statement added to the confusion slightly. I know we understand his logic, but you have to remember that the others were quite tired and concerned.

'Frogmorton's right,' added Elaine. 'We have to press on and contact the aliens.'

'They're coming back for me, you know,' was Rhona Willett's contribution to the debate.

'We've got to be careful, though,' said Susan Likely. 'There may be more people after us, and if they can track us down in a hired car, they probably know where we're heading anyway.'

'You think they're trying to stop us contacting the aliens?' asked Frogmorton.

'It certainly looks that way,' replied Susan Likely.

'But how are they likely to know about the aliens?' enquired Elaine. 'And if they know about them, why do they want to stop us?'

'They know about the aliens because of me,' piped up Gavin Woosner. 'And the reason they are trying to stop us is because they don't know the whole truth about them. They know about the message, but they don't know about the content. Even if they knew the content though, they wouldn't believe it. And I wouldn't be surprised if they're not at Jodrell Bank already – waiting for us to show.' There was a hint of resignation in Gavin Woosner's voice.

'What are we going to do?' asked Susan Likely.

'Look,' said Gavin Woosner, 'it's me they're after. I think it's best all round if I give myself up to the police. I broke the law by stealing NASA software, so I've gotta face the music. It will also take the heat off you guys and you can get to the radio telescope and send the message.'

'That's all very well,' said Frogmorton, 'but we can't send the message without you. We don't know whereabouts in space to aim the thing. After all, a decimal point in the wrong place in the trajectory could make us miss our target by several thousand miles.'

'So what are we going to do?' asked Susan Likely again.

'It's up to you, Gavin,' said Elaine and she gave him a desperate look that convinced him that risking his own life was the least he could do for the salvation of Planet Earth.

'To hell with it,' he said bravely, 'we've got this far. I'll take my chances. Maybe we can reason with these people.' To help him calm his nerves, Gavin Woosner started to cleverly fold a paper rhinoceros.

* * *

'This is getting to be more and more fun,' said Frogmorton's mother to Vanessa O'Mara as they made their way towards Jodrell Bank astride Mimi Sarchetti's scooter, 'but we ought to be wearing crash helmets,' she added in a moment of safety consciousness.

'Are you intending to crash this contraption?' asked the CIA agent.

'No.'

'Then what the hell do we need crash helmets for?' asked Vanessa O'Mara with what appeared to be reasonable logic. Frogmorton's mother was stumped for an answer and so, completely out of character, she said nothing.

The pain in Vanessa O'Mara's ankle was getting worse and she could see that it was getting very swollen. She just hoped that she could get this job done quickly and get her injury seen to. What had started out as a simple job seemed to be getting more and more complicated. Still, once it was over she promised herself that she would catch a plane to Ireland and immerse herself in her ancestral heritage.

'Can't you get this thing to go any faster?' she asked Frogmorton's mother.

In response, Frogmorton's mother opened the throttle a little further and the scooter reluctantly accelerated to sixty-five miles an hour, but no more. It was carrying more weight than it had done when the manufacturers were working out what its top speed ought to be recorded as being. Unless there was a jam ahead, there would be absolutely no chance of catching up with the car Woosner was in, but there would be no hiding place for the ex-NASA employee once they arrived at Jodrell Bank. Vanessa O'Mara allowed a faint smile to form on her lips until Frogmorton's mother wiped it off by driving over a pothole, causing a sharp pain to shoot through the CIA agent's injured ankle and nearly unseating the two of them.

Maybe crash helmets would have been a good idea!

Mimi Sarchetti was not a great fan of any kind of jazz music, unlike the driver of the car she had hijacked. The CD player was churning out jazz tunes one after the other, each becoming more musically complicated than the next.

'Can you turn that terrible noise off?' she demanded of the driver. 'I can't hear myself think.'

'It's not so bad once you learn to appreciate it,' said the hijacked driver defensively. 'In fact, it can be very soothing and is good for stress.'

'Well I don't like it,' said Mimi.

'You've probably never really given it a chance,' insisted the hijacked driver. 'Listen to it a bit more and I guarantee you'll forget all your troubles.'

'I don't have any troubles,' Mimi assured him. 'Now turn the damn thing off.'

'It's good for stress, I tell you,' assured the hijacked driver.

'I TELL YOU I AM NOT STRESSED!' shouted Mimi as she fired her gun destroying the CD player and half the dashboard. The noise of the gun going off clearly disturbed the hijacked driver and, considering the amount of stress he was feeling, I imagine he would have liked to have been listening to some jazz music at that point in time. They drove on in silence for a good few miles until the hijacked driver said, 'I need to pull in at the next service station.'

'Oh no. We're not stopping this car until we get to Jodrell Bank,' she informed him.

'But you don't understand ...' began the hijacked driver.

'Oh, I understand alright,' said Mimi Sarchetti, 'and I say you stay put behind that wheel and drive on. And I won't hear any excuses.'

'But...' said the hijacked driver.

'Button it – unless you want to end up like your CD player.'

'No – er... yes ... okay ... right.'

As they passed the Sandbach service station, it was obvious from his worried expression that the hijacked driver had a real need to stop there. He was about to appeal to Mimi Sarchetti again, but she anticipated his question by saying, 'No!'

Mimi was beginning to feel comfortable with the power she had and was smiling to herself about it when the car started to slow down and eventually ground to a halt.

'What's going on? Why have we stopped?' asked Mimi.

'I've run out of petrol,' explained the hijacked driver.

'What do you mean you've run out of petrol? We passed a service station a few miles back, why didn't you go …? Mimi's sentence faded in mid-flow as realisation dawned on her. It was her fault they'd run out of petrol.

'So that's why you wanted to stop at the service station?' Mimi asked.

It's always easy to be wise after an event, isn't it? Just like the ant-like alien land dwellers on Erith.

As luck would have it, the car had run out of petrol quite close to Junction 17, the junction where they were going to turn off the motorway, so Mimi walked up the slip road and extended her thumb at passing motorists. Being a woman was a distinct advantage when hitchhiking, and it didn't take long for Mimi to get a ride the rest of the way.

* * *

Frogmorton was very impressed with the sight of Jodrell Bank as it came into view. The massive Lovell telescope was an extremely impressive structure. He was overwhelmed by the size of it.

'Is that it?' Elaine said in a way that expressed that she was less impressed with the sight than Frogmorton was.

'It sure is,' said Gavin Woosner in the unimpressed manner expressed by impressive ex-NASA experts.

'It's not very big,' Elaine said. 'I was expecting something huge.'

'It is huge,' said Frogmorton still implying the impression of being impressed.

'The Lovell Radio Telescope has a diameter of 250ft,' said Rhona Willett.

They all turned their heads towards the madwoman. It almost seemed menacing when she was being coherent.

'That's right,' confirmed Gavin Woosner breaking the eerie silence. 'She sure is a big beautiful baby.'

'It still looks smaller than I thought it would,' said Elaine.

'Look,' said Susan Likely pointing at the mighty Lovell Radio Telescope, 'see that small dot up there?'

'Yes,' said Elaine after straining her eyes to see.

'Well that is someone walking across a gantry under the telescope,' said Susan helpfully.

'Wow!' exclaimed Elaine with a sudden surge of excitement. 'It really is big after all.'

'Well,' said Frogmorton, 'if we can't get a message through to the aliens on that I'll be most surprised.'

Everyone in the car fell silent whilst they completed the journey to Jodrell Bank, lost in their own thoughts, wondering what would become of them if they couldn't convince the aliens that the Earth was worth saving. All except Rhona Willett that is, who was simply wondering what had taken the aliens so long to return.

* * *

The first place that Korinyakov and Arthur Stubbins went to was the planetarium. After all, Jodrell Bank was all about space and it was a pretty big subject and the show in the planetarium was a good introduction. Then they started looking at all the exhibits and marvelling at it all. They were thoroughly enjoying the Jodrell Bank experience and wished they'd got there earlier, because there wasn't going to be time to fit it all in as the visitor centre was closing to the public in five minutes.

'Just our luck,' said Arthur Stubbins, 'it just starts getting interesting and now they're closing to the public.'

'It's probably just as well,' said Korinyakov. 'It means there will be fewer witnesses.'

A Jodrell Bank employee approached the two agents and said, 'I'm afraid we will be closing in a few minutes. Could you please make your way to the exit?'

Arthur Stubbins flashed the girl a smile and his identity card and said, 'I'm from British Intelligence; my friend and I will be staying behind after the other visitors have left. You haven't seen us.'

The Jodrell Bank employee nodded her bemused understanding of the situation and left the two men to continue their tour.

'Stop the car!' demanded Rhona Willet.

'What for?' demanded Frogmorton.

'Because we're sitting ducks in this thing,' she said. 'They'll be there waiting for us, so our best bet is to sneak in.'

'The madwoman's got a point, buddy,' said Gavin Woosner. 'If the people who are after us have got here first, they'll be on the lookout for this car. We can't risk getting caught before we send the message. You'd best do as she says and pull over.'

Frogmorton took the joint advice of the space expert and the homicidal lunatic and parked the car up, and the five of them made their way across the fields towards the huge radio telescope installation.

'We'd best keep as close to all the trees and bushes we can find,' suggested Elaine. 'They'll provide a bit of cover for us.'

'Does anybody else feel slightly stupid trekking across the fields like this when there's a perfectly good road we can follow?' asked Susan Likely who hadn't thought to put rambling shoes on before they set off.

'I'd rather feel stupid than dead,' Frogmorton informed her, and the rest of the party nodded in silent agreement.

* * *

Mimi Sarchetti waved goodbye to the nice man who had given her a ride to Jodrell Bank. A very charming half-Italian man who gave her his telephone number. Mimi decided that once she had taken care of the Woosner contract, eliminated any survivors from the helicopter crash and taken out the blackmailers, she would give him a call and invite him for dinner. She knew she would have to be careful from herein because she didn't know whether the people in the helicopter had any accomplices still on the case. She decided her best course of action would be to cut across the fields to avoid any possible confrontation before she got a chance to kill Gavin Woosner and collect the money for the hit. If Mimi Sarchetti hadn't climbed a fence and disappeared behind a bush when she did, she would have seen her old scooter roar by, being ridden by a rather large woman and a flame-haired beauty.

The pain in her injured ankle was troubling Vanessa O'Mara. She wanted to get this job over and done with and get it treated. How could such a simple mission turn out to be so difficult to complete? Obviously, Gavin Woosner was being helped somewhere along the way, but by whom? She knew the helicopter had been brought down and didn't just crash and she could see through the sight of her weapon that nobody in Woosner's car was responsible. So that meant an outside agency was involved. It was hard for her to believe that it could have been an American agency, unless of course by some miracle that ex-KGB fool Korinyakov had managed to follow them. It had to be the British government. They had a terrible habit of interfering in matters that were beyond their comprehension. It was time for Vanessa O'Mara to complete the job she had been given in spite of the opposition she was experiencing, and so she barked an order into Frogmorton's mother's ear.

'Turn off the road just here,' she said indicating a gateless field. 'We're going to cut across country and head them off.'

Frogmorton's mother was having far too much fun to argue with the injured CIA agent, and so she turned off the road as ordered with a resounding, 'Yeehah!'

Markham chuckled to himself about the ease with which he boarded the southbound train without having to buy a ticket. He had lost so much time in his pursuit of Frogmorton that he realised his former employee and his daughter would probably be on their way back home in a couple of hours, so he had caught a direct train home himself. If the Russians had collared Frogmorton all would not be lost. The diamond market was big enough for them and him. Perhaps he had been a bit hasty chasing after Frogmorton that way; after all, he was probably too dim to work a deal with the Russians in any case. His best plan of action now was to get back to Frogmorton's house and wait for him to arrive back home. Then he could make a mock apology to the idiot, reinstate him and then reap the rewards when the diamonds started rolling in. What a wonderful plan. He would gain untold wealth and give the appearance that he was being generous to Frogmorton. Markham was just reflecting on how perfect things were looking when he heard a voice behind him call out, 'Tickets please!'

* * *

Rhona Willett was singing 'The Grand Old Duke of York' in an effort to show that her repertoire wasn't limited to 'Baa Baa Black Sheep'.

'Rhona!' shouted Elaine. 'For the last time, will you keep quiet? We are trying to arrive unnoticed.'

'Oh, don't worry dear. When we get nearer I've got a secret weapon. Nobody will be able to see me.'

'Why's that Mrs Willett?' asked Susan Likely.

'Because the aliens gave me a cloak to wear that will make me invisible,' Rhona explained.

'Are you mad?' Frogmorton asked. 'What am I saying? Of course you're mad – I keep forgetting.'

'No, it's true,' Rhona insisted. 'They really did give me a cloak of invisibility.'

'Where is it then?' Frogmorton asked quite reasonably.

'Well, I'm not sure really,' replied Rhona. 'It's invisible. Invisible things are very hard to see, you know.'

'We've reached the perimeter fence,' announced Gavin Woosner, which brought an abrupt end to the invisible cloak debate.

'What do we do now?' asked Elaine, gazing directly into Frogmorton's eyes. This made him feel very important, and so he felt obliged to come up with an answer.

'We've got to get over, under or through it at some point and get our message sent to these aliens,' he said with the closest thing to authority in his voice that he could muster.

'What's that noise?' asked Susan Likely. Everyone stopped in their tracks for a moment to listen to the sound that Susan was trying to identify. It sounded like some kind of engine and Rhona Willet came up with a suggestion.

'It's them,' she said. 'They've come back for me.' And the smile on her face took on grotesque proportions at the prospect of the aliens' return.

The expressions on the faces of the others were far from huge grins. They wore the worried look of the doomed across their countenances.

'But they're too early,' protested Frogmorton as he heard the engine sound increase in intensity. Then, out of nowhere the motor scooter roared over the hedgerow and their heads, landed in the field, skidded and turned towards them and stopped a few feet away.

'Mother!' screamed a startled Frogmorton. 'What the hell are you doing here?'

'That's a fine way to greet your own mother who's travelled all this way to be with you. Far more interested in being with your lady friends than with the welfare of your own flesh and blood. Just like your father…'

'Don't start all that again, Mother,' interrupted Frogmorton. 'We haven't got time for that. We've got a planet to save.'

'And you think that's more important than me, do you?'

'Yes, I do,' said Frogmorton. 'Come on everybody – let's look for a break in the fence.'

'Shut up, you morons!' shouted Vanessa O'Mara to stamp her authority on the situation. 'Nobody is going anywhere.' And as if to emphasise the point she showed them all her magnificent weapon. Guns do have a way of grabbing the attention of people.

'Who are you?' Elaine asked.

'My name is Vanessa O'Mara – CIA. You people have put me

to a lot of trouble. It's going to be a real pleasure disposing of you all.'

'Look – it's me you want,' said Gavin Woosner. 'Let the rest of these people go. They haven't done anything.'

'On the contrary, Mr Woosner, these people have done something,' stated the flame-haired beauty.

'What?' asked Gavin Woosner.

'They got involved in matters that didn't concern them,' the beautiful CIA agent said with a wry smile.

'They concern everyone on the entire planet. Can't you see that?' pleaded Gavin Woosner.

'It's none of my concern who these matters concern. I'm only concerned with you and the people you are concerned with in this matter,' said Vanessa O'Mara ignoring the ex-NASA employee's pleas.

The rest of the group looked helplessly at one another in the vain hope that at least one of them had understood the CIA agent's last statement.

'We've got to get inside Jodrell Bank and get a message off to the aliens,' explained Frogmorton. 'I don't think you realise how serious this is.'

'I know just how serious this is, mister,' snapped Vanessa O'Mara. 'This whole simple business is turning into a nightmare for me. How serious is that? Very serious! I always take my work seriously and when complications set in the whole situation gets serious.'

'I'm not talking about things being serious for you, you stupid woman!' Frogmorton shouted. He was getting really cross with Vanessa O'Mara's attitude now. 'I'm talking about how serious it is for the whole planet. I'm not interested in the petty politics of NASA and the United States Government. But I am interested in stopping an alien civilisation coming to the Earth and laying waste to all life on the planet. Doesn't that mean anything at all to you?'

'Why should it?' said Vanessa, not used to being spoken to like that by any man. 'I'm not employed by all life on the planet. I'm employed by the United States Government and their requirements take first priority. And my priority now is to silence you people before you leak out any of this space alien nonsense.' So saying, the flame-haired CIA agent levelled her gun at Frogmorton's chest. Frogmorton just stood there open-mouthed. Elaine covered her eyes and screamed. Gavin and Susan looked on in horror, and Rhona Willet started skipping round in a little circle whooping to herself. Isn't hysteria a magical thing to watch?

Just as Vanessa O'Mara started to apply pressure with her trigger finger, a searing, unbearable pain shot through her ankle where Frogmorton's mother had kicked her. The gun flew through the air as the injured CIA agent fell to the ground in agony. There was a general air of relief as the others saw what had happened, although their jubilation was short-lived when the gun was snatched from its spiralling dance through the air by their favourite homicidal maniac, Rhona Willet. As she stood there holding the loaded gun with a maniacal grin on her face the others couldn't help feeling a little uneasy. Gavin Woosner rescued the situation by removing the gun from the madwoman's grasp and replacing it with a cleverly-folded paper rhinoceros.

'That was close,' Elaine said as she threw her arms around Frogmorton and embraced him.

'Mother,' said Frogmorton, 'I don't know what to say. You saved our lives.'

'I never did like that woman,' said Frogmorton's mother. 'She won't last long at C&A treating customers like that.'

Gavin Woosner walked up to Frogmorton and handed him Vanessa O'Mara's gun. 'Here,' he said, 'I think this could come in handy.'

'What do I want with it?' asked Frogmorton.

'Well, buddy,' Gavin Woosner explained, 'you're the head of this little group, and when we get inside I'm going to be rather busy with calculations and stuff. If we run into any trouble, you'll have to deal with it.'

'Right,' said Frogmorton gaining in confidence, 'let's get on with what we've come here to do then.' And he set off in search of a way through the perimeter fence.

'What about her?' asked Susan Likely indicating Vanessa O'Mara who was still writhing around in agony.

'Leave her,' said Frogmorton. 'She can't do anything now. We've got her gun and she's in no fit state to follow us. Come on everybody.'

They all trundled off leaving Vanessa O'Mara in a heap on the ground. The CIA agent did everything she could to make the pain more bearable and, as she saw the others disappear behind a hedgerow, she reached into the fabric of her jacket and withdrew a beautifully crafted but deadly miniature pistol.

* * *

Getting through the perimeter fence didn't prove as much of an obstacle as Frogmorton first imagined. This was mainly because the group came across a large break in the fence that the Jodrell Bank maintenance people had failed to get round to repairing. Once through the gap, they all headed for the cover of an outbuilding where they stopped to regain their composure.

'Did anyone bring a flask of tea?' Frogmorton's mother asked hopefully. Nobody bothered to reply. 'Oh well, never mind,' she continued. 'These sort of places usually have a café.'

'Mother!' Frogmorton said indignantly. 'We're here to save the world – we're not on a family outing!'

'Where are we headed for?' asked Elaine. 'The big dish?'

'No,' said Gavin Woosner, 'we've got to find the control room so that we can realign the dish and rig it up for transmission.'

'How long will that take?' asked Susan Likely.

'Once we find the control room, it shouldn't take long at all,' said Gavin Woosner.

'How are we going to find that?' asked Elaine.

'Well one of the best things about scientific establishments the world over,' explained Gavin Woosner, 'is that they label everything – including all their buildings and doors. It should be a cinch. All we need to do is look in the buildings away from the visitor centre.'

Just as they were about to start off again in search of the control room, a group of scientists came out of a nearby door, and they were lucky not to get caught. In fact, all over the installation scientists were coming out of nearly every available door and all heading in the same direction. The mysterious migration was solved when Frogmorton heard two scientists discussing the benefits of sausage, egg and chips – apparently an astronomer's staple diet. As luck would have it, it was time for the evening meal break, and so the control room could possibly be empty when they found it.

When the last of the scientists had disappeared, Frogmorton and friends started their search, and within ten minutes they had found what they were looking for.

'Is this it?' said Rhona Willet.

'What does it say on the door?' asked Gavin Woosner.

'Control Room,' replied Rhona Willet.

'Right everybody,' said Gavin Woosner, 'Rhona's found it – everybody in here.' And everybody piled into the room that Rhona had found.

Gavin Woosner started work immediately, feeding facts and figures into the computer. He started realigning the massive

Lovell Radio Telescope so that they could send their message to the source in space. Elaine and Susan looked on transfixed by the speed of his fingers on the keyboard. Frogmorton kept a careful watch on the door, holding Vanessa O'Mara's gun gingerly in his hand. Frogmorton's mother was teaching Rhona Willet 'Sing-a-song of Sixpence'

Elaine looked out of the window at the huge Lovell Radio Telescope and observed, 'It doesn't seem to be moving.'

'It doesn't have to move quickly under normal circumstances,' explained Gavin Woosner. 'I'll just make some adjustments in the program to hurry it up a bit.' So saying, his fingers attacked the computer keyboard furiously as he did his very best to speed things along. After several minutes the furious typing ended, and everyone gazed out of the window to see if Gavin Woosner's computer skills had worked.

'Your computer skills haven't worked,' commented Frogmorton. The giant telescope hadn't moved.

'I don't understand,' said Gavin Woosner. 'It should be moving.'

'Well it isn't,' said Elaine.

'Did you press the "enter" key?' asked Rhona Willet with more seriousness than was healthy in a homicidal maniac.

'What?' said Gavin Woosner almost absent-mindedly. He looked at the computer screen and realised that Rhona was right yet again. 'That's it,' he said triumphantly. 'You know Rhona, I don't know if you're a madwoman or a genius.'

'It's a fine line,' said Rhona Willet enigmatically.

Gavin Woosner stabbed his finger down on the 'enter' key and the giant Lovell Radio Telescope swung into action at a speed it was not designed to function at.

'Right,' said the ex-NASA man, 'now I'll hook up the telecommunications system to the telescope and then we're all set.'

Excitement was growing amongst Frogmorton and his friends, and they all watched as the giant Lovell Radio Telescope completed its realignment. Then Gavin Woosner said something that brought a deadly hush to the room.

'We're ready for transmission,' he said.

CHAPTER TWENTY

How to Eliminate an Alien Threat with a Well-known Book

All eyes in the Lovell Radio Telescope control room turned towards Frogmorton. Now was his moment. This was his opportunity to put the case for mankind to the alien civilisation that threatened humanity's continued existence. It was Frogmorton's big chance to save the lives of over six billion people and quite a few more other species. The atmosphere in that small room was tense as our hero moistened his lips and uttered the legendary words, 'I'm not sure what to say.'

'Think, Frogmorton,' urged Susan Likely. 'You have to find out why these aliens are coming here and put the case for mankind to them. Make it up as you go along.'

'Yes, Frogmorton,' encouraged Elaine, 'look upon this as a demonstration of a scientific project you've undertaken and pretend you're presenting it to my father.'

'Okay, okay! I think I have it,' said Frogmorton clearing his throat. 'Is it transmitting Mr Woosner?'

Gavin Woosner nodded to indicate that it was transmitting, and all eyes turned again towards Frogmorton Culpepper as he prepared to make the most important speech of his entire life. Frogmorton took a couple of deep breaths and then started his plea for mankind.

'Why...?' Frogmorton's oration was cut short at that point by the bullet that smashed into the computer equipment Gavin was using to transmit the Earth-saving message to the aliens, reducing it to a heap of useless electronic rubble. Everyone instinctively dived for cover.

'I thought you said that woman wouldn't bother us again,'

Susan quite rightly reminded Frogmorton.

'It can't be her. It must be someone else,' said Frogmorton – quite accurately as it turned out.

Another shot rang out and a bullet embedded itself in a filing cabinet about an inch away from Gavin Woosner's left ear.

'Well whoever it is seems to be gunning for me,' observed Gavin Woosner.

'How are we going to finish sending the message whilst people are shooting at us?' asked Elaine.

'We have finished sending the message,' replied Gavin Woosner. 'The system has been fried by that first bullet. We've done what we can to represent the human race.'

'So what message did you send in the end, Son?' Frogmorton's mother asked.

'I got as far as saying "Why?",' replied Frogmorton, feeling that he may have let the human race down a little.

'Well at least you responded,' said Susan Likely, 'which is infinitely better than not responding at all.'

'What do we do now then?' asked Frogmorton.

'If we ever get out of here alive,' suggested Gavin Woosner, 'our best bet is to go back to the hologram and wait.'

'Why back there?' asked Elaine.

'Because it's my guess that the aliens will use their point of transmission as a homing beacon and that their ship will end up in a point in space directly above the hologram,' explained Gavin Woosner, 'and if our response managed to get through to them at all, it might provoke their interest enough for them to make conventional contact.'

Another bullet smashed into office machinery above Gavin Woosner's head sending sparks everywhere.

'I don't like all this banging,' said Frogmorton's mother, who was about to stand up to see where the noise was coming from.

'Get down, Mother!' Frogmorton shouted. 'What are we

going to do, Mr Woosner?'

Gavin Woosner thought for a while. It was obvious that he was the intended target and he toyed with the idea of giving himself up to give the others a chance – but then he remembered the gun he had given Frogmorton.

'Listen buddy,' Gavin said in his calmest tones, 'whoever it is doesn't know we're armed, so we have an advantage. I'll lure them in here and as soon as you can get a clean shot – let them have it.'

Frogmorton looked a little unsure. 'Let them have it?'

'Yes,' confirmed the ex-NASA employee.

'I see,' said Frogmorton, still trying to work it out. Ignorance finally got the better of him and so he asked, 'What is it you want me to let them have?'

'Shoot them you fool!' Gavin said in a half-shouted whisper.

'Oh, right,' Frogmorton said hesitantly, 'of course, shoot them.' Frogmorton took the gun in both hands and tried to condition himself to the task ahead. Gavin Woosner tried to open a dialogue with the would-be assassin.

'Can't we talk about this?' the ex-NASA employee shouted, hoping that being shot at was negotiable.

'There's not really much to talk about, Mr Woosner,' said Mimi Sarchetti, 'but it would make things a lot easier and quicker if you could stand up and stop ducking behind things. Not to mention the expense. Bullets aren't cheap, you know.'

'Sorry,' said Gavin Woosner, 'it's a bit of an automatic reaction to being shot at, I guess. I'm not used to this sort of thing.'

'It's not your fault,' said Mimi Sarchetti. 'I imagine it takes a bit of getting used to. I'll try and make it as painless as possible.' Mimi Sarchetti decided that she would probably have to shoot Gavin Woosner at point blank range because of his annoying habit of taking cover all the time, so she gingerly walked through the door of the control room. Just as she did, Frogmorton seized the opportunity to let her 'have it' and the shot he fired blasted a fire extinguisher just to the left of Mimi, setting it off. The force knocked Mimi's gun from her hand and Mimi to the floor rubbing the foam from her eyes. The occupants of the room took the opportunity to run, and they made good their escape leaving the control room a smoking heap of debris behind them.

As they left the control room, Alexander Korinyakov carefully aimed his gun at Gavin Woosner's head from his hidden vantage point. Arthur Stubbins gently laid his hand on the ex-KGB man's weapon and said, 'Not now, Mr Korinyakov.'

'Why ever not?' asked Korinyakov displaying a little contempt for the British agent.

'There are bigger issues at stake here my friend. Too many people want our Mr Woosner dead and the British government want to know why. We believe this runs deeper than merely a few bits of stolen NASA software. We'll follow them and find out the bigger picture before we take any further action.'

Korinyakov was not happy, but he decided to go along with Arthur Stubbins' line of action – for the time being.

* * *

'Excellency!' boomed the very excited voice of SpaceTrooper (Fourth Class) Domr'k through the StarDestroyer's intercom system.

SpaceAdmiral Kratol was in the middle of a particularly erotic dream involving a number of Riludian dancers and was not too happy about his rude awakening.

'This had better be good Domr'k,' growled Kratol. 'You have just interrupted an important bit of space business.'

'It is very good, Excellency,' said Domr'k unable to hide the pleasure in his voice. 'Please come to the bridge as soon as possible.'

The moment with the Riludian dancers was never going to be regained and so Kratol reluctantly decided to go and see what was causing Domr'k so much obvious pleasure. Domr'k could barely wait for Kratol to step onto the bridge before he shouted out, 'They have responded!'

'What?'

'The people of Earth have responded, Excellency. They have sent a reply to our message.'

'What do they have to say for themselves?' asked Kratol.

'I will play back the message to you now, Excellency,' said Domr'k as he ceremoniously stabbed a couple of buttons on his console. Kratol placed both hands on the table and leant forward as if straining to hear and then the message started.

'Why...?' the message said – then silence.

Domr'k sat there with a stupid grin on his face, and Kratol still stood there leaning forward, straining to hear the rest of the message. After what seemed like an eternity of silence Kratol looked quizzically at Domr'k and said, 'Is that it?'

'Yes, Excellency,' beamed Domr'k.

'You mean to tell me that after receiving my very important message about the fate of their world all they can come up with in their defence is one simple word?'

'Yes, Excellency,' said Domr'k and sensing his superior officer's disappointment with the reply added, 'but it is an extremely good word isn't it?'

'It's pathetic!' remonstrated Kratol. 'Who ever heard of anyone getting anywhere or anything ever getting done by someone asking "Why?"?'

'Actually, Your Excellency, all the greatest scientific achievements in the Universe started with someone somewhere asking "Why?".'

'Did they?' asked Kratol unnerved slightly by the revelation.

'Yes, Excellency.'

'Oh,' said Kratol, 'well that sheds a new light on the message. Excellent. I think we may have made some progress here.'

'Does that mean that we can spare life on Earth, Excellency?' asked Domr'k.

'Certainly not!' said Kratol indignantly. 'Just because they come up with a clever message, doesn't mean they deserve to be saved.'

'But you will at least hear them out before you destroy them?' asked Domr'k, whose study of life on Earth had deepened his sympathies for the dominant species.

'I thought I did just hear them out,' said a confused Kratol.

'No, Excellency. That was just the start of dialogue between you and the representative of life on Earth,' explained Domr'k. 'It would be bad protocol to wipe them all out before answering their question.'

'Yes, of course,' said Kratol. 'I suppose you're right, Domr'k. I'd better go back to my quarters and prepare a statement in answer to their very clever question. It would do us both good to stretch our legs on the planet in any case. Carry on.' SpaceAdmiral Kratol retired from the bridge to prepare his statement and Domr'k allowed himself a little inward smile. He had a very good feeling about Planet Earth.

* * *

The conditions inside the hired car were very cramped on the return journey from Jodrell Bank. Frogmorton's mother was the bulk of the problem. In actual fact, Frogmorton's mother's bulk was the problem. There was a subdued silence in the car, a consequence of the shared knowledge that they had done everything they possibly could to get a message to the aliens and save all life on Earth from extinction.

Gavin Woosner eventually broke the silence. 'My guess is that we will have made them sit up and pay attention,' he said in an attempt to bolster everyone's spirit.

'I hope you're right,' said Frogmorton, 'that is if anything was transmitted at all.'

'We've got to put all that behind us now,' said Elaine. 'There's nothing more we can do about it. What we have to do now is plan for the next stage.'

'Annihilation?' asked Frogmorton.

'No!' said Elaine quite definitely. 'We've gone through too much already to fail. We've got to think positively and we can do this.'

'I'll do my best,' said Frogmorton.

'I'm just trying to get a few things straight for my article,' interjected Susan Likely at this point. 'I know the woman in the field who wanted to kill us was the woman from the helicopter and she was with the CIA, but who was the woman at Jodrell Bank who wanted to kill Gavin?'

'She was the woman on the roof of the car on the M6 who tried to kill us,' said Elaine helpfully.

'Yes,' added Frogmorton, 'but before that she was the woman on the moped who shot the CIA helicopter down.'

'That was fun, that was,' said Frogmorton's mother.

'Yes, but who is she working for?' asked Susan Likely, trying to tie up a few loose ends.

'I don't know,' Gavin Woosner answered honestly. 'The FBI maybe?'

'No,' said Frogmorton, 'that man my mother clobbered across the skull was FBI. And in any case, the FBI wouldn't shoot down the CIA would they?'

'I wouldn't put it past them,' said Gavin Woosner. 'There's a lot of inter-agency rivalry.'

'I need the little girls' room,' said Frogmorton's mother and in the interests of all the other passengers, Frogmorton made a hasty stop at the next services.

When they had stopped, everyone took the opportunity to take a break from the cramped conditions in the car and Frogmorton and Elaine went off for a little walk together.

'This is the first time we've really been alone since all this crazy business started,' Elaine said to Frogmorton as she took his hand as they walked along. He looked at her and smiled.

'I'm sorry I got you involved in all this,' he said.

'Well I'm not' she retorted. 'This is one of the most important events in mankind's history – I'm honoured to be involved. And I'm pleased you're here too.'

'Me? But I'm not much to look at...,' he said with a little embarrassment.

'I bet if you took these glasses off,' Elaine said, removing his glasses, 'and smoothed down your hair,' - she spat on her hand and smoothed down his hair - 'you'd look... er... pretty much the same. But looks aren't everything. It's your personality I've fallen in love with.'

'Love?' Frogmorton asked, thinking he had misheard her. 'You love me?'

'Yes, Frogmorton. I love you,' she said and closed her eyes waiting for him to kiss her, which he dutifully did. If you want more detail than that you should have bought a romantic novel!

After a break of twenty minutes everyone piled back in the car as best they could and they continued their journey south.

The main topic of conversation was, of course, the events at Jodrell Bank, but some thought was also given to what they could say to the aliens when they arrived. Frogmorton was still annoyed that nobody in authority would be there to handle the situation, but, as the others pointed out, there was no guarantee that the people in authority would know how to handle this situation either. Then Rhona Willet had an idea.

* * *

'Are you sure that an ice cream truck is a suitable vehicle for concealed surveillance?' Korinyakov asked Arthur Stubbins as they followed Frogmorton's hired car at what seemed a reasonably safe distance.

'We've never had any trouble in the past,' replied the British spy.

'It just seems to me that a plain, ordinary saloon car might be better suited to the task,' continued Korinyakov, who was blatantly trying to ridicule the British Secret Service.

'It might be better suited to the task in Moscow or New York, Mr Korinyakov, but here in the United Kingdom we've found that an ice cream van is the least conspicuous vehicle for pursuit or surveillance,' said Arthur Stubbins, feeling he had put the ex-KGB man firmly in his place.

'Excuse me, Mr Stubbins,' said Korinyakov with a wry smile on his face, 'but how can a large, brightly coloured vehicle sporting a nine-foot ice cream cone on its roof be less conspicuous than an ordinary saloon car?'

'Just take my word for it,' said Arthur Stubbins. 'The criminal fraternity and members of foreign espionage rings will always expect to be pursued by ordinary saloon cars. They come to expect it. So, an ice cream van is the last thing on the road they will suspect of tailing them.'

'I suppose there is some truth in that,' conceded Korinyakov.

'Yes. British know-how is the envy of the world, Mr Korinyakov,' smirked Arthur Stubbins. 'Rest assured that in this vehicle we are definitely not conspicuous.'

* * *

'Isn't that ice cream van a bit conspicuous?' asked Frogmorton's mother from the back of the crowded car.

'What ice cream van?' asked Frogmorton.

'The one that's been following us ever since we left that telescope place where everyone was shooting at us,' replied Frogmorton's mother.

Gavin Woosner glanced out the back window and said, 'I saw that ice cream truck when we stopped at the services. Do you think it's following us?'

'Don't be absurd!' said Frogmorton. 'What would an ice cream van be following us for? If we were going to be followed they'd do it in a plain, ordinary saloon car. They're less conspicuous.'

'I guess so,' said Gavin Woosner.

'What do you think to my idea then?' asked Rhona Willett with genuine interest.

'Rhona,' said Frogmorton in an understanding way, 'I'm not sure that seizing a visiting alien at gunpoint and holding him hostage is a particularly clever idea. Particularly when his friends have the capability to destroy the entire planet.'

'It was just a thought,' said Rhona who was trying her best to be helpful.

'We do appreciate your input, Rhona,' said Frogmorton, 'but we feel the subtle approach should be exhausted first before we go in with all guns blazing.'

'I wonder if he's got any choc ices,' said Frogmorton's mother who was still interested in the ice cream van several car-lengths behind them.

'Mother, will you stop going on about that ice cream van,' said Frogmorton. 'It's not as if you could stop him and buy one in the middle of the motorway, in any case.'

Frogmorton couldn't help thinking that saving the planet would be marginally easier without the homicidal lunatic and his mother to contend with. The car sped on ever southwards with Arthur Stubbins and Alexander Korinyakov in hot pursuit in the ice cream van.

* * *

Receiving a second audience with the President of the United States of America in such a short time meant that either the great man was very impressed with Rheingold or he took him to be a complete idiot. It doesn't take a genius to work out which is the case.

'Rheingold, you're a complete idiot,' the most powerful man in the world said, echoing our own thoughts.

'If you'll just give me a chance to explain, Mr Blessed-intent,' pleaded Rheingold.

'And don't start with all that confusing wrong name shenanigans. From here on in you refer to me as "sir" – got that?' said the President firmly.

'Yes, sir,' said a subdued Rheingold.

'British Intelligence informs us that your escapades have already resulted in helicopters being shot down and a gun fight at Jodrell Bank Observatory. What the hell has this Woosner fellah done, for you to go to all this trouble to get him?'

'Well, sir, I'm not really at liberty to discuss the case as a matter of National Security,' Rheingold said.

'This may come as something of a shock to you, Rheingold, but as President of the United States I think it's a pretty safe bet that my security clearance is a tad higher than yours – so cut the crap and tell me what the hell is going on here.'

'You mean the truth, sir?' asked an incredulous Rheingold.

'As near as you can get to it without lying to me,' replied the President.

'It all started, sir, when Woosner isolated a signal from space that confirmed the existence of extra-terrestrial intelligence,' began Rheingold.

'I thought I told you to tell me the truth, Rheingold,' warned the President.

'This is the truth, sir,' insisted Rheingold.

'Why wasn't I informed of this signal?' asked the President. 'Why weren't the American people informed of this signal?'

'I didn't think it was important, sir,' said Rheingold, 'and in any case, had the American people been told about the signal it would have resulted in riots and looting in the streets of our towns and cities.'

'Good move not to tell the people, Rheingold,' said the President, 'but you should have informed me. All the best Hollywood movies show the President being woken to be told about signals from extra-terrestrial intelligences.'

'Do they, sir?' asked Rheingold, unsure on points regarding Hollywood.

'Yes they do,' confirmed the President.

'Well it's not NASA policy to confirm the existence of extra-terrestrial intelligences, so the occasion never arose,' explained Rheingold.

'It may not be NASA policy to confirm the existence of extra-terrestrial intelligences, Rheingold, but were you able to confirm their existence?'

'Yes, sir,' confirmed Rheingold, 'the signal was the real thing.'

'From outer space?' asked the President for further clarification.

'Yes, sir,' confirmed Rheingold.

'And the signal was sent to California?' asked the President.

'No, sir,' said Rheingold, 'our calculations show that the signal was transmitted to somewhere in the South East of England.'

'England?' asked the President.

'Yes, sir.'

'England?' asked the President inwardly as if trying to locate a half-remembered memory from the depths of his mind. 'I've heard of England, isn't that one of our American outposts?'

'No, sir,' replied Rheingold, 'it's a small monarchy in Northern Europe. It makes up part of the United Kingdom. In the early part of the twentieth century the British Empire, controlled by England, covered a vast amount of the globe. We fought them in the 1776 War of Independence.'

'Of course we did,' beamed the President. 'Whipped their sorry asses too! So why did the extra-terrestrial intelligence send their signal to a bunch of losers like that for? Everyone knows that in all the best Hollywood movies, the signal from extra-terrestrial intelligences is always sent to the United States of America?'

'It's hard to say, sir,' admitted Rheingold. 'Maybe when they sent the signal there was a decimal point in the wrong place in their trajectory and everyone knows that a decimal point in the wrong place in your trajectory could make you miss your target by several thousand miles.'

'Good point, Rheingold,' the President said, satisfied with the explanation.

'The other explanation,' continued Rheingold, 'is that the extra-terrestrial intelligence chose a point on the Earth at random. But that is highly unlikely.'

'Agreed,' agreed the President. 'So, Mr Rheingold, what message was hidden in the signal from the extra-terrestrial intelligence?'

'Message, sir?' asked Rheingold.

'Yes. Message,' reiterated the President. 'Surely the signal was an attempt to communicate with us. What did they say and what response has been sent back?'

'I don't know, sir,' admitted Rheingold.

'You don't know?' asked an incredulous President.

'I didn't think it was relevant, sir,' said Rheingold.

'Mr Rheingold,' said the President, 'an extra-terrestrial intelligence transmits a signal which probably contains a message directly at the Earth and you don't think it is relevant?'

'Where is this leading, sir?' asked Rheingold uncomfortably.

'I don't know, Rheingold,' said the President. 'However, if we had some idea what the extra-terrestrial intelligence was trying to communicate to us we might have a better understanding of the situation.'

'What do you mean, sir?' asked a bemused Rheingold.

'Well,' explained the President, 'assuming that their message wasn't an unwanted advertisement for inter-galactic personal injury lawyers, they were probably trying to tell us something important, like, "Hi there, Earthlings, we'd like to be your friends" or "Warning Earth scum we're about to nuke you sorry sonsabitches!" You know, the usual heap of diplomatic crap.'

'I hadn't thought of that scenario, sir,' confessed Rheingold.

'No, Rheingold, you hadn't, had you?' said the President, 'and worse still, you are doing everything in your power to kill the one man who probably does know what the extra-terrestrial intelligence is trying to say to us.'

'Yes sir,' agreed Rheingold.

'Do you think that is the wisest course of action under the circumstances?' asked the President.

'Possibly not, sir,' said Rheingold.

'In order to try and bring this whole situation to a satisfactory conclusion, I've had you reassigned to a five-year research post on our Antarctic station, Mr Rheingold,' said the President. 'Close the door on your way out of my office.'

And so ended Rheingold's second interview with the President of the United States of America and his promising career at NASA.

The President picked up a phone and said, 'I want all United States Armed Forces in Europe on standby. Cancel all leave.'

Then he stabbed his finger down on the intercom on his desk. 'Get me the Prime Minister of England,' he said, feeling very powerful indeed.

* * *

Markham was starting to feel very sorry for himself. Nothing seemed to be going right. After being questioned at length by the British Transport Police, he found himself spending the night in the cells at Saffron Road Police Station on a charge of vagrancy. It was more a testament to his arrogance in the face of police questioning than the actual crime of being a vagrant. Nevertheless, at the back of his mind, Markham knew that once he got his hands on the diamonds, things would definitely take a turn for the better. This spell in police custody was just a minor setback.

* * *

Frogmorton's mother kept a steady stream of tea, coffee and biscuits flowing throughout the night. Everybody was too tense, nervous or excited to sleep.

Susan Likely spent the time writing her article of the events so far, and Frogmorton and Elaine were frantically going through encyclopaedias and searching on the internet in an effort to build a defence for the existence of mankind. Rhona Willett had withdrawn inside herself, and Gavin Woosner was making cleverly-folded paper rhinoceroses at a rate that could threaten a tropical rainforest or two.

Every now and then Frogmorton's mother would go to the window and peek through a small gap in the curtains and say, 'That ice cream van is still there. I told you it was following us.'

'It's probably a coincidence, Mother,' Frogmorton said in his best reassuring tones. He had bigger things to think about than ice cream vans.

'If he's there in the morning,' said Frogmorton's mother. 'I'm going to buy a ninety-nine from him.' She then shuffled back to the kitchen for further supplies of tea, coffee and biscuits.

'Where do we begin?' asked Elaine in frustration. 'How can we possibly summarise two thousand years of achievements?'

'Try not to mention all the wars,' suggested Gavin Woosner. 'That sort of thing might make them think we're hostile.'

'On the other hand, it might make them think twice about threatening us,' said Susan Likely.

'Aren't you all missing the point?' asked Rhona Willett.

'What are you getting at, Rhona?' asked Frogmorton forgetting Rhona's mental state momentarily.

'Not once have any of you questioned why these aliens are going to kill us all,' she replied half enigmatically and then she switched her brain off again.

'She might be mad,' said Susan Likely, 'but she does keep coming up with some excellent points.'

'So why do they want to kill us?' mused Frogmorton. 'Have you any ideas Gavin?'

'They must see us as a threat,' Gavin Woosner said.

'How could we possibly be a threat to them?' asked Elaine.

'They may have been monitoring the Earth for centuries,' explained Gavin Woosner. 'They could have seen how we have developed weapons of mass destruction. And now, of course, we are embarking on space travel. They're probably worried that we'll find their planet and nuke them.'

'I'm not so sure that they do regard us as a threat,' said Frogmorton.

'Why's that?' asked Susan Likely.

'If they regarded us as a threat, surely they would just come here and wipe us out. Why would they say that they wouldn't destroy us if we could come up with a good reason for us to live?'

'These are all questions that only these aliens can answer,' said Elaine.

The room fell silent as each of them reflected on the events of the previous days. The hours ticked by amidst endless tea and coffee and snatched moments of restless sleep. All the time, Kratol's hologram droned on and on about the impending doom for all life on Earth and the moment of truth was edging nearer and nearer.

* * *

Kratol strode onto the bridge of the mighty StarDestroyer Blagn'k to find Domr'k with his feet up on the main console, immersed in Beethoven's Ninth Symphony, which he was playing from the ship's database.

'What's that noise?' asked Kratol who had never heard Earth music before.

'It's the kind of music they listen to on Earth, Your Excellency,' explained Domr'k.

'It seems to me that we may be doing the Universe a favour when we purge the Earth, then,' said Kratol, amused at his own little joke.

'I rather like it,' said Domr'k.

'There's no time for that now, Domr'k. We will be arriving at the Earth shortly and I want to make sure the De-populator Device is primed and ready.'

'Aren't we going to respond to their reply then, Your Excellency?' asked Domr'k, feeling a little concerned about the fate of the inhabitants of Earth.

'Yes, we shall certainly respond,' said Kratol, 'but I'm just checking everything is working properly in case things turn out like they did on Gweelox 4. You can't be too careful about these things.'

'Quite so, Your Excellency,' said Domr'k.

At this point Kratol noticed that Domr'k was reclining in his chair with his feet resting on the console in front of him.

'What exactly do you think you're doing?' asked Kratol.

'Relaxing, Your Excellency,' explained Domr'k. 'It's something else people on Earth do, apparently.'

'Well, you're not on Earth yet, Domr'k,' growled Kratol, sweeping Domr'k's feet off the console. 'So set about your duties and stop all this relaxing.'

'Yes, Your Excellency,' said Domr'k and then he started to take readings from the navigational computer. 'Your Excellency,' he said, 'it appears that the constant corrections and compensations that the computer has been making to adjust for the increase in the ship's mass have resulted in our ETA being brought forward by several hours.'

'I see,' said Kratol. 'So when will we arrive above Planet Earth?'

'In about twenty minutes, Your Excellency,' replied Domr'k.

'Right, double-check the De-populator Device before we arrive. We don't want to take any chances.'

* * *

Squadron Leader Fligg was starting to get worried. The constant tractor beam acquisition and the intermittent problems he was experiencing with his flux grid were having drastic effects on his power cells. On several occasions, it had only been his very skilful re-routing of energy that had prevented the tractor beams from failing completely and hurtling the brave Muridaen into the vastness of space, which, as you know, is very big. Fligg wasn't sure how much longer he could hold out. He would soon have to make a decision to either try and hold on in the hope that the alien invaders' home-world was quite near or to fire his

Armageddon missiles at the alien invaders' ship and exact his revenge that way. The warning beeps and flashing lights on his systems array were starting to make the decision for him. His ship was breaking up. Fligg tapped a few figures into his tactical computer. The readout showed that in order to be a safe distance when the alien invaders' ship blew up, he would have to cut his tractor beams exactly two seconds before he fired his Armageddon missiles and then he would have to hit his retro-rockets. The destruction of the alien invaders' ship hardly compensated for the loss of his entire planet, but it looked like Fligg would have to settle for that. The brave Muridaen flicked the switch to arm his Armageddon missiles and stood by to cut his tractor beam.

'This is for Muridae,' said Fligg as he cut the tractor beam.

Fligg's plan would have worked in normal circumstances, but the moment he cut his tractor beam the mighty StarDestroyer Blagn'k arrived at its destination and stopped. Had he maintained tractor beam acquisition, Fligg would have stopped too. But he hadn't and he didn't. His ship was vaporised the moment it made contact with the hull of the mighty StarDestroyer Blagn'k.

The Muridaen Space Defence Corps now consisted of nothing.

* * *

The sudden appearance of a star-shaped alien spacecraft the size of a city above Frogmorton's house caused quite a stir, culminating in the postman falling off his bicycle. Dogs stood in the street barking at it and a gang of youths on the corner of the street started hurling stones at it.

The first indication that Frogmorton and his friends received that the aliens had arrived was when the hologram fizzled out and the sunlight streaming in through the windows was blotted out. Frogmorton's mother stuck her head out of the window, looked up at the mighty StarDestroyer Blagn'k, and announced to her son, 'I think your friends have arrived. Shall I put the kettle on again?' Everyone ignored her and filed out of the front door and into the street.

Aboard the mighty StarDestroyer Blagn'k Kratol and Domr'k studied the scanners and monitors.

'Where is the Earth's representative that sent us the message?' asked Kratol.

'Our message was transmitted to that small dwelling there, Your Excellency,' said Domr'k pointing out Frogmorton's house. 'So, I would imagine that one of the people who just came from there will be the Earth's representative.'

'Let's not waste any time. Set the De-populator Device to standby and let us go down to the surface and see what these people have to say for themselves,' said Kratol.

'Yes, Excellency,' said Domr'k, who was feeling very excited at the prospect of meeting people from Earth.

Elaine was the first to say anything. 'It's big, isn't it?' she said.

'Wow!' said Gavin Woosner.

Susan Likely was too busy taking photographs of the spacecraft to say anything, and Rhona Willett kept repeating to herself, 'They're back. They're back. They're back...' ad infinitum.

Frogmorton just stood and stared.

Arthur Stubbins shook Alexander Korinyakov's arm to wake him and said, 'Something seems to be happening.'

Korinyakov opened his eyes and stared in disbelief. And who could blame him.

The switchboard at Saffron Road Police Station was jammed with calls from people informing Sergeant Mills about the sudden appearance of a gigantic spaceship, a fact that the sergeant was only too aware of from glancing out of the window.

Throughout the South and East of England, USAF and RAF fighters were scrambled and a lot of military-type people spent a lot of time running backwards and forwards looking as if they were actually doing something.

The Prime Minister was kept informed of the situation and she in turn kept the President of the United States of America informed. In fact, the President could hardly believe that an alien spacecraft was hovering over South East England. 'What in hell is going on?' the President demanded to know. 'Everybody knows that in all the best Hollywood movies the alien spacecraft is supposed to hover above the White House.'

'Yes, I know,' said the British Prime Minister. 'And we all know what they usually do to the White House as well.' The Prime Minister cradled the hotline to the President and secretly wished that the alien spacecraft was hovering above the White House.

Rhona Willett was the first to notice the shuttle leave the mighty StarDestroyer. 'Look,' she said pointing at the shuttle, 'here they come.' Everyone looked up to where she was pointing and realised that the moment of truth for mankind had arrived. Would they be able to convince the aliens to spare life on Earth? Time would tell.

'Do you think they will be able to convince you to spare life on Earth, Your Excellency?' asked Domr'k.

'Time will tell,' replied Kratol.

From their shuttle the two Braakl'gians could see the immense number of people milling round in the street trying to make sense of the arrival of the StarDestroyer. They could also see the military planes closing in on reconnaissance sorties.

'They seem a little more organised than the inhabitants of Gweelox 4, don't they, Your Excellency?'

'If it looks like the situation is deteriorating, Domr'k. Make all haste back to the StarDestroyer and we'll activate the De-populator Device,' said Kratol.

'We've come this far, Your Excellency,' said Domr'k. 'The least we can do is hear them out.'

'Very well, Domr'k,' agreed Kratol reluctantly, 'but if this turns nasty, I'll hold you personally responsible.'

'Fasten your safety belt, Your Excellency,' said Domr'k. 'We are about to touch down on the surface of Planet Earth.'

Domr'k skilfully manoeuvred the shuttle and landed it in the street outside Frogmorton's house, playing havoc with the paintwork on Frogmorton's hire car in the process as the retro-rockets kicked in. Domr'k cut the shuttle's engines and an eerie silence fell on the street. The two Braakl'gians sat in the cockpit of the shuttle for a while whilst they gauged the mood of the crowd outside. After a few minutes the aliens decided that it was probably safe to come out and Domr'k lowered the steps so that they could go down and meet the Earth people face to face.

'You did check the atmosphere is breathable, didn't you?' asked Kratol stalling for time.

'Yes of course, Excellency,' replied Domr'k.

'Right,' said Kratol, 'you go first, then, Domr'k. I'll be right behind you.'

Domr'k didn't hesitate. He'd been waiting for this opportunity for days. He went down the steps two at a time and waited at the bottom for Kratol to join him. Kratol descended the steps with a little more dignity induced by nervousness. Once Kratol felt that they weren't in imminent danger of attack, the two Braakl'gians stepped towards Frogmorton and his group, and Kratol said, 'Greetings. I am SpaceAdmiral Kratol of the Braakl'gian Space Navy. Who is in charge here?'

I know, you've been wondering, 'How it is these aliens speak English?' It's a mystery to me too. They must have learned it at some stage. It would have been no use them trying to communicate with the Earth in Braakl'gian, would it? Especially here in England, because in general we British aren't too good at languages other than English. When we are abroad we are mortified when 'foreigners' can't understand our mother tongue. In order to be understood we just repeat what we had said earlier, only louder. We are just going to have to accept that the Braakl'gians have a working knowledge of the English language. So... back to the plot.

* * *

'I'm a representative of Her Majesty's Government,' said Arthur Stubbins, pushing through the crowd towards Kratol. 'Welcome to the United Kingdom. How may we help you?'

'Are you the one responsible for replying to our message?' asked Kratol.

'Her Majesty's Government always denies all responsibility for everything,' said Arthur Stubbins, 'but if you wish to send in a formal request in writing...'

'Silence!' demanded Kratol. 'I will only speak with whoever was responsible for replying to my message.'

'That would be me then, sir,' said Frogmorton stepping forward.

'Careful, Son,' said Frogmorton's mother, 'I don't like the look of him. He looks just like that little purple actor who fell out the back of the telly.'

'So,' said Kratol looking Frogmorton squarely in the eyes, 'you replied to my message?'

'Yes,' admitted Frogmorton, 'or at least I tried to. We had a slight... er... technical problem.'

'I was intrigued by your message,' said Kratol. 'Just one simple word. One word which you chose to use to save all life on this planet. The word "why".'

'I think we have a right to know,' said Frogmorton. 'We haven't done anything to you. We don't pose a threat to you. So why do you feel the need to destroy us?'

Kratol started to feel a bit edgy. 'It's turning out like Gweelox 4,' he said as an aside to Domr'k. 'Get back to the shuttle and start the engines up.'

'At least tell them why, Your Excellency,' Domr'k said. 'Surely we owe them that.'

Kratol turned back to face Frogmorton. 'You want to know why we have come to terminate Project Earth? It's because it has failed,' he said.

'Project Earth?' asked Elaine, 'What do you mean by Project Earth?'

Kratol held up his hand. 'Please!' he said. 'I only discuss this matter with the one who replied to my message. Address all your questions through him.'

'Ok,' said Frogmorton. 'What do you mean by Project Earth?'

'Project Earth is an evolutionary experiment set up by our employers – The Source,' explained Kratol, 'to see if life would evolve to the stage that The Source has reached.'

'And has it?' asked Frogmorton.

'No,' said Kratol, 'and that's why we are here to end all life on the planet and start again.'

This revelation sent a shockwave through the crowd that had congregated. This was the first any of them had heard about being wiped out. Arthur Stubbins and Alexander Korinyakov weren't too happy about it either. Arthur Stubbins started mumbling into the top of his pen.

'But you said you would spare us if we could come up with a good reason for being allowed to live,' said Frogmorton.

Gavin Woosner tugged on Frogmorton's arm to get his attention and whispered something in his ear.

'My friend has a good point, Admiral Kratol,' said Frogmorton. 'Evolution is a continuous process, so how come you've decided to intervene now? It could be thousands of years before we evolve into the same state that the... er... Source has attained.'

'It's out of my hands, I'm afraid,' said Kratol. 'Your planet was next on the list; so here we are.'

'What, just like that?' asked Frogmorton.

'I'm afraid so,' sympathised Kratol, 'but it's not just your inability to evolve properly. You're also irreversibly damaging your planet. If we let that go on we won't be able to start a new project when we've finally got rid of you.'

'In what way?' asked Frogmorton.

'You are depleting the ozone layer and increasing the greenhouse gases in the atmosphere. Your planet is going to die if this carries on unchecked.'

'But I know how to solve those problems,' said Frogmorton. 'I have invented a method of dealing with those issues. It can be cured.'

'You have?' asked Kratol slightly taken aback that the Earth's representative had an answer for that one. 'Oh... well I suppose we can scratch that reason out then.'

A large car screeched to a halt at the edge of the crowd and a large man in a large military uniform with a large row of medals on his chest pushed his way to the front.

'Alright everyone,' said the large military man, 'stand aside. The army is here now and I will handle the negotiations.'

Kratol didn't much care for the new arrival and turned to Domr'k and said, 'I don't like the look of this one, Domr'k. Do something about him.'

Domr'k pressed a button on the device he was holding and a

pink beam shot out of it and hit the large military man in the medals. The large military man instantly lost consciousness and fell to the ground in a heap.

'Have you killed him?' asked Frogmorton.

'No,' said Kratol. 'We have merely rendered him inoperable. I will only negotiate with you. It gets too complicated if too many people are involved.'

'So,' said Frogmorton, 'as the Earth is no longer under threat from us environmentally, I suppose you can spare us.'

'It's not quite that simple,' confessed Kratol.

'Why?' asked Frogmorton.

'That's your favourite word, isn't it?' said Kratol.

'The planet isn't in danger, so why would you want to kill us all now?'

Kratol had to think for a moment. 'Because you haven't been able to show me any real achievements. What has your species done of any note?'

A TV news crew arrived and started filming as Frogmorton ran back into his house to retrieve one of the books he had been using the previous night to come up with reasons for being spared by the aliens. He ran straight back out and handed the volume to Kratol. 'There,' he said. 'There are some of our greatest achievements.' Kratol started thumbing through the copy of *The Guinness Book of Records* that Frogmorton had handed him. He showed Domr'k and the two Braakl'gians were surprised at some of the feats they saw mentioned.

'That's quite impressive, Your Excellency,' said Domr'k. 'Do you think we will be able to spare the Earth?'

'These achievements are very impressive, Domr'k,' admitted Kratol, 'but I'm afraid rules are rules. Life on Earth hasn't evolved in a satisfactory manner, and it's up to us to terminate Project Earth and move on to the next planet on our list.'

'You can't dismiss an entire civilisation like that!' said

Frogmorton, showing his displeasure at Kratol's attitude. 'What right have you got to do this?'

'I'm only doing my job,' said Kratol. 'There's no need to take it personally. I've nothing against you, but you have to be destroyed. Farewell people of Earth and prepare to meet your doom.'

Kratol's speech didn't go down too well with most of the crowd, and panic set in with people running here there and everywhere. Frogmorton decided to take direct action and he lunged at Kratol gripping him in a half-nelson type grip. He pulled the gun out of his pocket and held it at Kratol's head.

'The Earth is not going to be destroyed today. Have you got that?' said Frogmorton.

'I knew this would turn out like Gweelox 4,' said Kratol. 'Disable him, Domr'k!'

'I'm afraid I can't do that, Your Excellency,' said Domr'k.

'That's right,' said Frogmorton, 'because if your friend there makes one false move, I'll blow your brains out.'

'We don't even know their brains are in their heads,' said Gavin Woosner, 'and what if his friends on board the mother ship start firing their weapons?'

'Wait!' said Domr'k. 'I may have a solution to this problem without anyone getting hurt and without any life on Earth being destroyed.'

'Why don't we move in and take over?' said Korinyakov to Arthur Stubbins.

'The situation seems to be well in hand at the moment,' replied Arthur Stubbins.

Frogmorton was interested in Domr'k's proposition. 'What have you got in mind?' he asked.

'Firstly,' said Domr'k, 'there are no others aboard our StarDestroyer, so you are safe from attack and secondly, I propose that I stay here on your planet and SpaceAdmiral Kratol is released.'

'But if he goes back to your ship he will destroy all life on Earth,' argued Gavin Woosner.

'No,' said Domr'k, 'he will not be able to do that. Braakl'gian law forbids us to take the lives of our own people. If I remain on this planet, he will not be able to activate the De-populator Device. It would detect my presence and shut down.'

'Domr'k,' said Kratol, 'this is treachery.'

'I would much rather be treacherous than spend the rest of my life destroying life on planet after planet. Surely you must tire of it too, Your Excellency.'

'But it's my job,' pleaded Kratol.

'Make a stand,' said Domr'k. 'Devote the rest of your life exploring new planets instead of sanitising them.'

'What about The Source?' asked Kratol.

'They have thousands of StarDestroyers in their employ,' said Domr'k. 'They are hardly going to miss one.'

'You mean there are more ships like this one?' asked Frogmorton nervously.

'Yes,' said Domr'k.

'Won't they come here to finish the job you started?' asked Gavin Woosner just as nervously.

'Probably,' said Kratol, 'but not for tens of thousands of years. Maybe your kind will have evolved properly by then.'

'So does this mean we live?' asked Elaine.

'Yes,' said Domr'k with a smile, 'for as long as I remain here you are in no danger from Braakl'gian StarDestroyers.'

'Domr'k,' said Kratol, 'I like your idea about devoting my remaining time exploring new worlds – but you forget one thing.'

'What is that, Your Excellency?' asked Domr'k.

'With you stranded here on Earth, I don't have any crew to pilot the StarDestroyer. Admittedly the controls are mostly automated, but a minimum crew of two is essential.'

'I had already thought of that,' said Domr'k. 'Choose someone from Earth to accompany you on your trek through the stars. Is there one among you in this assembly who would like to embark on a star trek?'

Suddenly Gavin Woosner realised that his boyhood dream was within his grasp. What he had failed to achieve at NASA could now happen for him with the arrival of these aliens from goodness knows where. His heart started beating a little faster as he realised the enormity of what he would be undertaking if he went with Kratol. The desire to ride through the Cosmos was too strong to be ignored, and he held his hand up high and said, 'I'll go. Take me. But I'm damned if I'm going to call him "Your Excellency".'

'You are a brave man,' said Domr'k, 'to leave your home-world on an endless trek through the Cosmos.'

'It's all I've ever wanted,' said Gavin Woosner who felt elated.

'Then all has been resolved here,' said Domr'k. 'Kratol and this man will go back to the StarDestroyer and Planet Earth will go on as it always has.'

Frogmorton released his grip on Kratol, and Gavin Woosner stepped up and joined the two Braakl'gians.

'What about me?' said Rhona Willett. 'Don't leave me behind.'

'Rhona,' said Susan Likely, 'they haven't come for you. These aren't the same people that took you before.'

'I don't care,' said Rhona Willett. 'I want to go with them. There's no future for me here. I know that. Let me go too.'

'There is plenty of room on the StarDestroyer,' said Kratol.

It was decided that Rhona could go too, not least because it would save a lot of explaining later if they took her back to the hospital.

'Is it all over yet?' asked Frogmorton's mother, 'because if it is, I'll go and put the kettle on.'

Domr'k came and took his place in the crowd as they all watched Kratol, Gavin Woosner and Rhona Willett climb the steps and into the shuttle.

'Who's going to be flying that thing?' asked Elaine.

'Don't worry,' said Domr'k, 'its flight pattern is automated. Even SpaceAdmiral Kratol could pilot it back to the StarDestroyer.'

Within a few minutes the shuttle had lifted off and was on its way back to the mighty StarDestroyer Blagn'k. The speed with which everything had happened was amazing, and Frogmorton, Elaine and Susan could hardly believe that the threat hanging over the Earth for the last few days was over. Then, barely half an hour after it first arrived above the Earth, the mighty StarDestroyer Blagn'k shot off into the unknown at speeds beyond our comprehension. The crowds in the streets just stood around wondering if it had all really happened or if last night's pizza had been off.

Vanessa O'Mara had seen it all from her vantage point and had decided that it would be in the best interests of the United States Government if she terminated the alien who had stayed behind. She had the perfect shot and was about to squeeze the trigger when she felt a man slip his arm around her waist. He whispered into her ear, 'Vanessa darling, I don't think that would be a very good idea.'

'Arthur,' she said, 'it's good to see you too.'

'Now,' said Arthur Stubbins slipping a pair of handcuffs onto her wrists, 'I need to talk to you about an unexplained disappearance that happened here a few months ago. I think you may know something.' And Arthur Stubbins led the flame-haired beauty to his ice cream van.

The press started closing in on Frogmorton, Elaine, Susan and Domr'k, and so they sought refuge in Frogmorton's house.

As they walked in, Frogmorton's mother produced a tray of

tea and biscuits. There was a lot of talking to be done and Domr'k had so many questions.

'What is your name?' asked Susan.

'Domr'k,' said Domr'k.

'It's hard to tell you are alien. You look so human,' said Elaine.

'We certainly are alike,' said Domr'k, 'until we blink.' And by way of illustrating his point Domr'k blinked and it was his lower eyelid that moved. Domr'k turned his attention to Frogmorton and said, 'I heard you say that you knew the solution to the ozone layer and greenhouse gases. Does it involve vast quantities of soot?'

'Yes,' said Frogmorton, 'and a high-powered laser beam.'

'Exactly how I would have solved it. Maybe we can work together,' said Domr'k.

'It would be a pleasure,' said Frogmorton. Chloe marched into the room at that point, looked carefully at everyone in the room, and then jumped up on Domr'k's lap and curled up and went to sleep. Frogmorton and his friends talked all through the night.

In the absence of a threat from aliens the military had been called off and life on Earth went back to normal and, oblivious of the events that had happened, Markham was released from police custody. He went home and changed before going round to see Frogmorton and offer him a research post at the university.

Nobody was more surprised than Frogmorton at the job offer, but he took it willingly. Especially now that he had Domr'k and Elaine to assist him in his work. Life was looking decidedly rosy.

CHAPTER TWENTY-ONE
Three Months Later

Three months later Frogmorton was ready to demonstrate his latest Project Earth. The time he had spent working with Domr'k meant that all the impurities had been ironed out. Markham was very excited at the prospect of his diamond 'mine' being ready and awaited the demonstration eagerly.

'Right Frogmorton,' he said, 'let's see what you've got for us.' Markham was already preparing an excuse to get rid of Frogmorton and take over the project himself.

Frogmorton started the fans going and introduced the soot and then he activated the laser beam. The experiment was perfect. It worked and the greenhouse gases were being converted to ozone. Markham waited for several minutes, and then his smile started to wear off. 'Where is the explosion?' he asked.

'I've eliminated all the flaws in the old Project Earth, Professor Markham,' explained Frogmorton. 'This experiment doesn't blow up, I'm pleased to say.'

Markham was dumbfounded. Frogmorton thought that Markham was feeling unwell, so he made his excuses and left. Markham just sat there gazing at the perfectly working experiment and muttered to himself, 'The diamonds! Where are my diamonds?' Unfortunately for him – they were no longer a side product of Project Earth. It's not nice watching a grown man cry.

* * *

Gavin Woosner was finding out just how big space really was and he was enjoying every minute of it. And so was Rhona Willett who had lost all appearances of being mad now that she was free and travelling through space. Just like Gavin Woosner, it had always been all she had ever really wanted. Kratol was enjoying the new experience too. It was much better to be exploring planets than laying waste to them, and the inhabitants were always less hostile when they were not being threatened. Kratol didn't drive his runabout at the droids very much ever since Gavin Woosner taught him a new skill. Now at every available opportunity the Braakl'gian could be found making cleverly-folded paper rhinoceroses.

The disappearance of Gavin Woosner meant that Mimi Sarchetti's first hit was unsuccessful. She decided to retire as a Mafia hit-woman before it was too late and went back to nursery school teaching. Mimi was never really sure which profession posed the greatest danger to her.

Alexander Korinyakov remained in the UK for the time being. He and Arthur had decided that they had so enjoyed their day out together at the Jodrell Bank Visitors' Centre that they would continue to meet occasionally for days out. Their burgeoning bromance had so far taken them to the National Space Centre in Leicester, Madam Tussauds in London and Chessington World of Adventures.

Vanessa O'Mara, on the other hand, was back in the United States, having mysteriously disappeared from custody and slipped back there via Ireland.

Susan Likely was nominated for Journalist of the Year for her interview with the alien Domr'k, whom it was rumoured she was having a secret affair with - which, of course, she was.

* * *

Frogmorton and Elaine walked into the kitchen and caught Frogmorton's mother in just her bra and pants ironing a dress.

'Mother,' cried Frogmorton, 'can't you wear a dressing gown to do that sort of thing?'

'It's a poor tale when you can't do what you like in your own house,' said Frogmorton's mother. Luckily she had finished ironing the dress and she slipped it on.

'We've got something very important to tell you, Mrs Culpepper,' said Elaine.

'What's that then?' asked Frogmorton's mother.

'Elaine and I are going to be married,' said Frogmorton unable to hide the pleasure in his face.

Frogmorton's mother stood there silently for what seemed an age, taking in what she had just been told.

'Are you happy for us, Mother?' asked Frogmorton.

'Happy?' asked Frogmorton's mother. 'After all I've done for you, this is how you treat me. Deserting your poor mother in her hour of need.'

'I thought you'd be happy,' said Frogmorton. 'All you've ever done for the last ten years is try to marry me off.'

'That's it,' said Frogmorton's mother. 'Just clear off and leave me on my own in my old age.'

And so the story ends. And the moral? You just can't please your mother all the time.

CORONA
BOOKS

Also available from Corona Books UK

Corona Books is an independent publishing company, newly established in 2015. We aim to publish the brilliant, innovative and quirky, regardless of genre. A selection of our other titles follows on the next pages. All our books are available on Amazon.co.uk and Amazon worldwide.

www.coronabooks.com

Please visit our website for the latest on other and forthcoming titles, and to sign up for our e-newsletter. We promise we won't bombard you with emails and you can unsubscribe at any time.

CORONA
BOOKS

The Great British Limerick Book

Lewis Williams

Surely it can't be done. But it has been done. For the first time in the history of mankind someone has been dedicated enough and fool enough to write a filthy limerick for every town in the UK which, unlike Leeds or Devizes, doesn't already have a classic filthy limerick to call its own.

From Land's End to John o' Groats, *The Great British Limerick Book* has a filthy limerick for your town, for your uncle's town, for your cousin's husband's ex-wife's town .... as long as it's in the UK and as long as it isn't one of those few places that are really impossible to find a rhyme for.

There are over 900 limericks in the book. A lot of them are hilarious. Most of them are very funny. All of them are filthy.

CORONA
BOOKS

The Oxbridge Limerick Book

Lewis Williams

Presenting the very finest in vulgar humour, *The Oxbridge Limerick Book* revives the ancient and noble art of the filthy limerick, injects it with a large dose of twenty-first century humour and applies it to the venerable institutions of Oxford and Cambridge, giving every college in the two universities a filthy limerick to call its own. The results will cause hilarity and provoke outrage, with what is quite possibly the best and most original little book of filthy limericks to be published since 1928.

About the author

Lewis Williams went to Darwin College, Cambridge (for one evening, that is, in 2015 for a dinner he was invited to.) On the other hand, he did genuinely work at Oxford University for a number of years. His ignominious departure from its employ had nothing whatsoever to do with his writing rude limericks concerning the place or its employees. He is the author of *The Great British Limerick Book* and *The Scottish Limerick Book*. He hasn't devoted the whole of his recent past to the art of writing filthy limericks, either. He is also up to over level 400 on Candy Crush.

Child of Winter

T. R. Hitchman

An old woman harbours a painful secret and meets a young man with a dark secret of his own; a narcissistic journalist learns that the camera can tell the truth in more ways than one; and a boy discovers horrors he never imagined when he set out to get in with the cool kids ...

Ten stories of love, loss and disappointment with a dark twist are the product of the imagination of writer, T.R. Hitchman, the new master of modern macabre.

About the author

T.R. Hitchman's first crush was on Christopher Lee. She grew up in love with the eerie stories of Edgar Allan Poe and, as a child of the eighties, was profoundly affected by being allowed to stay up late to watch *Hammer House of Horror* on TV. She has written for The Gothic Society and her acclaimed novella, *The Homecoming*, was published electronically in 2014. It is included here in revised form, along with nine other equally brilliant, dark and twisted tales in her debut story collection, *Child of Winter*.

Made in the USA
Columbia, SC
06 May 2017